The Sword Lord

Look for these titles by

Robert Leader

Now Available:

The Sword Empire

Sword Destiny

The Sword Lord

Robert Leader

A Samhain Publishing, Ltd. publication.

Samhain Publishing, Ltd.
577 Mulberry Street, Suite 1520
Macon, GA 31201
www.samhainpublishing.com

The Sword Lord

Print ISBN: 978-1-59998-811-5
Digital ISBN: 1-59998-173-4

Editing by Sarah Palmero
Cover by Anne Cain

First Samhain Publishing, Ltd. electronic publication: August 2007
First Samhain Publishing, Ltd. print publication: June 2008

Chapter One

The preparations for the wedding had lasted for twenty eight days, and Maryam, Princess of Karakhor, steeled herself to face her duty.

She had always known that, when it came, her wedding would be a political one, arranged by her father and his advisors in the best interests of the city and empire, and now, in her eighteenth summer it was time. Her mother had told her what was expected of her and what she must do. All that was left to her was to pray to the gods that the husband she had never seen would be young and kind and handsome, and that as the seasons passed they would learn to love each other.

Now her husband-to-be was encamped outside the city with a huge entourage of warriors, nobles, priests and chieftains, their bright pavilions filling the open plain beyond the blue river in a heaving patchwork of tents and men, cooking fires and chariots, weapon stacks and banners. They were a small army, too many of them to be housed in the city itself. The central pavilion occupied by the man who was to be her New Lord and Master was the most magnificent of them all, a splendid erection of blue and gold silks flying the savage Black Leopard banner of Maghalla.

Maryam could see it all from the window of her bridal chamber high in the swan neck tower of the west wing of the

Royal Palace, although she was too distant to pick out the faces of individual men. She did not need to, for since the arrival of her intended groom and his wedding party she had sensed the change in those around her, and she had heard whispered the name by which her lord-to-be was known.

"Sardar of Maghalla, Sardar The Merciless."

So he was not a kind and gentle man, of that much she was now certain.

For a while she had continued to pray that he might still be young and handsome, but even those hopes had quickly faded. Her mother and the other wives of Kara-Rashna, her sister and all her other attendants, had gradually become reluctant to reassure her on those matters, and had finally become so evasive that she had ceased to ask.

Since the arrival of the bridal party, she had seen nothing of her father or brothers or of any of the males of her household. Custom demanded that she remain in her bridal chamber in a purifying period of bathing and prayer, attended and visited only by other females. But the joy had gone from her mother's face and her visits had become less frequent, and Maryam had seen the wet tears in the soft eyes of her half-sister, Namita.

Inside the city, night and day, the sacred fires had burned constantly over the past four weeks, on all the altars before all the splendid temples, wafting the holy flames and smoke and sweet-smelling incense to the blue and star-lit heavens. The priests had prayed and made sacrifices and intoned the sacred mantas to *Indra, Varuna* and *Agni.* All that was due to the entire mighty pantheon of the known gods had been offered in incessant entreaty for their benevolence and favour.

In vain.

Maryam knew in her heart it had all been in vain. This was

her wedding day, and the gods were not smiling upon her.

One of her attendants, smiling faintly, offered her a hand mirror, and Maryam looked critically at her own reflection. She was beautiful. She knew she was beautiful because all those around her had always told her so. Her sister and her handmaidens envied her, the young men of the palace composed sonnets and heaped her with flattery and praises, and even her own brothers smiled and admitted that she was beautiful. But today there was a tinge of paleness to her flawless, dusky cheeks. There were faint lines of stress and tension at the corners of honey-brown eyes that lacked their normal sparkle. Her mouth was too grim. Her glorious black hair had been washed and oiled, scented and braided, and garlanded with white flowers, but still it seemed to lack its normal shine and lustre. Despite all her bridal finery—the pure white sari, the golden sashes and bangles, and the fortune in sparkling jewels with which she was draped and encrusted—she did not feel beautiful.

She turned her head to look at Namita, her younger half-sister who was also her chief bridesmaid. Namita, dressed in yellow and blue silks to honour Maghalla and almost as bejeweled as the bride, cast her eyes downward and could not meet her gaze.

Maryam smiled sadly. "Sardar is not handsome, is he?"

Namita hung her head mutely. Her shoulders made an attempt to shrug.

"Sardar is not young, is he?"

There was still no answer.

Maryam put her hand to Namita's chin and lifted gently. Wet gaze stared back at her and then Namita threw her arms around her sister and began to sob.

"Sardar the Merciless," Maryam said bitterly, "is old and

ugly."

The other girls who were her attendants, three daughters of the three noblest houses of Karakhor, drew back uncomfortably and exchanged distressed glances. Two of them also began to silently weep.

After a moment Maryam pulled a silk handkerchief from beneath one of her golden wrist bangles and tenderly dried Namita's eyes. "Tell me what you know," she ordered. "I must face my betrothed in an hour. In two, he will be my husband. It will be best if I go prepared."

Namita choked and cleared her throat. "No one knew," she whispered. "No one knew until he appeared at our gates. Even Jahan did not know. His spies send endless reports to tell him how many warriors Maghalla can raise, how many spears, how many war elephants, how many chariots. It is said that Jahan knows every word that is spoken in Maghalla's secret councils. But no one thought it necessary to tell him of this."

"That Sardar is old and ugly." Maryam grimaced. "Men would not think that such things are important. Men are fools who think only of war and politics."

"Our father is furious and so is Lord Jahan." Namita weakly defended them. "Kara-Rashna has sworn that those of his council who urged and advised this marriage will pay with their heads—and Jahan has threatened to whip every spy in his employ. Your brother Kananda wants war with Maghalla now, rather than see this marriage go ahead, and there are many who would unsheathe their swords beside him."

"But the marriage will go ahead," Maryam knew, and her tone was heavy with despair, "because Karakhor needs this alliance with Maghalla."

"Yes," Namita said wretchedly. "I have heard our uncles say that to cancel the marriage now will be a terrible insult to

Maghalla. Now that Sardar has arrived with his wedding party, we cannot send them away without their promised bride. It will mean a certain and terrible war. Even so, they are divided as to what we should do."

"And what does my father say?"

"Kara-Rashna rages. But he says that now the honour of Karakhor is also at stake. He does not fear war, but he will not lose honour."

"Our father was always a proud man, a noble king." Maryam spoke with a note of pride in her own voice, although her heart felt cold and dead as ice inside her breast.

Namita nodded, and again all four of the bridal attendants were helplessly weeping.

"Shut up, all of you!" Maryam snapped and stamped her foot. "I am a princess of Karakhor. I know my duty. And if this is what it must be, then I will do it." Her chin thrust defiantly forward, and with more courage than she felt, she finished bravely. "I will not be the first young bride who goes to an old and ugly husband. It happens more often than not."

There was a shuffling of feet, a drying of eyes, and reluctantly the girls continued their tasks, straightening folds in the silk sari and the fine lace shawls, loading her arms, wrists and throat with even more gold and jewels. The gemstones were all white diamonds and blue sapphires. They seated her gently to ease soft slippers onto her feet, and each one was almost invisible beneath its scintillating layer of fine blue stones. Maryam stared down at them gloomily, and reflected that each shoe was worth a fortune beyond the wildest dreams of almost all of her father's subjects, but that neither could buy back the lost days of her childhood and freedom. Suddenly, with an awful urgency and poignancy, all that her breaking heart wanted was to be a child again.

The morning sunlight streamed through the high tower window, and its passage round her chamber marked the moving hours of the day. The hours were passing too quickly.

I am a princess of Karakhor, she told herself resolutely. *I will do my duty*. She repeated the vow over and over in her mind, like one of the boring mantras of the priests.

Her hand-maidens worked in silence, and when they were satisfied that there were no more adjustments that could be made, they stood back and simply waited.

The inexorable line that divided sunlight from shadow continued its remorseless progress round the walls, lighting up the rich silk drapes with their embroideries, where deer and other gentle animals played and grazed, and birds and butterflies fluttered over glades of cool shade and running water. The line passed over the tall vases of fresh cut flowers and the wall niches where the statues of the gods were enthroned. The sunlight reached the impassive face of *Varuna,* the Supreme God above all others, and her time had run out. It was noon, the God had no reprieve to offer her, and her father's knock sounded on the door.

The girls looked at each other, and then slowly Namita moved to open it. The others helped Maryam to rise to her feet. She faced her father in the open doorway.

Kara-Rashna, King of Karakhor, Lord of the Golden City and the greatest and most far-flung empire that the world had ever known, still looked worthy of every one of all his royal titles. That is until he moved, for only then did the stiff right arm and leg show that he was no longer the strong young lion of his youth. His beard and moustaches, despite being carefully oiled and tinted, still showed touches of the grey that was now in his eyebrows and hair. His turban and tunic were resplendent with every known gemstone, the blood-red of rubies and the green of emeralds mixing with the white and blue of diamonds and sapphires, all of them set in pendants, rings and bracelets of gold. For gold was the symbol of Karakhor. Gold spoke of her immense wealth, which in turn spoke of her prestige and power.

Kara-Rashna was all-powerful, all-mighty, all-merciful, descended from the gods, and almost their equal. Yet today he was struck dumb. It might have been her own compelling beauty, Maryam thought fleetingly, or his own parental pride, but mostly she realized, it was pain and embarrassment.

"My daughter—" Kara-Rashna began, but then his words stumbled and failed him.

Beside him was Kaseem, the High Priest of Karakhor, the holiest of all the holy men and Brahmins who filled the many temples. Behind him, two more priests in their simple white robes and behind them, a small escort of the palace guard in gleaming bronze and leather. All of them looked uncomfortable.

Maryam steeled herself anew and drew a deep breath as she stepped forward and offered her right hand. The gold bangles shook only slightly on her slim wrist.

"I know, father," she said softly, "and I understand."

A tear glistened in the corner of his eye, but willpower held it back as he forced the grimace of a smile. He took her right hand in his left and turned. The priests moved aside. The guards parted to let them through. Maryam walked bravely beside her father and the small procession formed behind them as they reached and began to descend the circular stone stairway that led down from the tower.

I am a princess of Karakhor, Maryam repeated stubbornly in her mind. *I will do my duty.*

The silent vow was hollow and no longer gave her comfort. The face of her father, and the crushed and wretched face of

Kaseem, who had also loved her as devotedly as any uncle, all boded ill. She began to fear that Sardar was not merely old and ordinarily ugly. There was something more.

They reached the foot of the staircase and progressed along a stone-pillared corridor to reach the Great Hall of the palace. Here a great throng awaited them, her mother, her aunts, her uncles and her brothers, and all the great heads and nobles of the powerful bloodlines that made up the great houses of Karakhor. All of them wedding guests dressed in their most colourful finery. There were a few polite handclaps, a few forced smiles, but no real joy. She looked into the face of Jahan, the Warmaster General of Karakhor, an honourary uncle but the one whom she loved best of all, and although he met her eye without blinking, his grizzled face was a mask of iron. Beside him stood Kananda, her full brother, looking as though a caged tiger savaged his breast from the inside.

Maryam's heart sank even further. She looked away from them, through the avenue formed by their waiting bodies to the high arched doorway that opened out onto the courtyard at the far end of the hall. Outside in the courtyard, the wedding party from Maghalla waited with as many of their entourage as could be crowded between the enflanking colonnades. The musicians were playing and there was the sound of coarse laughter and merriment. The sacrificial altar burned with high, bright flames before the fountains in the center. She could see their glitter and the plumes of white smoke reaching into the blue sky.

Her father would give her hand to the hand of Sardar of Maghalla and speak the holy words of bride-giving. Kaseem would offer sacred prayers and blessings. The fires would flare and Sardar would lead her three times around the sacred flames and the ritual would be complete. Sardar the Merciless would be her New Lord and Master.

Maryam held her head high, gripped hard on the cold hand

of Kara-Rashna, and took the first step down the long hall to the open courtyard. *I am a princess of Karakhor*, her strong will insisted. *I will do my duty*.

Her procession swelled behind her and a trumpet fanfare filled the great dome ceiling and the arches above as the heralds stationed on either side of the doorway saw her approach. The sound was joyful, exhilarating, and fought bravely against the subdued silence of her family and courtiers behind her. The trumpeteers lining the walls above the courtyard took up the soaring fanfare, drums rolled, the conch shells blared, and Maryam stepped out into the sunlight.

She blinked, almost blinded by the glare. Her ears were momentarily deafened by the great roar of approval that rose from the massed throats of Maghalla. All her senses reeled: the smells of roasting meats, fresh flowers and fruits, incense and a thousand perfumes, all assailed her nostrils, and the sweet sting of the sacred smoke from burning sandalwood was a cloying taste in her throat. She swayed for a moment, recovered her balance, and opened her eyes.

A sea of faces stared up at her, cheering, shouting, pounding each other's backs or pounding fists into palms. The men of Maghalla were clearly not disappointed with their new princess. Their women laughed and clapped more politely, and some of them had the grace to look jealous. They were rough faces, many of them brutish, but Maryam looked for only one.

Sardar of Maghalla was unmistakable. He stood a pace forward of all the rest with a small knot of resplendent chieftains and lords behind him. He wore a tunic, a turban and pantaloons of blue and gold, and his jewels were blue sapphires and yellow amber. A huge curved sword and an equally wicked-looking curved dagger with ceremonial jewel-encrusted hilts were thrust through the red sash at his waist. His hands were planted on his hips with the stubby fingers spread wide to display a score of glittering rings. A mailed warrior who could have dwarfed an ox held the Black Leopard banner so that it floated boldly above his master's head.

Sardar was broad and squat, with shoulders even wider than his banner bearer, and his arms were long and powerful. There were tufts of thick black hair at his wrists and at the neck of his tunic, suggesting a hairy body that would be more like that of an animal than a man. He was not old, no more than forty years, but that was no consolation as Maryam stared at his face.

Sardar wore a fearsome grin on features that would have been ugly even before they had been brutally scarred. It was a face more ape-like than human, black and wrinkled with bloated lips and wide-flared nostrils. The deep set eyes were coal black in red-veined whites, and reminded Maryam of a wild pig she had seen once in a cage on the market. The scar tissue that gave the final touch of horror began just below the left eye, slashed through the corner of the mouth, and finished in an unnaturally deep cleft at the chin. It was a face that she could not have imagined in her worst nightmare.

The shock as the blood drained swiftly from her own face only caused more laughter from the crowd below. Sardar saw her repugnance and only grinned wider. She saw that his teeth were rotten and knew that his breath must stink. The brave words—*I am a princess of Karakhor. I will do my duty*—no longer echoed in her mind.

Stunned, she allowed herself to be led down the broad swathe of marble steps into the courtyard, until her father stopped her face-to-face with the horror that was to be her husband. Behind her, Kaseem was reciting a blessing and the other priests were chanting mantras, and in a half swoon the awful, sub-human face of Sardar seemed to dissolve, only to harden again as she forced herself to hold tight to her senses.

The pig eyes burned hotly into her own and she saw that there could never be love there, only a fierce, unbridled lust.

Her father had lifted her limp hand forward to place it in the rough, hairy palm of Sardar. Kaseem and the other priests fell silent, and even the crowd was hushed. The fanfare gave one last trumpet flourish and fell away into silence.

"Sardar, Lord of all Maghalla," Kara-Rashna began his address in flat and hollow tones. "This is my first daughter, Maryam, beloved of all Karakhor. Take her hand and walk the sacred circuits thrice round the sacred flame. Let her be, from this day forth, your own true and faithful wife."

The speech should have been longer, with more flowering phrases invoking the gods and extolling the virtues of both bride and groom, but Kara-Rashna had to pause as if to steel his own heart before he continued. Sardar was oblivious to such subtleties and to the responses he was expected to make. He tightened his grasp on Maryam's hand, clearly eager to lead her around the flames with no further delay.

Maryam stared into his eyes, and suddenly the iron will that had determined that she must do her duty turned a swift, soul-searching circle in her mind. She was a princess of Karakhor and she would not accept this cruel trick of fate. As firmly as she had determined to endure and obey only a few moments before, she now decided with death-defying finality that she would not. Like a flash of fire the word burned behind her eyes and was ripped from her constricted throat.

"No!" She shouted and tore her hand from the bestial grasp that held it.

She flung herself backward, but the crush of those behind her blocked her immediate escape.

"No," she shouted again, defiant and trembling. "I will not marry him."

There was a stunned gasp from the mass of on-lookers. Time froze. Kara-Rashna turned to stare at his daughter with a look of confusion. The face of Sardar grew black and even uglier with rage.

"What is this?" he snarled. "You are mine, woman. In Maghalla you will learn how to behave." He stepped forward, snatched her hand again and dragged her toward him. Maryam struggled but this time his iron grip was prepared and she could not break it.

"Leave her," a cold voice demanded. And suddenly her full brother Kananda was at her side. His left hand clamped upon her upper wrist, side by side with Sardar's. For a moment she thought that her bones would be crushed between them, and she heard the scrape of steel upon scabbard as Kananda's right hand half drew the sword at his waist.

"Gently, Lord Prince," Jahan hissed in Kananda's ear. The old warmaster's left hand was heavy upon Kananda's elbow, preventing him from drawing his sword and pushing it back a few inches into the scabbard. But Jahan's own right hand was resting on the hilt of his own sword.

Sardar stepped back, his face flushed now with rage. His own hand dropped to his sword-hilt and on both sides a score of blades cleared the first few inches of their scabbards. Maghalla and Karakhor backed apart.

"What insult is this?" Sardar roared, turning his anger against the flustered king.

Kara-Rashna was hesitant a moment longer, and then he sighed, it seemed, with relief. He stared from the grotesque face of the man who would have been his son-in-law to the white-lipped mask of his daughter, and then to his oldest and dearest friend.

"It seems our daughter shames us," he said quietly. The

reproach in his voice was for himself alone, and he too dropped his hand lightly on his own sword.

Jahan nodded, and in his eyes there was a smile. He glanced upward and both Kara-Rashna and Sardar followed his meaningful gaze. The trumpeters lining the courtyard walls had vanished, and from behind them ranks of archers had stepped forward. At Jahan's almost imperceptible nod, each man nocked an arrow to his bow. As always, the warmaster general had been ready for anything.

"A trap," one of Sardar's chieftains snarled, his anger laced with fear.

"No trap," Kara-Rashna reassured them all. "Just a misunderstanding."

"I think," Jahan said politely to Sardar, "That our daughter is unwell. You can see for yourself how pale she is, how near to fainting. We regret that, for today, the wedding must be postponed."

"If there is no marriage, there is no peace," Sardar bellowed. "This insult can only be wiped out with blood."

He glared hatefully at his intended bride, and Kananda carefully handed his sister back to her attendants and their mother. The ranks of his brothers and uncles re-formed behind him. Maryam stared at their defensive backs and listened to Sardar's vile threats and cursing.

With tears in her eyes and her heart beating wildly, Maryam knew that she had won. Her father had relented and Karakhor would not force her into this marriage. She found her feet and fled back into the palace with her mother and her attendants running behind her.

She had failed in her duty and had been reprieved, but at what terrible cost for the future she could not even begin to know.

Chapter Two

Kananda, First Prince of Golden Karakhor, halted his war elephant on the crest of the jungle ridge. He was less than an hour's march from where the Tri-Thruster command vessel lay hidden in a wooded valley, although as yet he was unaware of the spaceship's presence. The intrusion from another world was three days old, but still unknown to its local inhabitants.

For a moment the first-born heir to city, kingdom and empire paused, soothing the slow-moving elephant with a soft word of command. The great beast stood patient and solid, its wrinkled eyelids drooping. A fearsome iron spike, its needle point tipped with red, protruded from the massive leather head harness and below that the long and powerful ivory curves of the sharpened tusks were painted with white and gore-crimson stripes. Terrifying in charge and battle, the elephant was temporarily content to half slumber. In the heat, even the effort of reaching its trunk for the nearest branch of tender green leaves was too much.

To the south, the jungles thickened, a rising plateau of gloomy forests and wild, tangled gorges where strange beasts and strange men dwelt in half-darkness and primitive savagery. Further south rose a vastness of foreboding mountains, and beyond, the great, wild Godavari River, of which Kananda had heard but never seen. The tribes of these regions were subhuman, more like monkeys than men, shambling brutes too poor and ignorant to be worth taming, but dangerous enough to be kept at bay. An occasional show of strength was needed here on the southern edge of the lands of Karakhor.

The real danger was to the west, far beyond the visible horizon, where the rising power of Maghalla was growing in arrogance and strength. The Maghallan tribes had begun their invasion from the northwest two generations before, forcing a route between the Great Thar Desert and the trackless foothills of the mighty Himalaya ice-peaks that formed the northern edge of the known world. They had subdued the passive plains people who lived between the Chambal and Narmada rivers and their settlements had grown into the crude but war-like kingdom which now had the boldness to challenge Karakhor.

Kananda's lips tightened as his gaze focused on the far hills that formed the border lands. In the cruel reign of Sardar the Merciless, the very name of Maghalla could conjure fear and trembling in the breasts of women and babes, and even for a royal prince, fearless in his manhood, youth and pride, it caused a grim bracing of both his physical and spiritual self.

Then pride became the dominant emotion, a warm glow that filled his breast and expanded his being, and Kananda smiled as he thought fondly of his sister, Maryam. He recalled those fateful, blood-pounding moments almost a year past when the first royal princess had bravely spurned the arrangements for her marriage to Sardar and Maghalla, which their father's soft-stomached advisers had briefly entertained. Such an alliance, it was now realized, could only have polluted the royal bloodline of the house of Karakhor and could only have been envisaged by the weak council of men who had never seen the half-human ugliness of Sardar.

Mighty had been the wrath of Sardar, and now Maghalla and Karakhor prepared for war. Sardar saw himself as the recipient of the gravest insult that could only be wiped away in blood.

From behind the young prince, disrupting his thoughts, came the sounds of the advancing hunt. Wild birds fled shrieking in flashes of incandescent colour and startled white-faced monkeys scattered through the sun-lanced treetops, hurrying away from the shouted voices of huntsmen, trackers and warriors. Spotted deer leaped more gracefully into the distant gloom and the crash and tear of breaking trees heralded the trampling feet of the war elephants.

Kananda turned as the foliage parted noisily behind him, and a second war spike protruded through the tangle of green. Then the elephant carrying his brother, Ramesh, forced its way up the hill to stand beside him. Both princes wore high leather helmets, embroidered with golden thread and encrusted with jewels around the diamond sunburst insignia of their rank. They wore heavy necklaces of gold and precious stones, armbands and bracelets of gold. Bright sashes of royal scarlet supported their simple white loincloths, and on each prince, the hilt of a jeweled dagger. Their calf-high boots were of soft deerskin, fringed with red and silver tassles, and soled with hard leather. Their weapons, bows and arrows, swords and javelins, were hung on the harness of the elephants, close at hand where they were mounted on the broad necks of the huge tuskers.

Ramesh was younger, his handsome bronzed features a more boyish and care-free mirror of Kananda. Not yet as hard-muscled in physique, as confident in manner or as skilled in warfare as his elder, he still carried himself with all the promise and pride of a Karakhoran prince. His eyes sparkled and he was anxious to move on, his heart too joyful to be afraid.

"Well, Kananda," he demanded. "Where is the tiger you promised me? Our hunt is three days old and again the sun is near to noon. And as yet I have not seen so much as a whisker of a striped cat."

Kananda laughed and briefly touched the necklace of tiger teeth that lay upon his own bare breast. It was the only difference of apparel between them. "Fear not, little brother. Twice the trackers say that we have only just missed a cat that has escaped from our path. The third one cannot be so blessed by the gods. Soon we will find a beast worthy of your spear. Perhaps *Indra* is even now driving toward us the mightiest tiger of them all, especially for you."

Ramesh drew his hunting spear from the thong that held it against his elephant's neck. "Mighty *Indra*," he shouted to the sky. "God of thunder and of storm—God of the lightning's flash and all the forces of thunder—send me a mighty beast that I might slay it and prove my valour."

"And boast of it to the fair maidens of the city forever and a day," Kananda finished impiously for him. "May they swoon at your glory, and heap garlands and kisses at your feet—and perhaps other select parts of your noble person."

The two princes laughed uproariously until a third elephant toiled up to rest on Kananda's left flank. This beast wore no war spike and carried both a driver and a passenger on a swaying seat high on its back. The driver was naked but for a brief and simple loincloth, but the passenger sweated in swathing white robes, despite the shade of the white umbrella above his balding head. The wrinkled lines of his ancient and normally gentle face were now registering deep shock and anger.

"Noble princes, you forget yourselves," the old Brahmin spoke fiercely. "Your mockery ill befits you, and the gods are not partial to such scorn. Rest assured that your impiety will not go unanswered."

Ramesh flushed with embarrassment, while Kananda bowed his head in momentary shame. “Tonight we shall make due obeisance to Mighty *Indra*,” the elder said carefully. “We will light the sacred flame and make due sacrifice.”

“It may not be enough,” answered Kaseem, his tone reminding them that he was both the high priest and holiest of the holy men of Karakhor. And he voiced another grumble, “You are also both reckless with your lives and earthly duty. We hunt here in the southlands not only for a tiger to raise the fame of Prince Ramesh. Our main purpose is to show our strength to the savages and impress upon them the folly an alliance with Magahalla. Such a duty will not be served if you get yourselves slain by riding too far ahead. You must rein back and stay with our warriors and the hunt.”

Kananda sighed. His impulse was to forge ahead, but Kaseem held their father’s mandate when Kara-Rashna was not there to supervise his own sons. They were irritated by the old man’s caution, but respected his years and his wisdom.

“Your chastisement is deserved,” Kananda said. He briefly bowed his head again but not before Kasseem had seen that the twinkle of merriment was not quite dimmed in his eyes.

Kaseem frowned, preparing himself to deliver a sermon, but the princes were saved by a wild cry from the right flank of the hunt. It was a cry taken up and repeated by a great swell of excitement, echoing in the hot, languid air from a hundred throats.

“Tiger! Tiger! *Tiger*!”

“Tiger!” Kananda added joyously to the sudden uproar, and upon his face there flashed a brilliant smile. “The gods are not angry, Kaseem. They forgive us. Come, Ramesh!”

Prodding their huge mounts with javelin and spear butts, the two princes plunged together down the ridge, steering to the right where the first cry had sounded. The blare of a hunting horn now marked the centre of the chase and the whole line of mounted nobles and running warriors was swinging in that direction. Behind them Kaseem clasped his hands and offered a brief prayer to heaven, while his driver, knowing well his master's temperament, goaded the third elephant more cautiously in pursuit of the hunt.

On this chase only the princes and the priest rode elephants. The sons of the other noble houses of Karakhor rode horses, having left their chariots behind on the plains. Now the riders were moving out to the flanks of the long line of running warriors and huntsmen. Their task was to forge ahead and contain the great cat in the running V of the hunt, and finally when it had tired, to turn it back to the centre of the line where the fates ordained it must die upon the ready spear of the Prince Ramesh.

The hunt had turned and reformed on the run with a fluid efficiency that gladdened Kananda's heart. It swept down from the ridge and swept westward along a shallow valley. Three horns now answered each other with exhilarating blasts that echoed between the low hills on either side. The short, deep blasts from the head huntsman marked the path of the fleeing tiger. A succession of longer, higher notes marked the position of the young lord Gujar, forging ahead on the right flank. From the left a more vibrant fanfare attested that there Jayhad, son of the old warmaster Jahan, was boldly leading the field.

Side by side, Kananda and Ramesh urged their thundering tuskers onward. Twice they almost trampled the racing foot warriors in their path, and only the quick wits and agility of the men in danger enabled them to save themselves. Both elephants were trumpeting fearsomely in their excitement and had become all but uncontrollable. Kananda saw the green helmet of Hamir, the head huntsman, bobbing through the shoulder high grass and foliage and turned his mount to follow on the man's heels. In another moment he would have run the man down and he hammered the butt of his javelin desperately between the elephant's eyes in the signal to slow it down. The tusker blundered almost to a halt, all but pitching the young prince forward over its head. Behind him Ramesh's laughter rang wild and free.

There was still no glimpse of the striped beast, but the keen eye of the huntsman marked the trail. Hamir moved at a fast crouch, tracking on the run with a skill that was unmatched throughout the empire. In one hand he held the hunting horn that was constantly at his lips, in the other a short-handled but long bladed spear. He swerved suddenly, taking a new course that led up the slope of the hill to the left.

Kananda yelled at the hunt and his elephant to bring them all on the turn. There was a general confused floundering and crashing of bodies through the undergrowth. A peacock fled screaming through the grass and the elephants trumpeted again in their toiling frenzy. From the right the pursuing shouts became edged with anger and frustration as hunters and warriors realized that their quarry had broken away from them. From the left the yelling voices became diffused into gasps and panting as the men on that side turned to ascend the slope. From the top of the ridge there came a blood-chilling death scream which Kananda could not identify as coming from a man or an animal.

Kananda froze. The blood that had pulsed hot in his veins seemed to pause in mid flow. His mind was suddenly crystal-clear, sharpening to a new alertness, and his soul quailed. Instinctively he knew the gods no longer smiled. The elephant carried him on and a moment later they crashed through a flimsy screen of small trees and onto a bare patch of the ridge top. Kananda saw a crushed circle of yellowed grass that was bloodied with gore. A black stallion was flung to one side of the circle with its throat and flank ripped wide as though *Indra* Himself had slashed it open with a mighty sword-cut. The crumpled body of the young lord Jayhad lay just as raw and red and obscene on the far side of the circle. Of the tiger there was no sign.

The awful cry had been that of man and horse blended together. Kananda knew that now and he tasted his own fear mixed in with the rich, sweet smell of the fresh gore. His heart lurched, but then anger steeled his heart and mind. He and Jayhad had been boyhood friends. They had played together, and raced each other on foot, in chariots, and as swimmers across the broad Mahanadi. They had thrown dice together, got drunk together, and competed for the smiles of the same young girls. Jayhad had been almost as much a brother to him as Ramesh, and suddenly this was no longer Ramesh's tiger. Jayhad's blood cried out for vengeance and with a fierce cry of grief and fury Kananda answered the call.

Hamir reached the hilltop at the same time as Ramesh and three of the horseman who had accompanied Jayhad. The old huntsman's experienced eye swept the scene and his weathered face paled as if confirming a dark suspicion that had been forming in his mind. His trackers had flushed the big cat by chance without first finding and examining its spoor, but now he was certain that this was no ordinary beast. He shouted a warning to Kananda, but in the turmoil of angry and fear-filled voices he was drowned out. The First Prince of Karakhor was voicing his own cry in the same moment and was already urging his tusker down into the next valley.

The hunt and the horns were behind him now and Kananda trusted blindly to fate and the gods and the charging elephant beneath him. If it was *Indra's* will, he might yet catch up with the escaping tiger.

ଔ

The five-strong crew of the Tri-Thruster had learned to relax. Their mission was to make friendly contact with the largest and most civilized population of the planet, and so the great pear-shaped subcontinent of the southern hemisphere had been the obvious choice. There had been signs of habitation around the Fertile Crescent beside the island-dotted inland sea to the west, and again to the north where long rivers wound across the vast land mass that lay behind the planet's highest mountains. But here, on the wide, lush plains below that towering white barrier, bisected by a dozen major rivers in a warm tropical climate, lay the widest areas of cultivation and the only signs of large cities and towns that they had been able to observe in seven orbits.

However, caution had decreed that they should make their first landing somewhere remote from the nearest settlement so that they would have time to rest and acclimatize themselves to the planet's slight atmospheric and gravitational differences before they attempted to make contact. The cramped, eighty-seven day journey through the solar system had left them all tense and strained. Space travel, between the traumas of launch and landing, was an infinitely tedious process that led to irritation and short tempers among the best of crews. And on this trip they could not afford to have their peace mission turn into confrontation through some simple lack of diplomatic tact.

Zela, Commander First Class of the Alphan Space Corps, commander of the ship and leader of the Alphan expedition to the third planet, lay at ease in the cool shade of a bamboo grove. Her eyes were closed and her thoughts drifted peacefully as she listened to the soft gurgling of the nearby stream. Her one-piece silver zip-suit was open for comfort and beneath it she wore only a brief pair of pants. Her arms were stretched back, her hands clasped behind her head, and even in that semi-flattened position it was clear that her breasts, like those of all Alphan women, were firm, round and voluptuous. Her flawless skin was a light golden colour, a few shades paler than her long, golden hair.

In one ever-responsible corner of her mind, she marked the positions of her companions. Blair, her energetic First Officer was upstream, almost certainly absorbed in the scientific analysis of more of the planet's flora and fauna. Cadel, the Engineering Officer, was back on the ship, forever checking and testing, writing up his log books or reading his manuals. Only Kyle and Laurya had any sense. Her Weapons and Communications officers were together on the far side of the stream, out of sight and out of hearing, at the very least holding hands, and more likely stealing another opportunity to make love.

Zela smiled wistfully at the mental image and felt a brief touch of jealousy. Her loins felt sensuous and she wished that she were some exotic wild woman, and native of this beautiful blue-green planet. Perhaps then Blair would find a scientific interest in her. Blair was not unhandsome to look at, and at least he had a first class body. Or perhaps if she were robotic, with an internal system of electrodes and microchips, then Cadel would find her an object worthy of his love and fascination. She chuckled aloud at her thoughts. She should not be thinking these things, she told herself. A commander should remain a little bit aloof. Love encounters at her level were not good for discipline.

The tiny wings of a dragonfly beat a gentle murmur close to her ear. There was a drone from other insects feasting on the nectar of a profusion of scarlet and yellow flowers but they did not bother her. A single ray of direct sunlight found its way through the green blades of bamboo and warmed the bare nipple of her left breast. Zela closed her eyes and drifted toward sleep. She heard the splash of fisher birds darting in and out of the stream, a dove cooed, a lark warbled, and somewhere faraway there sounded a faint, shrill scream.

Zela was abruptly awake and alert. She sat up, her head cocked and listening. They had chosen this valley because, although there was a clear glade where the ship could land beside the stream, it was otherwise thickly wooded with tall trees and screening jungle to keep them hidden. However, from the pre-landing survey, she knew that the land rose in a long hill to the south, and it was from the direction of the ridge top that the sound had come. Now she faintly heard other sounds that were not in tune with her sylvan surroundings, far-off human voices and the harsh notes of some kind of musical instrument.

Zela reached for her belt pack and deftly fastened it around her waist. In its neat pockets the belt held emergency food, medical and tool kits, her communicator and a lazer hand weapon. She used the communicator to call the others back to the ship, and without haste began to move in that direction herself.

Something was definitely disturbing the forest to her left. Birds and monkeys were now shrieking in flight through the treetops. Zela hesitated and drew the lazer weapon with her right hand. For a moment she was uncertain whether to hurry ahead or to wait for Blair. Then the panicked scream of the trumpeting elephant assailed her ears. The tusked beast was descending the steep ridge too fast, its huge bulk slipping and sliding as it flattened every obstacle in its path. Its scream and the thunderous crashing of its approach focused Zela's attention too far back along the line of the pursuit and she was facing the wrong direction as the tiger leaped out into the glade fifty yards ahead of her. As it landed, it opened its throat to let out a great roar of rage.

Zela pivoted on her heel, half turning and catching her boot in a tangle of grass. She fell sideways on her right hip and elbow, her eyes wide in horror at what she saw. The huge red-and-white striped beast was twice the length of a man and almost as high at the shoulders. A fearsome sabre tooth curved down from each side of the snarling jaws that already dripped with blood. The eyes burned and the cat roared again, and then launched itself toward her in a running charge.

Having landed on her right elbow, it was impossible for Zela to aim the lazer weapon in her hand, but she fired it anyway. The bolt of white light missed the bounding fury of fang, fur and claw, but struck a tree close to the animal's path. The tree was felled as though by a clean axe-blow and simultaneously burst into flames. The cat turned, startled and screaming, to bound back in the direction from which it had come.

The forest parted with another mighty crash of breaking trees and branches and the war elephant lumbered into view with Kananda still clinging precariously to its neck with his knees. The Hindu prince had exchanged his lightweight throwing javelin for a heavier hunting spear, which was poised in his hand. But events were moving too fast for him and springing too many surprises. He saw a brief glimpse of the golden-haired woman in the silver suit, and then tiger and elephant met in a gigantic clash of hurtling tusk and tooth and claw. For the first time, Kananda realized that he had been chasing a sabre-tooth, twice as large as any ordinary tiger, and as dangerous as one of the wrathful gods themselves.

The gods were with the tiger. As it leaped upon the elephant, it missed impaling itself upon the tusks and the war spike and crashed against the side of the elephant's head. One great paw raked the elephant's eye, blinding it instantly on the one side. One razor-edged claw from the other front paw laid open Kananda's thigh and the young prince was knocked backwards. As he fell, he thrust with his spear and wounded the tiger's shoulder.

Hurled from his mount, Kananda landed on his back and shoulders, his fall mercifully broken by a clump of bushes. He was bleeding and bruised but quickly struggled to his feet. The sabre tooth still clung to the head of the roaring elephant, snarling as it slashed with fang and claws. Half blind and mad with pain, the elephant backed up, dragging its tormentor with it. Kananda steadied himself and with his spear braced in both hands, he ran forward to plunge its blade into the tiger's side.

The great cat wheeled, screaming now with pain of its own, leaving the elephant to attack the challenging man. Kananda withdrew his spear with a wrench, knowing that if the shaft was snapped off he would be defenceless. He wielded the weapon in desperate fury to fend of the flailing claws and the monstrous jaws.

Zela was on her feet now and running forward, her composure partially recovered and her hand steady. But the man blocked a clear line of fire. She had to wait as man and beast fought with awful ferocity, and then the whirling conflict presented her with a chance. She fired and her second bolt hit the tiger in the side, the energy-charged beam burning its way deep into the huge body and scorching the red-and-white fur. The tiger howled but was still not finished. Kananda was flung aside and the sabre tooth turned again to charge at the woman.

Zela held her ground and fired her third bolt. Three was the most these small hand-held weapons could discharge without losing lethal power and the third beam lanced full into the spitting jaws. Still, its charge carried the beast forward and Zela went down beneath it. The great cat was dying but there was enough strength left in it to make a final kill. The sabre-toothed jaws loomed over her within inches of closing on the soft golden throat. Then Kanada made his final charge and his spear penetrated the cat's neck. The thrust was deep and the monster arched backward in its death agony. Kananda pushed with all his strength and the cat fell sideways, its fall pulling the bloodied spear from his hands.

The man and woman from different planets gazed at each other in bewilderment and wonder. Beside them, the muscles and limbs of their mutual enemy still writhed in lingering death spasms, and after a moment Kananda reached for the woman's arms and tugged her clear. Then a great dizziness came over him, his head reeled, his body swayed, and he collapsed beside her.

Chapter Three

Zela lay breathless, temporarily stunned and in a state of shock. On the edge of the clearing, Kananda's dying elephant had sunk to its knees, weakened by its terrible loss of blood, and it raised its trunk in one last anguished, gasping bellow, before it toppled sideways and expired. Then the clearing was still and silent. There was only the sickly reek of the blood that was soaked and spattered everywhere over the crushed grass and foliage, from the elephant, from the tiger, from Kananda and, Zela realized as her senses began to swim back, from her own left arm. Her suit and the flesh beneath had been slashed from shoulder to elbow. Pain began to seep through the initial numbness, and as she struggled to push herself up onto her right elbow, she had to clench her teeth against the need to cry out.

Through the mist of tears in her eyes, she stared at the sabretooth. Even in death the size of it made her shudder. The savage jaws that had almost snatched her head from her shoulders were still open wide in its final snarl. There was still menace in the red-stained sabres that were like two curved ivory daggers, and only the now-dulled eyes reassured her that she was safe. At first she was fearful that they might blaze again, that the tiger might still possess some last flicker of life, but at last she turned her head slowly to look at the strange earth native who had been her ally in the unexpected battle.

The man was as tall as any man of her own race, perhaps an inch taller than Blair who was the tallest in her crew. He had the body of a trained athlete, fit and supple with firm muscles and no body hair. His skin was bronzed, a richer, more reddish gold than her own. His face was handsome, and even though he had fainted it still hinted at strength of character in the clean lines of the bone structure and the firm jaw. His jeweled helmet had rolled away to reveal dark hair that was cut short, tousled and wet with sweat. His courage he had already proven in their fight with the tiger, and fleetingly she wondered how he would make love.

She banished the thought as she realized that his leg was bleeding badly, more so than her own arm. There were more practical things to think about and her hand moved to the medical kit in her belt pack. Then she cautiously became still as the silence was broken by the crash of more approaching beasts and men.

The second elephant blundered noisily into view with Ramesh mounted on its neck and urging it forward. As the green tangle of jungle parted, the young prince gaped with amazement at the scene before his tusker continued to plunge forward, and then, realizing that he was about to trample his own brother, Ramesh yelled at it to halt. His spear butt banged on the huge forehead and his mount stopped with one giant foot poised to throw its shadow over Kananda's face. The elephant was well trained, but in the excitement of the hunt it was baffled and confused. It hesitated, but then the training won and, responding to the urgent commands of its rider, it eased back a pace and stopped. Ramesh stared down, sweating, and he too was bewildered by all that he saw.

More arrivals burst out of the forest. Three of the horse riders who had accompanied the unfortunate Jayhad reined their steeds alongside the war elephant and their prince. The head huntsman and a dozen warriors arrived on foot, and with every moment more warriors and hunters flooded out from the barrier of green. All of them were armed with raised spears. They formed a startled, but threatening circle behind Ramesh and the young lords.

Blair reached the clearing from the opposite side, a lazer weapon ready in his hand. Zela saw the silver flash of his suit from the corner of her eye and spoke without turning her head.

"Wait, Blair, do not alarm them."

Blair stopped, motionless at her command, but the lazer was still pointed and ready. The warriors recognized a fighting stance and the sharper-witted suspected rightly that the stranger held a weapon. Spear arms tensed and a dozen voices spoke in warning. With Kananda fallen they looked to Ramesh for a lead. The young prince bit his lip uncertainly. He was not ready for this level of responsibility. At the same time he was a Karakhoran prince and with Kananda unconscious, he was the only acting member of the royal line present. He looked down at Kananda and read the signs. The dead tiger told its own tale.

"Wait," Ramesh decided. "He is only one man."

"There are three."

Ramesh looked up as Kasim, one of the horse-riders, spoke at his side. He saw two more of the strange silver-suited figures wading across a small stream. They too held mysterious weapon-like implements in their hands. Kyle and Laurya came to stand silently beside Blair, the former putting a cautionary hand on his companion's weapon arm as he saw that the situation, although tense, was not desperate.

"They are dangerous," Kasim said nervously. "We should slay them all before more appear."

The head huntsman was looking over the dead sabretooth with a practised eye. His fears were confirmed and he was only surprised to see the beast dead.

"Sire," Hamir said slowly, speaking in Hindu which Zela and her companions could not understand. "There is a wound I do not understand in the side of the beast. It was not made by a spear. The flesh and fur are burned as though by fire."

"Perhaps that is what those weapons do," Kasim suggested. "We should kill these people, before they kill us as they have killed Kananda and the tiger."

A dozen voices shouted assent, and a dozen spear arms were poised to throw, but still they awaited the royal command. And still Ramesh hesitated. Then another elephant pushed its way up to his side.

"There is no burn wound on the Prince Kananda." The high priest Kaseem made the solemn observation from the lofty perch of his canopied seat on the elephant's back. "If these people slew the beast, then perhaps it was to save our prince."

Ramesh glanced at the old Brahmin with relief. "What do you advise?" he asked in a rare moment of complete deference.

Before the old man could answer, a new voice chose to make itself heard, booming above the assembled heads as though coming from the sky itself.

"Zela." The voice was Cadel's, amplified through a communication speaker from the ship. "I have the ships main battle lazer targeted on your new friends. Ready to fire on your command."

Prince and priest, warriors and hunters, all drew back in sudden terror from the sound. They stared upward with bloodless faces, and then a chorus of gasps, whispers and exclamations focused their gaze further down the valley, where the Tri-Thruster command ship stood tall and graceful against the green jungle and the brilliant blue sky.

"A black temple—a temple of steel." The words were choked

hoarsely from the ashen ranks of the Hindus. "These must be the gods—the gods speak—the voice is *Indra !*.

"Cadel." Zela used their moment of confusion to speak into her communicator. "Do nothing." She looked up to Kaseem and Ramesh and smiled as warmly as she knew how. Their languages were different, but a smile was a universal sign of friendship, or at least she so hoped. "We are your friends," she said quietly. "Please let us help you." She knew they could not understand, but trusted that the tone of her voice would add to the reassurance of her smile.

Ramesh could only gape, while Kaseem suffered an internal turmoil of mental struggle and physical emotion. The old priest was torn between faith and doubt, fear and ecstasy, and hope and despair. These beings were nothing like any of his dearly held images of the gods. They were only the size of men, and they lacked the multiplicity of arms and hands essential for the multiplicity of tasks involved in maintaining the whole of creation. They did not wield thunder and lightning, like mighty *Indra*, the god of the elements and of war. Their feet were firmly fixed upon the Earth. They did not reign in the far blue heaven where the god *Varuna* was emperor and overseer of all that happened in the universe. And they were not wreathed in sacred flames like the fire-god *Agni* who carried the smoke and incense of sacrifices to the two great gods. At the same time, the strange voice from the sky had rolled like thunder, and the tiger had been burned with fire. Perhaps only a lightning bolt could have killed such a devil beast. If these beings were not deities, it seemed that perhaps they did have their powers. Perhaps they were messengers of the gods.

The old man closed his eyes in anguish and swayed dizzily. His tormented mind simply could not cope and deep in his heart he was not sure that he wanted to meet the gods. As a physical reality he was not even sure that he had ever believed in them, he had often thought of them as symbolic of a reality that was essentially spiritual and metaphysical. Perhaps he was wrong and *Indra* had sent these messengers to punish him. The thought stabbed him with a soul-struck fear, and he would have fallen if Ramesh had not been close enough to reach a steadying hand for his shoulder.

Zela saw that the old man was temporarily incapable of decision and gambled that the others would not act without his lead. She turned to her companions and kept her voice calm and gentle as she issued her orders.

"Relax and put the lazers down on the ground. Laurya, their culture seems male-dominated and so they will probably have less fear of a woman. Come to me slowly."

Cautiously, Laurya crossed the open glade. Like Zela, she was golden-haired and golden-skinned, although a few inches shorter and slighter of build. Her silver suit hugged her figure tightly and the contours of breast and hip were clearly defined. She stopped beside her commander who was still resting on her good elbow on the reddened grass. Zela held up her injured arm.

"Treat this, but do it slowly, and do it so that they can all watch what you are doing."

Laurya nodded, and conscious that almost every eye was fixed on her movements, she took the medical kit from her belt pack and began her task. Carefully, she cut away the bloodied silver sleeve, and then cleaned the long gash on Zela's arm. Then, holding the two edges of the cut together, she used a combined anaesthetic and sealing spray to dull the pain and close the wound. Finally she administered an injection against infection.

When the job was done, Zela rose to her feet and showed her arm to both Kaseem and Ramesh. The old priest had now opened up his eyes, giving up the hopeless struggle to understand, and simply watched with wonder. Zela displayed her arm on all sides, and then, trusting that she had made her point, took out her own medical kit and knelt over Kananda. There was an immediate rustle of spears and movement among the alarmed warriors.

Kaseem was still at a loss. He stared into the face of Zela, and then at Laurya who had cautiously moved back one pace. He realized that the backward step was meant to be reassuring and non-threatening, and for the first time he took full notice of the gently smiling face of the second of these strange females.

Laurya's eyes were green under fine golden lashes, the deep cool green of a forest pool fringed with golden rushes, or the bright flash of green in the gold of a sunbird's wing. And they were another violent shock to his already over-loaded nervous system, a sharp emotional upheaval that seemed to leap up in his very soul. It was as though he had seen those eyes before, even though the woman was an alien deity.

The thought was impossible and again he almost swooned. The tree tops and the spires of the black steel temple all seemed to revolve slowly around his head. With them, the nearest warriors swam in and out of his vision. They were still awaiting his word, spears raised, muscles tensed. Ramesh was looking to him desperately. One of the spear arms moved back another few inches, the last move before the throw.

"No," Kaseem croaked. His reasons were conflicting but the command came through. He felt instinctively that these strange gods were trying to help. If not, then mere human arms with spears and swords were probably powerless against them. But most of all, something inside him knew that he had to protect the green-eyed woman, even if the other was a threat to his prince. He realized that he could hardly hear his own voice and struggled to speak again.

"No, hold your weapons."

Ramesh still looked uncertain, but the warriors heard and obeyed.

ଓ

Zela made sure that all her movements were as clearly visible as Laurya's had been, and it was while she was cleaning the fearsome gash on his thigh that Kananda came slowly to his senses. The first thing he saw was her face, the smiling, beautiful face of an administering angel, framed in its glorious cascade of rich golden hair. Her eyes were a deep, magical blue, a colour unknown among his brown-eyed people, with curling golden lashes. His gaze flickered to the open silver suit, still revealing those magnificent, plumply rounded golden breasts, and he was a man with a soul lost in wonder and a body lost to desire. In his mind there was none of the priest's doubt and confusion. To Kananda she could only be a goddess, and he did not need to be told that she came from the stars.

He tried to rise, supporting himself on one elbow and reaching out one hand toward her. Pain stabbed through his thigh and made him wince. Zela leaned forward and gently pushed him down.

"Do not try to move," she advised softly.

Her words were alien to Kananda, but her voice sounded like sweet music to his ears and her meaning was plain. He looked down at the dressing on his thigh. He saw that the linen was of a different colour and texture to the wound wrappings that Kaseem carried in his saddle bag, and so understood that the strangers had treated his hurts. He remembered the goddess helping him to fight off the tiger and saw the beast lying dead. He gave her a grateful smile.

"I am Kananda," he told her, "First Prince of Golden Karakhor." He launched into the full list of his titles and then saw from her blank look that she could not understand him either. He laughed at his own folly. "Kananda," he repeated more simply and touched a finger to his own forehead.

Zela still looked uncertain. Kananda repeated his name and the gesture. Then he pointed to Ramesh and Kaseem, stating their names in turn.

Zela understood. She placed a forefinger on her own temple and said, "Zela."

Kananda repeated the name three times until its pronounciation rang true. Again he named himself, Ramesh and Kaseem. Zela entered into the spirit of the exchange and named Blair and Kyle and Laurya. Kananda's enthusiasm outran itself and he began naming the entire hunting party. He stopped and laughed at himself again as he realized that this was all too much. There were smiles all round and the original tension was broken.

Only Ramesh remained still uncertain. "We should return to the main camp," he suggested. "There Prince Kananda can rest until his wound is healed."

"No," Kananda said immediately. He had no intention of being parted from his administering angel. "We can camp and rest here."

Ramesh looked to Kaseem for support and the old priest deliberated.

"We should stay," Kaseem said at last. "We have no chariots here, and to seat the prince on a horse would restart the bleeding from his leg."

Ramesh looked sulky at being opposed, but Kananda was delighted with the decision.

☙

The days that followed passed pleasantly in the shaded palm grove. Kananda's leg healed quickly and cleanly, and it was not long before he could hobble with the help of a spear, but the wound was deep and needed time to heal fully. Except for a small party whom Kaseem had sent back to the plains with their news, the hunt had made camp. There was clean water in the stream, and plenty of fruit and game, pheasant's eggs and bee's honey, in the surrounding forest. Zela and her crew were well pleased to have made friendly contact, and they found more than willing collaborators in Kananda and the old priest as the two parties endeavoured to understand each other's language. The encounter with the tiger, and the time-consuming delay provided by Kananda's wound was a perfect opportunity.

Kaseem was torn between continued mental discomfort and fascination. His logic slowly told him that these people were not gods, for they had to eat, sleep and function like mortal men and women, and yet he could not be sure that they were not from the gods. There had been no more voices from the sky, but the black temple of steel was a mighty edifice with three needle-pointed spires that were twice as high as any temple he had ever seen in stone, and he could not see how the hands of mortal men could have shaped it. The whole fabric of his philosophy and beliefs was under brutal attack and he performed his regular ablutions and sacrifices with the desperation of uncertainty.

Even so, his thirst for knowledge held him fast, and he would not willingly have left the valley until all his questions were answered. Always a humble Brahmin, he did not see himself in any brave or noble light, but only as an old and unworthy priest who had been chosen by capricious fate to meet this new challenge to learning. He prayed endlessly as he struggled to understand the meaning of this new wealth of experience.

Kananda was locked in a simpler, more fatal fascination. That of a young man's awakened passion for a rare and lovely young woman, as ideal and mysterious as any vision from his wildest dreams. He hardly dared to admit his immediate infatuation for Zela, even to himself, for it would have taken the boldness of a god to declare his love for a goddess. Even so, he knew that he loved her, and constantly pricked or pierced his own flesh to determine that he was not dreaming.

The bulk of the warriors and hunters, as their first fears diminished, were content to loaf and be idle. They stared often at the spaceship and its silver-suited crew, but eventually their attention turned more and more to gambling with the dice cubes that every soldier carried in his pack.

Only Ramesh was dissatisfied with the unending delay. He fretted and pouted and nursed a grievance, for the tiger that Kananda and the woman had slain should have been his by right. The sabre teeth should even now be adorning his youthful chest, but he could not wear a trophy he had not killed. He felt cheated and more and more frustrated as it became painfully obvious that neither Kananda nor Kaseem were in any hurry to renew the hunt.

☙

Kananda had many times visited the port of Baneswar, where the great river Mahanadi opened out into the heaving blue waves of the Indian Ocean. The main port and channel of trade for the empire of Karakhor, Baneswar was a proud bustle of inns and commerce. At its wharves lay ships that plied between the far coasts with silks and gold, timber and ivory, spices and salt, and a hundred other cargoes. On one visit, the young prince had seen a three-hulled trimaran lifted out of the water for scraping and repair, and he was reminded of that proud sailing vessel as he looked up at the sleek, rakish lines of the Tri-Thruster. The spaceship stood erect, but like the trimaran, its main hull was much taller than the wing pods of its subsidiary rockets. It was designed for atmospheric as well as deep space flight, and so its long, smooth curves were aerodynamic. Kaseem had likened it to a bird, a mighty black raven poised for flight, but Kananda could still see the resemblance to the trimaran. He could imagine the ship sailing between the stars on the heavens as the trimaran had sailed on the waves of the ocean.

Three of them walked slowly around the ship: Zela, Kananda and Kaseem. The other members of the spacecraft's crew had formed their own friendships among the Hindus, and due to their combined and determined efforts the language barrier was slowly breaking down. Kyle and Laurya, always inseparable, were trying their skill at archery and spear-throwing, much to the amusement of Gujar and a group of his companions who had loaned their weapons. Blair was somewhere in the forest with the head huntsman, having recognized that the man had an almost encyclopedic knowledge of the planet's terrain and wildlife. Cadel was rolling dice with a circle of warriors, and was wryly trying to calculate mathematical probability against chance.

Kananda and Kaseem had ventured inside the ship at Zela's invitation, but they had found the interior cramped and claustrophobic, and the bewildering array of dials, screens and switches was totally beyond their comprehension. They had been apprehensive and relieved to escape again to the blue sky and fresh air, but they never tired of walking round the ship and gazing up at its triple spires in awe-struck wonder. With difficulty Kananda asked where were the sails which enabled the vessel to make a passage between the stars. He imagined that they must be folded away inside the hull, together with the masts, although he could not see where they might emerge, nor fathom out how.

Zela smiled when she grasped the question, although she was perplexed as to how best to answer it. The ship's main propulsion was derived from a nuclear pulse rocket engine, in which pellets of deuterium and helium-3 were ignited by electronic beam energy to create controlled fusion. The secondary engines used for atmospheric flight, together with the lazer banks, were all powered by energy converted from the intense friction heat that was generated by each planetary orbit during space launch and re-entry. All of this she could have explained in explicit technical detail in her own language, with an expertise equal to that of Cadel or the engineers who had designed the ship, but there were no equivalent earth words to explain these things even in simplified terms to the Hindu prince.

There are no sails," she said carefully. "When we leave your world to travel to our world there is no air and no wind. There is nothing to move sails."

"Then how does this ship move?"

"Perhaps it flies," Kaseem suggested. He was still thinking of its likeness to a bird. "Perhaps the wings move."

"It does not fly in that way," Zela told him. "Even a bird needs air in which to fly." She saw the priest's brow wrinkle even more deeply with hopeless concentration on her words, and sought for some descriptive example. A shout of applause caused her to glance to where Laurya had just shot an arrow into a target and she seized on the inspiration it gave her. "It flies like an arrow." she said awkwardly, "Without the flapping of wings or sails."

Prince and priest were still baffled. Kananda stared up at the towering height of the spaceship, and then searchingly at the jungle all around. There was a long silence while Kananda considered what Zela had just said, and Kaseem found his own gaze drawn back to where Laurya was still surrounded by the laughing circle of young men. He felt the now familiar surge of anguished emotion, anguished because he could not understand it.

She was the other reason for his indulgence of Kananda's obvious attraction to Zela. He had not spoken to Laurya directly, and deliberately chose to avoid her. In fact he hardly dared to look into her eyes. Forest pool or sunbird's wing, he still could not decide, but they were *familiar.* He *knew* her, or at least, he *knew the soul behind the eyes.* It was an insane thought and he wondered if he were on the edge of madness. Until these last few days he had not even been sure that he had believed in souls. He had taught the doctrine of the *Atman,* the Divine Self that was in all things, and all beings, but like all his teachings of the gods, and the whole body of his religious belief, it had been an act of faith which rose dominant over a partially open mind.

He finally heard Kananda speak and forced his attention back to their present conversation.

"But where is the bow?" Kananda had asked.

Zela laughed, understanding his mental predicament. "There is no bow, Kananda. Your language does not have the words for me to explain. But the ship shoots into the sky—as if it were shot from a bow."

"Like an arrow that is shot without a bow? And it shoots all the way to the stars?" Kaseem tried to concentrate, fearing to say that her words were false and yet unable to believe her.

"Not to the stars," Zela said. "The stars are like other suns. Our world is like your world, it circles this sun."

Their faces were blank. Zela was momentarily at a loss, but then she broke off a twig of foliage and, began to draw a sketch of the solar system on a patch of smooth earth. "Here is the sun," she pointed to the, small circle in the centre of her map. "There are ten worlds that circle the sun." She drew in the ten orbits like rapidly widening ripples round a pebble. "Your world—this world—which you call Earth—is here. It is the third world from the sun. Our world, which we call Dooma, is here. It is the fifth planet from the sun."

The old man and the youth both crouched to stare at what she had drawn but their faces showed no enlightenment. Then Kaseem reached tentatively for the twig. He drew his own map, in which there was just the central pebble and one orbiting ripple.

"Our world," the priest insisted, pointing at the centre of his universe. The twig sketched the single orbit around it once again and then he pointed upward. "Our sun."

"No," Zela said, and again she went over the details of her own map. Kaseem scratched his head and then squinted his eyes against the glare of the sun. This new idea was an almost impossible one to accept.

Zela tried again, describing the solar system for the third time, and struggling to explain its relationship to the stars and galaxies. Kaseem shared the struggle with her, the old priest desperately wanted to understand. But Kananda was losing interest in these dry scratchings in the dust. The frontal zip on Zela's silver suit was almost imperceptibly sliding downward as she talked, and he could see again a tantalizing and gradually expanding view of her breasts. He began to wish fervently that

Kaseem would shut up and go away.

The old man was oblivious to the desires of youth. He squatted with his robe clutched tight around him, listening intently with his gaze moving constantly from the drawings to the woman's face, but to his frustration he comprehended little. The woman was talking about the stars, but in among the Hindu words she had learned were strange words from her own language which had no meaning for him. In the end he gave up and changed the subject to one that was dearer to his own heart.

"You are from the gods," he challenged her. "Do you know the gods? Are they in the stars?"

Zela sighed. "You ask difficult questions, friend Kaseem. No, we are not gods. Nor are we messengers from your gods. We are people like yourselves, from another planet in this solar system which is much like your own."

"But you know the gods," Kaseem insisted, almost fiercely. You know *Indra*, the god of war and thunder and storm. You know *Varuna*, the high god of heaven who is Lord over all."

"We do not know the names *Indra* and *Varuna*," Zela said carefully, knowing that this was an area where she might easily offend, or worse, turn the old priest into a deadly enemy. "But I think these are two different names for one god, and on Dooma we do believe in one God."

Confusion registered on the old man's face. He frowned and scowled, and then dared to look her directly in the eyes. "If you do not know *Indra* and *Varuna*—then who is your God? Do you worship fire, or sky, or Earth? Or do you worship monkey totems like the primitive tribes of the forest?"

"Please, Kaseem, let me explain." Zela tried to calm him with a gentle smile and by resting a light hand on his bare shoulder. "Our world is much older than your Earth. Because it is further from the sun the oceans cooled more quickly and intelligent life began to develop there long before it did here. Our recorded history on the continent of Alpha goes back for ten thousand years. During that time our ancestors fought endless battles and wars, most of them for power and conquest, but always with the followers of one saint or god fighting the followers of another. Religions and gods always divided our people, and those divisions always enabled the power-hungry to mobilize the masses for war."

"Tell me about your gods." Kaseem was not willing to be side-tracked into history.

"We had many gods," Zela admitted wryly, "And many religions. But their names and doctrines are only of importance to the individual subscribers of that particular belief. What our philosophers gradually came to realize was that if any god existed then there could only be one God, and that this was a spiritual and not a physical reality. It became clear then that we fought only over names and definitions of that which could never be finally named or defined. From this it followed that all religions worshipped the same god, even though they did not realize this truth, and that if the god-names and the doctrines were not of prime importance, then it must be faith itself which leads all believers to the One God. Once we had reached this understanding—that all religious faiths must lead inevitably to the One God—then it became easier for the different religious groups to tolerate each other. They did not have to accept other doctrines or god-names in place of their own, but only to understand that other groups worshipped the same spiritual reality in a different way."

Kaseem had only understood part of what she had said. The parts of each other's language they shared were not yet sufficient for a full exchange of such complex ideas. But he was trying hard. His ancient face was anguished as he asked, "But how can you worship a god who has no name or shape or form?"

"Most of our people still worship the old names and the old concepts in the traditional ways. There is a human need for religious faith to be expressed, and the old ways still serve those needs. What we now understand is that behind all those old names and concepts is the same reality and purpose of that which is divine. Our philosophers hold the conviction that the universe is a balanced structure of hidden order, and that the rise and fall of men, and kings and empires, is as ordained as the cycles of the seasons. It is all part of the balancing laws of nature. This underlying belief in one God, and the Divine Purpose of hidden order has led to the development of the First Enlightened Civilization of Alpha, where we have unity and harmony in place of all the old religious conflicts. Alphan civilization has at last reached its golden age of art, music, peace and prosperity for all."

This ideal was again too difficult to comprehend. In Karakhor there were king and priests, lords and nobles, warriors, artisans and slaves. Beyond the city walls there were farmers and fishermen, hunters and serfs, and in the wild lands beyond the kingdom there were naked and near-naked savages. The Hindu social structure was a carefully tiered and guarded system of ranks and privileges and responsibilities, from the many-titled and jewel-bedecked glory of Kara-Rashna himself, right down to the untouchable misery of the lowest dung-collector. It was surrounded by a sea of rivals and enemies, and to imagine all of this necessary human diversity sharing in peace and prosperity and a belief in only one god was inconceivable.

"You say that *all* on your world share in these things, and that *all* believe in only one god?" Kaseem asked in astonishment.

It was Zela's turn to frown. "Not all," she had to concede. "All the people of Alpha are now united in this way, but not all the people of our world. On Dooma there is another great continent, from which we are divided by a vast ocean. The continents of Alpha and Ghedda are on opposite sides of our planet, and for thousads of years they have developed separately. Now Gheddan philosophy, if you can call it such, is the antithesis of belief on Alpha. They deny the existence of any god and see the universe as formed by only chaos and chance effect. They acknowledge no concept of a spiritual realm, or of any ideas of design, purpose or morality. To the Gheddans "Might is Right" and there is no higher power or law than their own naked swords. Theirs is a harsh, barbaric continent, where the strong rule and indulge their own selfish pleasures. For them death is the end. Nothing exists beyond this moment. They hold no hope for any life beyond this one, and consequently they are untroubled by any fear of final retribution."

She paused, and for the first time a note of bitterness and anger crept into her voice. "On Alpha we have triumphed over the foolishness of war and diversity, but only to find ourselves facing a much more terrible foe in the form of the Gheddan Empire."

She looked back into the uncertain face of the old priest and her fingers tightened painfully on his shoulder.

"When you pray, friend Kaseem, you would do well to pray that it will never be your misfortune to encounter a Sword Lord of Ghedda."

Chapter Four

Golden Karakhor had earned its far-flung fame from the beaten gold leaf which adorned the roofs of its sumptuous palaces and the rich homes of its lords and nobles. The city gleamed in the dazzling sunshine, its silhouette of yellow domes, spires and cupolas all mirrored in the clear blue waters of the Mahanadi. Its thick outer walls and ramparts were of red sandstone and the streets of its shopkeepers and artisans were shaded with bright, multicoloured awnings of red and yellow, blue and green. The great palace of Kara-Rashna overlooked the green lawns and terraced flower gardens of the river bank, while on the north side it faced the central plaza that was flanked by the three great stone temples to *Indra*, *Varuna* and *Agni*. Each temple soared like a man-carved mountain into the vivid blue sky, in rampart upon rampart of ascending red sandstone climbing up toward heaven and the gods. The temples were not adorned with golden tile, marble screens and silken drapes as was the palace. They were bare and spartan inside, designed for worship and not for comfort, but the walls and ceilings of the buildings themselves were sculpted with a fantastic array of friezes, panels and figures. Here were all the gods and mythology of ancient India, mingling with men and beasts in war, sport and play. The building and carving of each temple had been in itself an act of worship. The ultimate spires of the temples to *Indra* and *Varuna* reached higher than the golden dome of Kara-Rashna's palace, while the temple dedicated to *Agni* was only slightly less magnificent. All around the city there were smaller temples to a score of lesser dieties, all piercing the skyline with their spires and pinnacles.

In a secluded corner of the royal gardens, protected from common eyes by high walls on three sides but with a clear view down the lawns to the river, two young girls played with bats and a coloured ball. Both were in the first flush of womanhood, and both were richly dressed and beautiful. Their saris were of the finest silks, the older girl in white and gold, the younger in white and blue. A diamond pendant graced each dusky forehead, and golden chains linked the jeweled rings and bracelets that adorned their hands and wrists. The princess, Maryam, first-born daughter of the first wife of Kara-Rashna, wore around her throat a necklace of eight strings of alternating emeralds, diamonds, rubies and pearls. Her half sister Namita, the first-born daughter of Kara-Rashna's second wife, wore around her throat a necklace only slightly less magnificent, of six strings instead of eight. The distinction of rank had to be observed.

At nineteen, Maryam was the older by two years, and normally she was the better player at the many sports and games at which they passed much of their time. Today her mind was preoccupied and she missed a fast return from Namita which sent the ball flying into the shrubbery behind her. Swearing crossly she hurried after it, but by the time she had pushed through the fragrant tangles of frangipani and bougainvillea the ball had bounced down onto the terrace below and was rolling down toward the river.

Both girls chased after it, but they were too late. The ball splashed into the river and was gently swirled away. Maryam stopped at the river's edge and reached for the clasp of her sari. Her intention was clear for she was a strong swimmer, but then

Namita restrained her.

"'No, Maryam, not without a proper bathing suit. Look, there are young men on the far bank."

Maryam looked across the water. A group of young warriors stood on the far side. The young men waved, and one hero quickly threw off his weapons and dived in after the ball. Reluctantly Maryam watched him as he splashed around the curve of the river and out of sight. He was swimming strongly but clumsily, and moving no faster than the ball he pursued. His companions lustily cheered him on.

"I could have caught it," Marym complained. "And from that distance how could they tell whether I wear a bathing suit or just my underclothes."

She turned away and walked gloomily back toward the palace. Her behaviour was out of character and Namita frowned. The younger girl cast a fleeting glance across the river, where at least one of the young warriors could be considered as almost handsome, but then she ran after Maryam once more.

"What is wrong?" Namita asked. "You do not usually play so badly."

Maryam paused. "Don't you know? Haven't you heard the palace talk?"

Namita blushed. "It is unseemly to listen to other people's conversations."

"Perhaps," Maryam conceded. "But we are women, and if we do not we will never know what is going on. The men will not bother to tell us."

"But what is going on?"

Maryam took her younger sister's arm and led her to a shaded bench where they could sit and talk. "Kanju is aligned to Maghalla," she whispered fiercely. "That is what is going on."

"But how do you know?"

"Old Jahan has many spies in the capitals of Kanju and Maghalla. And in the towns of all the other kingdoms I should imagine. Merchants and traders bring him information and news from innkeepers and prostitutes and others that they meet on their travels."

"What are prostitutes?"

"Women who sell their bodies for sex. They make the best spies because men are vain creatures who will always boast to the women they make love to. Everyone knows that."

Namita looked shocked. "I have never heard such things."

"You do not listen enough."

"But why should Kanju make an alliance with Maghalla? The king of Kanju is one of our father's oldest friends."

"I do not know why. I only know that it has happened. Kanju and Maghalla are united. Together they stand against Karakhor. Perhaps now other kings and kingdoms will join them."

"But why should they? Karakhor has no enemies, except Maghalla."

"Karakhor is rich, Namita. Our wealth is the envy of all the other kings and kingdoms. While we are the stronger, they are our friends. But if enough kingdoms unite against Karakhor, then greed will sway the rest. They will all want their share of plunder."

"How is it that you hear so much?"

"I listen, and I ask questions. There are many young nobles and guard captains who like to air their knowledge, especially when they think I am impressed by their bold talk and their promises to protect me and our city with their lives. It is not necessary to use sex to make a fool of a man, Namita. The coy flutter of an eyelid is usually enough."

"Maryam, you are shameless."

"Perhaps," Maryam smiled a little, but then the smile fled and her troubled face became serious again. "Oh, Namita, this is all my fault. What am I to do?"

"But how is it your fault?" Namita clasped her shoulders and looked into her eyes. There were tears in the gold-brown depths and suddenly Namita was afraid. "How can you be responsible for what happens in Kanju? What are you talking about?"

"It is my fault that Karakhor is threatened. If I had not refused Sardar then Karakhor and Maghalla would be united. There would be nothing to fear from a unity between Maghalla and Kanju."

"But you could not forsee that Kanju would betray us."

"It is still because of me that Sardar has declared war, and any fool could see that Maghalla alone is not powerful enough to destroy Karakhor. Sardar would have to seek allies."

A tear rolled down Maryam's cheek and splashed onto her gold–and-white sari. Her anguish was deep and overflowing. Namita clutched her older sister helplessly, not knowing what to do or say.

"I should have agreed to the marriage," Maryam said bitterly. "Because of my refusal all of our people—all of Karakhor and Maghalla, and Kanju, perhaps all the world—all must now suffer the horrors of war."

"But Sardar was so old—and ugly—his face must have been repulsive even before it was scarred. You would have been married to a cruel old monkey."

"It was my duty," Maryam insisted. "To our father. To our people. To Karakhor." She bit her lip to stop it from trembling and her teeth drew a small globule of blood. “Perhaps it is not too late. Perhaps our father could send messengers to Maghalla—to tell Sardar that I will go through with the marriage. It is a woman’s privilege to change her mind. Men can accept that.”

“Kara-Rashna will not accept this change of mind. Not now. And neither will Karakhor. We have all seen the ugly face of Sardar. We all understand and share in your repugnance for the monster. Kara-Rashna will not send you to Maghalla. Our brothers would not allow it. There is not a noble house in Karakhor where the young men would not gladly die fighting rather than see you forced into a union which they all know you will abhor.” Namita shook her head sadly and now there were tears in her eyes also. “It is too late to change things, Maryam. There is nothing you can do.”

Maryam bowed her head. “Oh, how I wish Kananda were here,” she cried desperately. She did not know how her brother would help or counsel her. She only knew that in times of crisis he was her truest friend and greatest comfort. But Kananda was not here, and she could only rest her head upon Namita’s shoulder. The two princesses held each other and wept together.

☙

In the high-columned, gold-tiled audience hall of his palace, Kara-Rashna sat on blue silk cushions on his marble and ivory throne. Two huge, elaborately carved elephant tusks, formed an arch at the back of the throne, and two smaller tusks formed its arms. The monarch wore loose robes of white, with a broad crimson sash across his chest that was emblazoned with the rising sun insignia of Karakhor set out in a thousand diamonds and other precious stones. A simple, jeweled turban sufficed for his head, the ceremonial crown being much too heavy and uncomfortable for everyday wear. He was a man of sixty-five, strong in will, but failing now in health. His physicians had diagnosed the sharp chest pains he had recently suffered as warnings from the gods. One severe attack that had rendered him temporarily unconscious had also left him partially crippled in his left leg and with limited mobility in his left arm. With his right hand he could still wield a sword, but the attacks had aged him and carved his face with deep pain lines. He tired easily and was often irritable, more with himself than with those around him, although it was those around him who bore the brunt of his irritability. A tyrant might have been removed at this weakened stage, but Kara-Rashna had generally ruled wisely and not too greedily or harshly by the standards of other monarchs. Prince Kananda, his natural heir, was strong enough to block the line of succession, but was possessed of love and a strong sense of loyalty to his father that curbed his own ambition. Also the king had staunch friends in the High Priest Kaseem, and in his senior general, Jahan, the Warmaster of Karakhor.

It was Jahan who had brought the news that had aged Kara-Rashna's face by another ten years in half as many minutes. The warmaster general was a man of sixty, grey and grizzled, but still as tough as teak and as sharp as the great, ruby-hilted sword that was slung at his left hip. The purple sash across his blue tunic was embroidered with the head and shoulders of a snarling tiger, and the clasp that secured the front of his purple turban was a single red gem-stone, as hot and fire-bright as a tiger's eye. He was tested and experienced in a dozen battles, both in single combat and in the direction of a widespread military campaign. The far-flung web of his intelligence-gathering operations had always ensured that when he spoke he spoke with certainty as well as authority, and his words were rarely doubted in the palace councils. Now Kara-Rashna was torn by doubt, and the tumult of emotion within him forced him to voice it.

"Jahan, can there be no mistake in this news you bring me? Kumar-Rao, the King of Kanju, is one of our oldest friends. I would have trusted him almost as I trust you. I cannot believe that he would align with Maghalla against us."

"It is true, sire." Jahan bowed his head and his voice rumbled deferentially but firmly. "I have waited until the news has been confirmed by almost a score of my most trusted sources. It is common knowledge in Kanju and Maghalla. The prince, Zarin, oldest son of Kumar-Rao, has been married to the princess Seeva, one of the daughters of Sardar."

"But why would Kumar-Rao do this?"

"I think, sire, that the king of Kanju has been tricked." Jahan chose his words with care. The news was carried to Kanju that Sardar was to be married to the princess Maryam. What was withheld from Kumar-Rao was the later news that Princess Maryam had refused Sardar, and that the marriage had not taken place. My sources suggest that Kanju's king was deceived into believing that Karakhor and Maghalla were already alligned. Kumar-Rao then believed that he could safeguard Kanju, and his friendship with Karakhor, by making his own alliance with Maghalla."

"But how could Sardar succeed in such a deceit?"

"Unaided, he could not succeed." Jahan frowned and now he was angry. "There is intrigue in the palace halls of Kanju. Bharat, Kumar-Rao's brother, aspires to Kanju's throne. And Bharat is the favourite uncle of Prince Zarin. In peace, Bharat can never hope to rule, but in times of war, kings and princes may die upon the battlefield, and bold men can make their own opportunities. One of my reports says that Kumar-Rao sent messengers to Karakhor to invite Kara-Rashna and his queen to attend the wedding ceremony of Prince Zarin, even though he could not understand why his old friend had failed to invite him to attend the wedding of Princess Maryam. I need not tell you that those messengers never arrived in Karakhor. It is my belief that they were slain in the jungle somewhere along the way. And I smell more than the hand of Sardar in all of this. I smell the hand of Bharat."

Kara-Rashna groaned and held his head in his hands. "Is there no way we can resolve this situation?"

Jahan shrugged his massive shoulders in a hopeless gesture. "The marriage was properly performed, with all due sacrifice and ceremony. It is blessed by the gods and cannot be undone. Prince Zarin is now a prince of Maghalla, he is duty-bound to stand with Sardar, and Kanju must stand with him. Kumar-Rao will resist, he will counsel peace and reconciliation. But if Sardar is adamant, and we know that he will be, then Kumar-Rao cannot avoid entering the war. Unwittingly Kumar-Rao committed Kanju when he sanctioned the marriage with Maghalla."

There was a long silence in the audience hall. In addition to the king and his chief general there were a dozen men gathered there, not counting the guards, slaves and priests. The noble houses of the city were all represented; the princes Sanjay and Devan, younger brothers of Kara-Rashna were there, looking grim and angry, while the princes Rajar and Nirad, the younger sons of Kara-Rashna by his second queen, stood together like two resplendent young fighting cocks both burning to be unleashed.

It was Rajar who spoke first. "Why do we wait for Kanju and Maghalla to attack?" he cried fiercely. "If Kanju has formed this alliance against us, then let us attack Kanju now. We can easily strike at Kanju before Maghalla can come to their aid. Kanju alone cannot stand against Karakhor. And once Kanju is defeated, we can deal with Maghalla in their turn."

"No." Kara-Rashna lifted his head sharply and half rose from his chair. "If Kanju comes against us with Maghalla, we will fight them both. But I will not strike Kanju first. I will give Kumar-Rao time to find his own way out of his dilemma."

"But if Kumar-Rao cannot find his way out?" Prince Devan shrugged and left his sentence unfinished. He was a strong fighter with little imagination and less faith in the politics of peace. In his own heart and mind he knew there would be war.

Kara-Rashna glared at him and repeated, "I will not strike the first blow against Kanju. We owe that much to our oldest friend."

Prince Sanjay was a tall lean man, famous as a charioteer, from which he could throw a javelin as accurately as any man in Karakhor. He looked to Jahan and asked calmly: "How will Karakhor compare, matched against the combined forces of Kanju and Maghalla?"

"We have eight hundred war elephants and almost as many chariots. And we can field up to five thousand foot warriors." Jahan had the facts ready at his fingertips. "Kanju has four hundred war elephants, some six hundred chariots and can field three thousand foot warriors. Maghalla has three hundred war elephants, four hundred chariots, but can field almost seven thousand foot warriors. We are outnumbered in chariots and warriors but numbers do not win battles. Many of our warriors and charioteers are highly skilled in battle."

"Kanju may be soft," Devan reflected, "but the Maghallans are renowned for a cruelty and ferocity that makes up for their lack of skill."

"We can defeat them," Jahan predicted confidently.

"Providing they do not find any more allies." Rajar would not defy his father by repeating that they should attack Kanju first, but his tone conveyed as much.

Kara-Rashna beat his fist against his forehead. "All this talk of war with Kanju is madness. I still cannot believe that this is happening." A sudden nameless but vaguely identifiable fear lanced through his heart and he put it, unthinking, into words. "I wish we had not sent Kananda and Kaseem to the South. I wish Kananda were here."

The young prince Nirad was only eighteen and prone to quick speech, which he often regretted almost immediately. "You do not need Kananda," he blurted. "You have Nirad—and Rajar. We are your sons too. We are as brave as Kananda."

Kara-Rashna turned on him swiftly, but then let tolerance mellow his reply. Pride and boldness, even when they were out of place, were qualities to be carefully nurtured in young princes. "I mean you and your brother no slight," he reassured the boy. "But in this hour of danger, Karakhor needs all her sons."

"And you are right to be concerned, sire." Jahan had no time for sibling rivalries and kept to the point. "Now that Sardar has won Kanju to his banner he will be more open in his search for more allies. If so it may prove a mistake to have sent the princes Kananda and Ramesh to fly our banners along our southern borders. Sardar may be tempted to attack our hunting party, and if he can make a successful attack against two royal princes, then that will impress the monkey tribes. Kananda and Ramesh will not know of these new events that will make Sardar more audacious. They may be in grave danger."

"Then we must recall them," Kara-Rashna decided.

"If they returned in haste it would be taken as a sign of weakness," Jahan advised. "'Let them be warned, so that they may be vigilant, and return without any apparent haste as soon as the prince Ramesh has killed his tiger."

There was a murmur of approval, and the monarch nodded his agreement. Only Nirad and Rajar looked displeased. With Kananda absent from the city the crisis might have proved their opportunity to shine more brightly.

The debate would have continued, but at that moment there was a terrifying interruption. A faint growl of thunder filled the hot, still air, growing swiftly in power and volume until it vibrated through the entire city. The fearsome sound echoed like a monster's roar beneath the golden domes, and the slender columns of the audience hall shook and trembled. The assembled faces turned ashen as the blood drained away from every man. The guards stood transfixed. The priests sank onto their knees and prayed. The slaves fell on their bellies and faces to whimper and cower. Kara-Rashna made a great effort to struggle up from his throne, but then slipped feebly back again.

Jahan moved slowly on leaden feet, as if in a nightmare, and stared out through the arch of an open window. Even with his own eyes as witness, he had no comprehension of what was happening, but what he saw descending from the sky was a five-clustered pinnacle of steel that slowly lowered itself on a red pillar of fire. The hand that had automatically rested on the ruby hilt of his great sword went dead. Like the rest of his body, it was nerveless with shock.

The princes Sanjay and Devan had moved reluctantly to stand behind him. All were equally numbed, their mouths agape, their minds reeling. They watched as the spaceship came to rest on the far side of the river and shock waves like those of a minor earthquake rocked the very foundations of the city beneath their feet. The pillar of red fire became a bowl of orange flames and boiling black smoke in which the ship briefly nested and then the fire slowly died and the thunder ceased.

The city became still again. As still as though every heart had stopped and every soul was frozen.

A Gheddan spaceship had landed.

Chapter Five

From space the third planet had appeared as a perfect marbled sphere, thickly veined with diffusing colours of ocean blue, the white of polar ice caps, and the green and brown of its continents, revealed in patches beneath swirling white clouds. Apart from Dooma, it was the only other inhabitable planet in the solar system. If Dooma was to ultimately destroy itself, as many of the leading scientists and thinkers of Alpha believed was inevitable, then there was only the third planet to offer any possible hope of refuge to the survivors.

Ghedda did not hold to the Alphan view that the home planet would disintegrate in a full scale nuclear and lazer beam war between the two continents. That was a soft-stomached Alphan ploy designed to hold off the superior military might of Ghedda, which the craven hearts of Alpha so desperately feared. It was also a smokescreen to cover the real reasons for the Alphan expeditionary flights to the third planet which they undoubtedly had hopes to colonize. Ghedda had no fear of war with Alpha, or of its consequences, but the Gheddan Empire was concerned with the possibilities of inter-planetary conquest. To deny the Alphans a bolt-hole and to reap the rewards of conquest for Ghedda—these were the twin aims behind the presence of the Gheddan warship.

The ship was a Class Five Solar Cruiser, its design

incorporating a central rocket with four smaller, finned booster rockets. Like the Alphan ships, it was nuclear-pulse powered. It carried a crew of six and these were all male. There was no sexual equality on Ghedda.

The six men wore white uniforms which contrasted with the pale blue of their skin colour and the darker blue of their hair. They also wore wide belts of chain mail, together with cod-pieces and outer vests of the same fine linked steel, which could protect their vital organs from dagger and sword thrusts. Two of the six, Caid and Landis, were engineers. Garl and Taron were the two lazer gunnery officers. The cold-eyed, cold-faced Thorn, who had twenty sword duels and twenty sword deaths to his credit, was Deputy Commander and Navigator. In overall command of the space cruiser was Raven, Commander First Class of the Gheddan Space Force and a Sword Lord of Ghedda.

Even Thorn, as skilled and defiant as any Gheddan swordmaster, was proud to serve with Raven. Raven had thirty-seven sword duels, and thirty-seven kills to his credit, including two of his own brothers. Now, no one dared to challenge him.

They had studied the computer screen with its selected images of the land mass terrain recorded on their initial orbits. The major populated and cultivated areas were easily identified and so they had chosen the flat plain beside the largest city of the great pear-shaped subcontinent for their first dramatic landing.

☙

Maryam had watched the landing in mortal terror, holding Namita so tightly that she had violently bruised the younger girl's shoulders and arms. Her own arms were also black and blue where Namita's clutching fingers had dug into the bone, but she had not felt a thing. For long minutes she was petrified, but after the fire and sound had stopped there was nothing. The earth no longer heaved and the river flowed as calmly as before. There was just the strange, towering monument of black steel standing against the far forest and sky, where before there had been nothing.

Moisture returned to her dry throat. She felt the movement of her own and Namita's breathing. They were alive. The city was still here. Voices were beginning to sound from behind the palace walls, voices tinged with fear, edged with panic.

Her heart was suddenly beating very fast. By regulating her breathing she gradually controlled it. She realized slowly that she was dry-eyed, and that although there was now fear in her heart there was no longer the frustrated anguish that had so recently caused her to weep. Something new had happened, something totally different from anything that had ever happened before. This visitation must have some tremendous new meaning. Perhaps it portended some cataclysmic change in the order of the world, in the whole order of creation. Perhaps the gods had come themselves to aid, or to punish Karakhor. Whatever the meaning it pushed the issues of Kanju and Maghalla into insignificant proportion.

Borne on impulse and a mixed wave of fear and hope Maryam scrambled to her feet. She pulled Namita with her and hurried into the palace. Her sister was still in shock and she handed her into the care of two equally distressed slave girls, trusting that the three of them could comfort each other. Then, pulling her lace shawl over her head, she ran swiftly to the audience hall where she knew her father was in conference with his advisors.

ॐ

The rulers of Karakhor had rallied themselves, recovering some of their courage and composure. Kara-Rashna had been helped to the window where he could see for himself the great steel spire that stood taller than *Indra's* temple. As the silence lengthened, he had cursed his stiffened arm and leg and agreed that Jahan should lead a party out of the city to investigate this incredible phenomenon.

"Should we go in strength?" Sanjay wondered. "Or to pay homage?"

"We will go in strength," Jahan answered, "but we will go prudently, with priests in the forefront to pay homage."

The attendant priests turned a shade paler at the thought, but the monarch nodded his approval. "Let the priests light their fires and give blessings to the city, then let them be mounted on war elephants to lead the way. But take as many chariots and warriors as you can muster."

Jahan nodded and turned to issue his orders to the priests and to the senior nobles who also served as military commanders. Sanjay and Devan hurried away to don their weapons and harness their chariots. The young prince Rajar stepped forward to face his father and gathered up all his faltering courage.

"Sire, as you cannot sally forth, then I should represent you. As the eldest son present of the royal line, I should lead our forces on this task."

Kara-Rashna frowned, but then smiled faintly. "Well-spoken, my son. Your day of glory will come, Rajar, but I think it is not yet. In this hour Karakhor has need of a wise old head as much as proud young blood. Jahan has my royal mandate in this matter. He will lead our forces. You must stand by him well as I know you will."

Rajar was only slightly mollified, and then to his increasing annoyance there was another interruption from behind him. Maryam had arrived, breathless but determined, and in the general confusion no one had thought to bar her from the room.

"Sire," she said bravely. "The first royal line should be represented, the true royal line. Prince Kananda is not here, so let me go in his place."

"There is no place for a woman in this." Rajar glared at her, but in the presence of their father did not dare rebuke her further.

Maryam shot him a look of anger, but then turned more beseeching eyes upon her father. "Sire, if anything happens to Kananda—and may the gods forbid that misfortune should befall him—then one day I may rule Karakhor as her queen. It is my right and duty to attend these important matters."

The ailing king was unable to escape the fervent intensity of her gaze as he considered. She had all the sweet, woman's wiles of her mother he realized, but surely the strong independence of spirit within her was a reflection of his own. She warmed his heart, and he did not know whether he wanted to keep her here to protect her, or grant her the favour she desired. Finally he nodded his head. "If Lord Jahan will consent to take charge of you, you may go."

Maryam smiled, knowing she had won. She had always looked upon Jahan as her favourite uncle, and she knew that as long as she behaved sensibly he would not refuse her.

Kara-Rashna recognized the smile and wondered if he had been too indulgent.

ꟹ

It was an hour before all the necessary sacrifices and ablutions had been performed, and all the due supplications made to the gods. The priests would gladly have taken longer, but at last they were purified and ready, and a dozen of them were mounted on elephants to lead the way across the carved stone bridge that spanned the river. As they passed through the main gateway of the city and onto the bridge they were all praying loudly, their eyes closed and their white-knuckled hands clasped piously before them.

Behind them came two score of chariots, flying as many different brilliant banners that fluttered defiantly in the light breeze that had now sprung up along the river. First the proud purple banner of Jahan, with its snarling tiger emblem. From the chariot beside him Maryam flew the rising sunburst banner that would have been Kananda's if he had not been absent. A golden hawk clutching a javelin was the proud standard of Prince Sanjay. A lion's paw with reddened claws unfurled over the chariot of his brother Devan. The princes Rajar and Nirad raised standards depicting a silver falcon and a silver boar. The double-bladed axe of the House of Gandhar was there, the black orchid of the House of Tilak, the blue raven of the House of Bulsar. The jostling banners of the lesser houses were almost as splendid, and every charioteer was armed for war. Behind them tramped a great mass of foot warriors, carrying their own war banners before them.

The great cavalcade spread out into a broad front after it had crossed the river, and then approached slowly with the elephant-borne priests and the jostling mass of chariots in the centre. They took courage from their own sheer weight of numbers, their own bristling display of spears and axes, swords and maces, and from those bold and trusted banners of their proven champions. They also took courage from the fact that only one man, human-shaped and human-size, stood alone to meet them.

Raven had walked fifty paces away from his ship and stood with arms calmly folded as he awaited the coming of the earthmen. A sword was slung at his left hip, and a lazer hand weapon was holstered at the right. The brief, but strategically tailored sections of his chain mail armour gleamed golden bright against the pure white of his high-tunic uniform. He smiled at the size of the company that had issued from the city to challenge him, and it was the smile of a man who had to deal with the innocence of children. The simple fools did not know whether to be belligerent or cautious, but they would soon learn.

The cavalcade stopped at what they thought was a safe distance. The elephant drivers would go no further, and the priests would not interrupt their praying to urge them. The chariots ground to a halt, but after a brief confusion, Jahan drove between two of the elephants to halt in front of them. The other princes joined him, and not to be outdone Maryam pushed her chariot through to stand by her uncle. They all stared at the lone man, and then at the towering rocket ship behind him, wondering what they should do next.

"He is a god," Rajar said suddenly. "Look, the colour of his skin is blue."

Maryam stared in wonder. In all the pictures she had ever seen of the gods they had all been depicted with a multitude of arms and legs, and always with skin of light, radiant blue. This man had only one set of arms and one set of legs, but his face and hands were definitely a soft, pale blue. Surely he had to be a god. She stared at him and realized that he was also a handsome god, and an extremely sensual god. He was standing with feet apart, and her gaze flickered back and forth between his sardonic face and that loin-draining bulge of gold chain mail between his thighs, and she felt herself go faint and near to swooning.

The princes looked to Jahan for a lead. The old general looked back to the priests and saw that none of them would be of any practical value. Not one of them had yet dared to open his eyes. Feeling certain only of his duty to do something Jahan lifted his reins to coax his horses a little closer, and then he stopped again.

Raven had moved, unfolding his arms slowly from his broad chest. Lazily he extended one hand and pointed to his right. A great pile of boulders stood there, as high as the walls of Karakhor, and timelessly cloaked in tangles of green creeper and yellow lichens. As the signal was given a fierce beam of white energy lanced down from the nose cone of the spaceship behind him, blasting into the giant tumble of rocks. The creepers and lichens were burned off in the first split second of the flash of fire, and then the rocks themselves slowly shrank and melted.

There was pandemonium among the ranks of Karakhor. Horses bolted with their chariots and warriors fled or fell screaming. The mighty elephants trumpeted in alarm, turning away and toppling their burdens of praying priests to the ground. Prince Rajar found himself bruised and choking in the dust, while his chariot and that of his brother Nirad vanished back toward the city. Those who stood fast held their plunging horses with difficulty as the sound and heat of the terrifying spectacle washed over them.

Raven half-turned and extended his left hand. There he pointed toward a low hill, and the agonized watchers saw the top of the hill sliced clean away by a second shaft of white-hot light. More men and horses panicked, and more threw themselves prostrate on the earth.

Behind the spaceship was a belt of young forests and there

Raven pointed for the third time. Taron fired a third lazer blast and incinerated half the forest. A fearsome tunnel of fire sped through the shriveling trees, and then the flames began to roar hungrily and eat their way through the forest on either side.

The demonstration was over. The proud banners of Karakhor were scattered and demoralized. A dozen chariots were overturned and it would take days to re-capture the stampeded elephants. Those who had held their ground could only stand dumbly now and wait.

Briskly Thorn, Garl and Landis, descended from the ship to join their commander. Raven led them forward to where only a handful of chariots now waited. He looked at the frozen faces of the men, and then at the white face of the woman. She had held firm when all but the boldest of her menfolk had fled, and she was both ripe and beautiful. He noted her soft, awe-filled eyes, the high-held chin, and the full-curved heave of her bosom. Here was a woman who might make worthy sport, even for a Sword Lord. He stepped up beside her, took the reins from her faltering hands, and then turned the horses to race the chariot back to the city.

Thorn had calmly climbed up beside Jahan. Garl and Landis took their places in the chariots of Sanjay and Devan. The warmaster general and royal princes exchanged doubtful glances, and then accepted their passengers without question. They, too, wheeled their chariots to follow Raven and Maryam.

As they passed through the walls of the city, Maryam dared to look up into the hard but handsome blue face of the man beside her. Raven chose that moment to glance down and he could afford a smile to calm her trembling.

Maryam returned the smile and touched the firm blue hand that held the reins. It was warm. He was warm-blooded after all, perhaps a god in human form. She felt weak but there was an overpowering excitement swelling up within her breast, almost smothering the painfully rapid beating of her heart.

God or man, he was clearly far more powerful than all ordinary men, perhaps more so than all ordinary gods. And he had chosen her. He rode beside her as though they were god and consort. Now, at last, she knew exactly where her duty and her destiny lay. A union with this leader-of-gods would atone for all the trouble she had caused by rejecting Sardar, and would more than satisfy her duty to her father and her people. An alliance with these super-beings from the sky would give Karakhor far more power and security than any petty joining with Maghalla.

Oh, Kananda, she thought passionately, *I wish that you could see me now.*

ଓ

At that precise moment in time, Kananda had more pressing problems on his mind. He stood by the Alphan Tri-Thruster with Zela and Kaseem, listening to the bad news that had just been brought to him by the young lords Kasim and Gujar. His brother Ramesh was missing, along with a dozen other young men, and their absence had just been discovered.

“They must have left secretly, of their own free will.” Gujar offered his opinion cautiously. “They could not have been taken from the camp without an alarm being raised. Also it cannot be coincidence that the missing men are all close companions of the Prince Ramesh, together with his personal guard.”

“Damn him for a foolish young cub,” Kananda said angrily. “Where would he go?”

“I think our head huntsman can answer you.” Kasim pushed the man forward as he spoke. Hamir shuffled his feet and bowed his bare head. His green helmet twisted anxiously in his hands.

“Speak!” Kananda ordered.

“Sire, Prince Ramesh came to me two days ago. He asked me to lead him and his companions on a hunt of their own. I told him I would gladly do so if you sanctioned the hunt, but that without your sanction I could not. Prince Ramesh was very angry, but said no more.” The man hesitated and then finished nervously, “Now I have learned that one of my assistants is with the missing party.”

“He has gone on his own tiger hunt.” Kaseem wrung his wrinkled hands in priestly anguish. “I should have forseen this. Prince Ramesh is impatient and reckless. I knew he fretted. May the gods forgive me.”

“We must go after them.” Kananda’s gaze was still fixed on the huntsman. “Which way would they go?”

“My assistant is familiar with good tiger country to the south of here. I think he will lead them in that direction.”

“So, they head closer to the wild lands,” Kananda said grimly. “We must catch them quickly, before they run into trouble.” He put his hand on Gujar’s shoulder. “Our elephants will be too slow. I would borrow your horse, my friend, and take another small party for speed. You will take command here in my absence, defer only to Kaseem.”

“I would sooner go with you,” Gujar said loyally. “But your will is my command.”

Kananda smiled, and punched him lightly on the shoulder. Then he turned to Kasim. “Gather the horsemen, and for foot soldiers we will take only a dozen of the strongest runners.” His attention fell again on the head huntsman. “How fast can you run?”

“As fast as any man, sire. And I will run until I drop.”

"Then you will track for us. Make ready."

The men dispersed to saddle the horses and don their weapons. Kananda buckled on his own dagger and sword. Then Zela touched his arm and said calmly, "If you can spare me one of your horses, I will come with you."

Kananda stared into her deep blue eyes. She gazed back at him, unflinching.

"There could be danger," he said uncertainly. "The monkey tribes are savages but there are many of them. We ride toward their country and a smaller party may tempt them to attack."

"We fought the tiger together," she reminded him.

"The tiger attacked us both. But why this? For you there is no need."

"There is our friendship," Zela said softly. And her eyes said much more.

Kananda laughed then and called for a horse for her to mount. Zela called Kyle and ordered him to bring her own sword and lazer. Blair was close and frowned a little.

"Is this wise, Commander?"

Zela smiled at his concern. "It is a politically sound decision. We have made much progress here and it could all be lost if Prince Kananda fails to return. That would be a foolish waste when a single lazer shot could settle any conflict that might arise on this planet. I can provide good insurance for our friends with little risk."

Blair was not fooled. He had noted that his commander and the Hindu prince had taken far more pleasure in each other's company than was politically necessary. He had noted the growing intimacy of their smiles and the exchanged looks and body signals. With every day that passed, they touched more often, and the moments of touching became more lingering.

"Be careful," he advised. But he refrained from designating those areas in which he felt that she needed to take extra care.

ↂ

They rode hard for three hours, the horsemen scouting ahead in all directions, but then they had to stop and rest the running men. Kananda was sorely tempted to race ahead with his mounted companions, but Hamir could only track at ground level, and without him they might miss the trail altogether. It was only from the signs that his keen eyes could read that they could be confident that they had not already gone astray.

They dismounted and Kananda sat with his back to a tree, his right leg stretched out full length and throbbing dully. The wound from the tiger's claws had healed, but this was the most severe test he had yet given it. He drank sparingly from his leather water bottle and then offered it to Zela. She too drank slowly, like a seasoned soldier, and handed it back after the second swallow. "How long before we can hope to catch them?" she asked as she sat beside him.

Kananda shrugged. "It depends upon how fast Ramesh moves and how much distance he feels he needs between us before he stops to hunt. He must have at least half a day's start."

Zela made herself comfortable, unselfconsciously sliding down the zip of her suit to allow the cooling air to circulate around her bare breasts and beneath her damp armpits. Kananda sought to avert his gaze and looked instead at the sword on her hip. It was the first time he had seen her with such a familiar weapon.

"I thought your people only fought with lightning bolts," he said curiously.

"For many centuries my people fought with swords and other weapons similar to your own," Zela told him. "Today, for many Alphans, the sword is but a ceremonial weapon, but a few of us are skilled in its use. Among the Gheddans, the sword is the only true weapon of honour and only a single combat sword kill holds genuine prestige. That is why some Alphans still practise with the sword—to be able to meet a Gheddan on equal terms and fight at their level."

"This seems strange when you have the lightning bolts." Kananda saw that some of the runners still needed to catch their wind and continued: "Tell me more about Alpha and Ghedda. If they remained unknown to each other for so long, then how did they come to discover each other?"

"Dooma has three moons of different sizes and in different orbits," Zela told him. "And so the great oceans that divide our two continents are subject to violent tides and tidal waves. They are also ravaged by fierce magnetic storms. Because the oceans are so unpredictable and dangerous, Alpha and Ghedda were kept apart. Our ships did not dare to venture far from the safety of the continental shores. It was not until we built large ships and developed fire and steam as a means of propulsion more reliable than wind-driven sails that Alphan navigators first discovered the continent of Ghedda."

She smiled ruefully. 'That was only a few hundred years ago, and it would have been better if they had left that barbaric place undiscovered. Once the Sword Lords of Ghedda realized that our planet held another continent, one that was rich in wealth and soft and ripe with peace, they began immediate plans for conquest. A mighty Gheddan war fleet was put together and sailed to loot, rape and enslave us. The natural barriers of the ocean depleted the Gheddan war ships, but many of them got through. The survivors were defeated in battle off the coast of Alpha, but at a terrible cost."

"And all this was before you developed the lightning bolts?"

Zela nodded. "May God forgive us, but it was the threat from Ghedda that pushed forward the development of more and more fearsome weapons. Our scientists saw an urgent need for self preservation and defence. They discovered the power of explosives for propelling vehicles and firing weapons. Then they discovered atomic power. And then nuclear power. Next came thermonuclear bombs and missiles, and nuclear-pulse rocket engines. And finally the lazer-beam energy weapons that you call lightning bolts."

Again her talk included many words that had no equivalent in Hindu, but Kananda had grasped the concept of growing power, even though it was in forms that he did not understand. "With all this power, surely you could destroy these Sword Lords and their land of Ghedda?"

"There were times when such action might have been possible, when we were far enough ahead in the arms race to have made a first strike that would have devastated their homeland. But it was not our way. We had found peace and a belief in one God. We believe that the Gheddans are also children of that God. Many missionaries sailed alone or in small groups to Ghedda, but those who reached those savage shores were almost all killed in sport by the inhabitants. What we had failed to perceive was that the Gheddans had no belief in God, in any form or forms, nor did they believe in any spiritual realm. It is true that their ancient history spoke of religious wars and conflicts much the same as ours, but in time they had come to the opposite belief—that there is no god, and that any such belief is just the refuge of the mentally crippled and the weak. Ghedda has believed for two thousand years that all that we are becomes extinct at the moment of death, and so for them, the only meaning of life is to squeeze out of it as much personal power and pleasure as is possible while it is there."

"But now that you know the godlessness of Ghedda—surely now you can destroy them?"

"Now it is too late, for Ghedda is as powerful as Alpha. The Gheddans have always been far more experienced in the arts of warfare, espionage and deceit. Alphan scientists have made all the important advances of the past three hundred years, but Ghedda has always been able to steal them or obtain them in some other manner. Many of our greatest scientists and thinkers have believed that we hold a moral responsibility, given by God, to share the peaceful benefits of each new technological step with Ghedda. It is only by trusting the Gheddans, so they have argued, that we can help them to learn to trust us. So in many cases our secrets have been given away."

Zela paused, and her faced mirrored a confusion of inner feelings, ranging from anger and disgust to sorrow and despair. Then she concluded, "Ghedda has always been behind Alpha in the arms race, but now we are in a nightmare situation where both sides hold an arsenal of weapons so powerful that to use them would cause the total destruction of the entire planet. Our scientists have calculated that if only the weapons of one side were used, then the chain reaction of released energy would rip Dooma apart. Where our proud planet now orbits the sun, there would only be a smoking belt of asteroids and radio-active rubble revolving between the fourth and sixth planets of this solar system."

"You could destroy your world?" Kananda was shocked, and despite the hot sun, he felt cold at the thought.

Zela nodded. "That is one of the reasons why we wish to make friends here on Earth. Alpha will never use those weapons but we fear the Gheddans will. So we pray that you may make the survivors of our race welcome, if the madness on Dooma should ever reach the suicidal peaks of planetary oblivion."

Kananda stared into her face. "You are welcome," he said. "In Golden Karakhor where I shall one day rule." He still believed her a goddess, but boldness had been growing in him and at last he dared to reach for her and hold her close. For the first time they were free of the ever-watchful presence of Blair or Kaseem, and for the first time she seemed vulnerable to him. Zela leaned against him and it seemed that their hearts beat in unison. She raised her face to him, her gaze searching his, and then slowly their lips met. It was a brief kiss, uncertain and half-fearing on each side. Then her mouth softened under the pleasurable contact and moved sensuously against his own. In that moment of time, Kananda knew that this was ordained and approved by all the gods in heaven.

After a moment, they separated. There was work to be done and there were still too many of their companions too close for comfort.

"We should be thinking of finding Ramesh," Zela said reluctantly.

Kananda nodded and got to his feet. He swung up into the saddle of Gujar's horse and gave orders. The party moved forward once more. A few of the foot warriors grumbled but soon settled into a silent, loping run. They were crossing a broad plain of long grassland, scrub bushes and patches of low trees. It was possible tiger country, but the signs indicated that Ramesh had still been travelling fast when he passed this way.

The trail continued south, toward a blue blur of distant hills that darkened into thickening forest and black mountains. They were leaving the frontiers of Karakhor and pressing toward the untamed wild lands.

Chapter Six

They caught up with the hunting party late in the afternoon of the second day, where the land broke up into low, jungle-clad hills on the very edge of the black forest. In a shallow valley between two of the hills, they found the first body. One of the young lords who had ridden with Ramesh lay in a crumpled sprawl, with sightless eyes staring up at the sky. A spear blade had pierced his heart and his throat had been cut. The carrion birds that had led them to the spot circled overhead, crying angrily at the interruption.

Kananda looked down from his horse and felt sick in his stomach. He had feared the worst and it had happened. They were too late. Emotion tore at his heart and battered at the portals of his mind, but he knew he had to maintain a clear head. He sucked in a deep breath to hold down the waves of anger, grief and frustration. Then he rose to his full height in the saddle to survey the landscape all around. They had been moving with ever-increasing caution and this was no time to relax.

There was nothing to be seen or heard except the circling vultures, and yet Kananda sensed that they were not alone. He lowered himself back into his saddle and said grimly, "We will dismount to search this area. A man on horseback is too easy atarget. But we will stay in one group. No man is to move out of sight of the rest of us. And be prepared to defend yourselves at any instant."

The horse-riders dismounted and the majority of the party drew their swords. A few of the soldiers chose to unsling their bows and notch an arrow in readiness. All of them had been wearing arm shields since the start of the day.

Zela hesitated a second and then drew her sword in preference to her hand lazer. The lightning bolts, as Kananda chose to call them, were best held in reserve.

The search quickly located a score of bodies. Twelve of them were from the hunting party, three more scattered and pierced with arrows where they had fallen alone, and the others slain in a group where they had valiantly stood to defend themselves. The rest of the dead were wild men, naked but for a belt of monkey skin supporting the bark-cloth pouch that held their private parts.

Within ten minutes, all of the missing hunting party had been accounted for except Ramesh. Of the young prince there was no sign.

"They would know his rank from his apparel," Kasim offered hopefully. "Perhaps they have taken him alive."

"Perhaps," Kananda answered in a hollow voice. There was no real hope in his heart, just the crushing feeling of having lost his brother and of failing terribly in his duty. However, he knew the direction in which his duty lay now. "Bring me our huntsman," he ordered.

While he waited, he studied one of the dead savages. The corpse had long, tangled black hair, and its dark face and skin were painted with coloured clays and berry juices to give it a ferocious aspect. The face was coloured chalk white with large red circles drawn around the mouth and eyes. The lips were painted with black triangular teeth to give the impression of a mouth within a mouth.

"This is a war design," Kananda told Zela who stood beside him. "The extra teeth are painted on to frighten enemies. So this was not the case of one hunting party falling foul of another."

Zela said nothing, but she sensed his suppressed emotion and her hand was a comfort on his shoulder. Then Kasim returned with Hamir. The man expected to be blamed and was trembling as Kananda straightened and turned to face him.

"The attackers have taken Prince Ramesh,"' Kananda said calmly. "Alive or dead we do not yet know. Can you tell which way they have taken?"

"The signs point down this valley, sire, and then into the forest." Hamir swallowed hard and then added, "But, sire, I think we are being watched."

"I think so too. But only one pair of eyes, perhaps two. If there had been enough of them to attack, they would have done so." He paused thoughtfully. "Can you track the main party at night?"

"Tonight there will be a moon. If there is not too much cloud, I can follow the sign down the valley. But in the jungle? If there is a path, it may be easy. If not..." He shrugged and spread his hands.

"Then let us hope for a path. We will leave here now and return at nightfall. The watchers will see us go, and they will run back to their village before dark. These wild men are afraid of the darkness. They believe that the night is haunted by the spirits of the forest and of their dead. That will be the best time to move against them."

Kasim looked toward the remains of the hunting party. "Have we time to bury our dead?"

Kananda shook his head. "It galls me to leave them, but if those who watch us have sent a runner after their main party, then those who attacked Ramesh could return and surprise us before we have finished. It is best if we leave now."

There was no more argument. The riders swung up on their mounts and the small force began an apparently dejected retreat.

☙

Two hours passed before the sun began to set behind the western hills. The sky flamed briefly pink and gold, and such was Kananda's state of mind that his imagination saw it as a dying funeral pyre for his lost brother. The flames dulled, like a glow from red embers, and then they were gone. The shadows closed in, a few stars pricked through the darkening heavens, and a half moon rose in the north. They rode for another ten minutes until a hundred stars were shining in the night sky. Kananda felt certain then that they were no longer being followed and he called a halt.

They rested for an hour and then turned back. Some of the foot soldiers moved reluctantly, but none argued. They stayed in a close group, and in the soft moon and starlight, Hamir was easily able to retrace their route. Two more hours and they were back in the shallow valley where the dead still lay unburied.

There was a scuffling sound, as a jackal or some other scavenging animal was disturbed from its feast, but then stillness. Kananda and his party stood motionless, all their senses alert, their hands softly muzzling the horses, but there was nothing to alarm them. There was no longer the sensation of being watched.

Kananda nodded to the huntsman and he continued to lead them down the valley, past the scene of the ambush. The band of savages who had attacked the hunting party could be estimated at between thirty and forty and their trail was clear to follow. It led through the hills to where the forest loomed as a black, tangled wall in front of them.

Hamir scouted ahead and came back.

"There is a path." His voice was caught somewhere between relief and fear. "It is narrow, but we can follow it into the forest."

Kananda dismounted and the others did the same. "We will go into the forest on foot," he decided. "If the gods are smiling, their village will not be too far inside the forest and we will recover Ramesh before dawn. Two men will stay here with the horses."

They entered the jungle footpath with swords drawn. The huntsman led, with Kananda at his shoulder. Zela came next, then Kasim and three more of the young nobles. There were ten soldiers to follow them. They were seventeen strong. The odds against them were unknown, but at least twice their number had attacked Ramesh and his hunting party. If they were to succeed, then the elements of surprise and darkness had to weigh heavily in their favour.

The jungle closed around them, suffocating and threatening in its almost total blackness. There would have been no room for the horses here and they kept to the footpath only because there was no other way. The path was like an invisible tunnel through the seemingly impenetrable tangles of foliage on either side. There was a constant low rustling, chirping and buzzing from the small nocturnal animals, birds and insects that hunted unseen on the forest floor. Leaves and creepers continuously touched their faces or dragged across their bodies like cold, caressing fingers.

Their progress was slow and nerve-wracking, and for the first time Zela began to concede that Blair might have been right. Perhaps this was not a wise course of action on her part. A hand lazer might be an effective weapon in a stand-up battle between two human forces, but it would be of little use against the fangs of the cobra that might be coiled in waiting beside this jungle path or against the prowling leopard that might be even now stalking them through the lower branches of the trees.

Her right hand tightened on the hilt of her sword, and her left hand tightened on Kananda's shoulder. It was an involuntary shudder of apprehension, but then Kananda's fingers reassuringly touched her own. Zela smiled then in the darkness. Blair might be right—probably was right—but this was where she wanted to be. Kananda needed her and that was enough.

It was difficult to judge time and distance and so they could only guess at how far they had penetrated into the forest. It seemed like forever, but at last there was a break in the blackness ahead. The red glow of fires cast a flickering light and they could smell the woodsmoke. The trees thinned out on either side and they discerned the faint silhouettes of some low, conical huts.

Hamir stopped. Kananda gently drew him back and signaled the others to wait motionless. He moved silently forward, intending to reconnoitre alone, but Zela and Kasim moved equally silently beside him.

Kananda stopped them after a few more paces. They were on the edge of a wide clearing that contained the native village. The huts were crude constructions of grass and leaves, plastered with mud onto a framework of branches. They formed a large circle around the perimeter of the clearing. In the centre of the clearing was a large black tent, big enough to comfortably sleep a dozen men. There was a smaller tent on either side of the big one, and these were more simply constructed of wild animal skins. A large wood-fire burned in front of each tent and a few smaller cooking fires flickered in front of some of the perimeter huts. The village appeared to be asleep. The only inhabitants awake were the guards standing in pairs in front of each tent.

All this Kananda saw at a glance, but then his gaze was riveted upon the tall pole that had been erected in the centre of the clearing, just in front of the central fire. A body was displayed on the pole, suspended head downward by lashed feet. The arms hung limply, stained with red streaks from the spear wounds in the bare chest. The firelight played on the once-proud face, still distorted in its final agony. The body no longer looked like that of the young prince Ramesh, but Kananda knew that it was his brother.

"We are too late," Zela whispered softly with her mouth close to his ear. "I am sorry."

"It is as I expected." Kananda kept his voice low, although he wanted to scream his fury. His knuckles gleamed white around the hilt of his sword. "But we cannot leave Ramesh there on display for the sport of these animals. I must retrieve his body and return it Karakhor."

"It will not be easy," Kasim murmured. And he pointed to the black banner that fluttered over the large tent.

"I have seen it," Kananda answered bleakly. He turned to Zela and explained, "The black leopard banner is the emblem of Sardar. Our enemy, the king of Maghalla, is here. See the banners above the other two tents, the black monkey and the red monkey? They are the chief clans of the monkey tribes. Their chieftains are here also. This can only mean that Sardar has already made his alliance."

Kasim breathed fiercely between his teeth. "We must warn Karakhor."

Kananda nodded. "That is vital, but I will not leave without

Ramesh." He laid his sword carefully on the earth in front of him and unslung the short bow from his back. He pulled an arrow from his quiver and checked its straightness against the starlight before notching it to the bow. "We need five more of our best archers," he instructed softly.

Kasim moved back to the main group and returned with four of the soldiers. All had their bows unslung. Kananda pointed out each man's target and they knelt in a line. "When my arrow flies, they all fly," he commanded. "Then, no matter what happens, I shall cut down Prince Ramesh."

His five companions nodded silently. Kananda drew back his arrow and took aim on one of the guards standing outside Sardar's tent. The Maghallan wore a black loincloth and turban and his upper torso was protected by a leather waistcoat that was partially unlaced at the chest. Kananda aimed for the spot that was a finger's breadth to the left of the breastbone. He looked to see that the others had also taken aim, and then loosed his arrow.

The soft twang of the bowstring was the signal that launched the other five arrows. The first Maghallan fell dead with Kananda's arrow piercing his heart. His companion staggered a moment with Kasim's shaft through his neck and then he too fell. The four savages guarding the monkey banner tents were the lesser danger. They were half asleep, and probably only placed there in mimicry of Sardar's efficiency. However, three of those also fell dead. The fourth stumbled back against the tent he guarded, his eyes popping open and his mouth dropping slack as he stared dumbly at the arrow embedded in the joint of his shoulder.

Kananda was already moving, slinging his bow across his shoulders and snatching up his sword as he raced to the centre of the clearing. He reached Ramesh in seconds, wrapping his left arm around his brother's cold shoulders as he reached up with his sword to slash through the ropes that secured the feet. With the second stroke, Ramesh fell free from the pole and dropped over his left shoulder.

The surviving guard found enough of his wits to scream. The sound was choked into a gurgle as Kasim's second arrow plunged into his cheek, but it was enough. The guard's fall against the tent had disturbed the occupant and the half-cry brought the man out to raise the alarm. He was a squat, hairy creature wearing a necklace of monkey skulls. His hair was woven into long black braids, and from each braid there dangled the skull of a bird. He carried a spear and, with a fearsome shriek, he charged full tilt at Kananda.

Kananda noted that the monkey skulls were painted a bright red and that the man had emerged from the tent with the red monkey banner. The chief of the clan, he guessed, and there was a grim satisfaction in him as he deflected the spear thrust and skewered the man through the middle.

He backed up swiftly, but by now the camp was in uproar. A dozen Maghallan warriors came running from behind the black tent with Sardar's banner, armed with swords and axes, while from all sides the wild men were pouring out of their huts with clubs and spears.

Another volley of arrows from Kananda's small force of archers slowed the Maghallans, and Kananda glanced over his shoulder to see the rest of his soldiers rushing to join him. Among them was Hamir, the huntsman. Hamir was not a trained fighter, but a brave and loyal man and a strong, fast runner. Kananda slew another Maghallan with his sword, and then passed Ramesh back to the huntsman.

"Take your prince back to the horses," he shouted.

He could only trust that he was obeyed, for there were swords and spears thrusting at him from all sides. Blows rained on his arm shield and his defending sword blade, but then he was no longer alone. Kasim was on his left and the slim silver figure of Zela on his right. As one sword became three, defence became attack, and they carried the fight back into the ranks of Maghalla.

Kananda fought as he had never fought before, his sword whirling an avenging dance of death before him. Kasim was no mean swordsman and Kananda could have chosen no better man to stand beside him. But even in these hot and bloody moments, as their sword blades flashed and reddened in the star and firelight, he found time to marvel at the prowess of Zela. Her speed and skill were equal to his own and she fought with all the fury and splendour of a true goddess.

The three held the foreground while their companions held the flanks, and the Maghallans gave way. This strange silver woman with the flying gold hair and the death-singing blade was beyond their comprehension. They, too, feared that she was more than mortal, a demon perhaps, in human form.

Kananda gave an order and the Karakhorans fell back, retreating in an orderly group toward the path that led back through the forest. The lull in the battle and Zela's unnerving presence might have given them their escape, but then the king of Maghalla and a group of his senior commanders burst from their black tent.

Kananda recognized Sardar immediately. The short, broad body with the powerful chest and long arms was one he would never forget. Disturbed from his sleep, Sardar wore only a black loincloth, but in his hand was a long sword. His face was a startled mask of bestiality, slashed with that dreadful scar tissue from beneath the left eye and across the corner of his mouth to the cleft of his chin. He had a high, ape-like forehead and flared nostrils and his eyes burned with black rage.

Recognition also flashed in Sardar's eyes. At their last meeting, they had faced each other over half-drawn swords in Kara-Rashna's palace hall, but now their blades were free and naked and the weight of sheer numbers was with Maghalla. Sardar swung up his sword and, with a mighty roar, he attacked.

Kananda sprang to meet him. Here was a god-given chance to avenge his brother, to put an end to Sardar the Merciless, and perhaps to the whole threat of war. If he could succeed in this, then he would not have failed in his duty.

Both sides recognized a battle of champions and stayed their hands. Steel met steel in a crash of sparks and the night air echoed with blow after blow in ringing succession. The blades of Kananda and Sardar whirled faster than the eye could see and for a full minute both men held their ground. Then Sardar slipped and drew back.

Kananda thrust for the kill, but was foiled by one of Sardar's lieutenants. The man hurled himself between them to protect the body of his king, and died as Kananda turned his blade, first to deflect the assailant's axe-stroke, and then to back-cut across the man's throat.

The moment of single combat was past. The Maghallans threw themselves forward and surrounded Sardar. A dozen blades flashed against Kananda, but then Zela and Kasim were beside him again. Kananda strove furiously to reach Sardar and three of the Maghallan bodyguards died in as many seconds before his wrath, but there were more Maghallans to take their place. The Maghallan camp behind Sardar's tent was much larger than Kananda had realized. Sardar was swallowed up behind the bodies of his guards and saved from Kananda's ferocious reach.

The weight of the battle swung against them. Four of the

Karakhoran soldiers and two of the young nobles were dead. The survivors fought for their lives against ever-increasing odds. The wild men had found their courage and pressed in from both sides to avenge their dead chieftain.

It was now or never, Zela realized. She pressed forward with another lightning display of swordsmanship that cleared the ground before her, and then in the few seconds breathing space, she stepped back. She transferred her sword neatly to her left hand and with her right she drew the hand lazer from her hip. She fired directly into the loose knot of warriors that confronted Kananda and Kasim.

The bright, white shaft of the energy beam lanced through the mob, killing three and scattering the rest in mortal terror. It hit the black tent of Sardar and transformed it instantly into a red burst of roaring flames. Maghallans and wild men fell back together in shock and confusion.

Zela fired again, the beam scything through the close-packed tribesmen on their left flank and turning the tent with the black monkey banner into a second inferno. The howls of hate that had issued from the savage throats now became howls of gibbering fear. Those who did not faint or throw themselves to the ground turned and fled.

Kananda searched for Sardar, but his enemy had disappeared. He would have launched himself in vain pursuit, but Kasim's hand restrained his arm and Zela called on him to fall back. He ground his teeth in bitter frustration, but knew that they were right. Zela's hand weapon could only hurl a limited number of the lightning bolts and they had to use the respite she had given them to escape.

He gave the order and the survivors from Karakhor backed up to the path that had brought them here. Then each man in turn dashed back through the invisible tunnel into the thick darkness. Kananda held the rear, but there was no challenge. He stared at the running backs of their enemies who were fleeing in the opposite direction. Then he looked up at the black leopard banner above the burning tent and saw that it too was being eaten by the ravenous flames. It gave him a moment of satisfaction but it was not enough. Again he searched for Sardar.

Zela pulled at his shoulder and she urged him to hurry. Kananda swallowed his frustration and turned to follow her and Kasim through the jungle. The fierce glow of flames was quickly left behind them.

They were blind here, but they ran as fast as possible knowing that there might be other jungle paths where the wild men would be able to get ahead of them. The unseen foliage that had softly caressed them as they slowly moved in now whipped and slashed at their bodies and faces as they raced back. When any one man stumbled, the others automatically blundered into him or over him in an undignified heap. Where their courage had held fast in the face of battle, it now waned as they felt themselves lost in this hellish, tangled blackness. The retreat had become a rout, but mercifully they were not pursued.

They finally emerged from the forest bruised, battered and bleeding, but with an infinite sense of relief at finding that they were once again beneath the familiar patterns of moon and stars. Kananda saw with relief that the huntsman was waiting for them with the two soldiers who had stayed with the horses, and the body of Ramesh was already secured on Kananda's mount.

"He is alive," Hamir said hoarsely, but there was hope and elation in his voice.

Kananda stared at the huntsman, hardly daring to believe

what he had heard. Ramesh hung like a corpse, face down in front of the saddle, and slowly Kananda lifted the slack head and looked into his brother's ghost-white face. As he leaned closer, he felt the faint movement of breath on his cheek. He had been so certain that his brother was dead that he could barely believe it. He turned to stare joyously at Zela.

"He breathes. He lives! We must tend his wounds."

"There is no time," Zela answered firmly. "We must get further away."

Kananda stared at her, and then realized bitterly that she was right. The pursuit would be hot behind them and if they stayed, they might all be lost.

They had left four of their number behind, so the party now numbered thirteen, together with Ramesh who had to be carried. Kananda ordered the horses to be ridden double, and the four men who still had to run to be rotated as soon as the runners flagged, and in this manner they continued their escape at a good speed.

☙

It was mid-day before Kananda dared to allow a stop. He knew that even though the monkey tribes might be demoralized by the death of one of their chieftains, Sardar would almost certainly pursue them as soon as it was light. They were still only just within the frontiers of their own empire, but the horses had to be rested and the men needed to eat and drink to rally their strength. Also he could no longer delay his own desperate need to examine his brother. After the hard riding of the past few hours, he was again unsure whether Ramesh was alive or dead.

They laid the young prince tenderly on the ground, and

with Hamir and Zela beside him, Kananda carefully checked his wounds. Hamir had made a hurried attempt at dressing the two deep gashes in the naked chest and Kananda peeled away the rough bandages and the handfuls of leaves that the huntsman had used to plug the open wounds. They were spear or sword thrusts, ugly but mercifully shallow. One thrust had skidded off the ribcage, tearing the flesh in a long, ragged slice. The other had pierced between two ribs, but the thrust had lacked power and had been stopped by the ribcage itself before penetrating any vital organs.

"I think he suffers mainly from shock and loss of blood," Zela offered. "Fortunately you cut him down before he could fully bleed to death." She took the medical kit from the broad belt at her waist and quickly began to clean and dress the wounds. Ramesh remained unconscious, but at this stage there was no more they could do.

While they shared the meagre rations from their saddle packs, Zela again sat to eat beside Kananda. When they had refreshed themselves, they were silent for a while, and then Kananda struggled to find the words to thank her.

"We are friends," Zela said. But her smile was troubled and she continued, "I am glad your brother lives, but we lost four men in exchange. Was it worth it?"

"Ramesh is a royal prince of Karakhor," Kananda said slowly. "We showed that an attack on the royal household will not go unpunished, and that retribution from Karakhor can reach even into their forests. We killed one of their chieftains and burned the leopard banner of Sardar. All of this may force the monkey tribes to think again, and they may yet turn back from their alliance with Maghalla. If we have achieved this, then we have done what my duty demanded."

He paused to glance at the still figure of his younger

brother. "In all of this, Ramesh was more than a man. He was more than my brother, even though I would war against all of Maghalla to avenge him. He was a symbol. He carried the name of Karakhor and flew her golden banner. And it is always in the nature of men to die for their names and their banners. Even if Ramesh dies, even if he had been dead as I first feared, all of what we have done would still be worth the sacrifice and the effort."

Zela nodded her understanding. They watched a hawk hovering in the blue sky to their left, and when it swooped out of sight, Kananda spoke again. "You are skilled with the sword, Zela, more so than any man I have ever seen. And yet I thought your people only wore swords for ceremony?"

"I did add that some of us do practise the art," she reminded him. "And with good reason." Her face hardened with another grim memory, and then she explained: "Once, I too had a brother, whom I loved as dearly as you love Ramesh. Lorin was my elder brother, a splendid young man, and when I was a little girl I worshipped him almost as though he were a god. I also had two younger brothers. We all used to play together. One day, when I was only ten years old, we were playing in a boat on the lake near our home. Suddenly a terrible storm blew up..."

☙

The memory was ever painful in her mind, a mental pain her thoughts would return to like a tongue to a nagging tooth. The fateful day had started with hot blue skies, the warbles of birdsong, and the light slapping of the wavelets on the small gold sand beach below their father's house. Laton, their father, was absent as usual, having left early in his sky-car for the City of Singing Spires where he taught philosophy and unified learning in the Academy of Knowledge. Zara, their mother, had died in child-birth when Larn, the youngest of Zela's brothers had been born. Larn was five now, Logan was seven, and Lorin was thirteen. Only Zela and Lorin could remember their mother, and for Zela it was a memory of feeling loved and cared for and secure rather than any visual image. She knew that Laton loved them and cared for them just as much, but he had to spend much of his time at the academy, and some of the security, and something that was unique and beautiful, had gone forever. Or perhaps not forever. Sometimes Zela had wanted to die, just to know whether she and her mother would be together again, as Laton had promised.

Rena, the nurse-housekeeper who had looked after them since their mother's death, was always busy, and as Larn and Logan became more agile and adventurous, and Lorin more capable and responsible, they were all left much to their own devices outside the hours of schooling. So they had played hunt and chase on the beach, climbed as high as they dared on the rocks, bathed at the edge of the lake, and finally, tiring of all the land-bound games, they had launched their small boat with its bright disc of orange sail.

They had been told never to sail more than fifty paces from the shoreline and they had no intention of disobeying the rule. Lorin had cast out a large, roped stone that served as an anchor and they had commenced fishing. The sail disc had been tipped to its horizontal position above their heads so that it now provided them with shade instead of catching the wind, and they became absorbed in their sport. The lake was filled with a rich variety of fish. The most plentiful and the most delicious to eat were the red-finned silverbacks and today they were close inshore in shoals and they were hungry. The slippery pile of fish grew quickly in the bottom of the boat, wriggling and sliding over their bare feet and filling them with excitement and enthusiasm. With their attention concentrated on their hand-held lines, they failed to notice that the sail had tilted slightly and was catching some of the strengthening breeze from the shore. The crude anchor was dragging on the lake bottom and inexorably they were being carried out to deeper water. The silver, solar-panelled dome of their father's house was growing darker as the storm clouds gathered, becoming smaller in its nest of blossoming fruit trees.

It was then that Lorin's line had hooked a blackfin. The blackfins were a much larger fish, less pleasant to eat, but vigorous fighters. The blackfin was a true sporting fish and Lorin fought and played it while the others cheered and all but fell overboard in their misguided efforts to help. The small boat began to rock dangerously, partly from their reckless movements and partly from the increasing size of the waves.

Several things happened almost simultaneously. The water became deeper than the length of their anchor rope, and suddenly the stern of the boat was dipping because the stone was pulling them down instead of dragging on the bottom. The boat began to move even faster and further from the shore and the squall hit them in a violent lashing of wind and rain. The sail tilted almost to the vertical to catch the full force of the wind. Lorin's line broke, the blackfin escaped, and all four of them became abruptly aware of their position of danger.

In moments they were drenched and terrified. Lorin struggled manfully with the sail, fighting the wind in his efforts to get the sail-frame back and secured in the horizontal position. Zela hauled in the now useless anchor, while Larn and Logan huddled together in the bottom of the boat. By the time Lorin had the sail made fast, they had been blown another hundred paces from the shore and the waves had slopped into and half-filled the tiny boat.

Lorin took up the oars and tried to row them back to the shore, while Zela found a drinking cup and desperately tried to bale out the water that was sloshing around their ankles. The squall had become a gale, the waves towered fearsomely all around them and lightning split the black sky with a deafening crack of thunder. Larn began to cry, but his whimpering was quickly lost in the nightmare of falling water.

Lorin's efforts with the oars were futile and Zela's frantic baling even more so. The boat was water-logged and sinking. Suddenly it tipped with the thrust of a wave and they were all tossed helplessly into the lake. Zela saw Larn and Logan still clinging together, their faces agonized and screaming then the waves sucked them down. She was sure she was going to drown with them, but then Lorin's arm was around her waist and he was pulling her with him as he swam bravely for the shore. Only Lorin could swim and he could only try to save one of them. And, Zela realized in anguish, he had chosen to try and save her.

It seemed to Zela like forever that they were in the water, and a thousand times it seemed that she must have choked and drowned in the roaring black tumult of the waves. Each time, her head somehow emerged again and, despite her bursting heart and lungs, she managed to gulp down enough air to keep her alive. Lorin was tiring, his struggles becoming weaker, but still he would not let her go. Zela tried to beg him to save himself but her mouth filled with water and she could only splutter and gasp. In that moment she would have preferred to go with her mother and her brothers, but Lorin's hold on her was unbreakable.

She closed her eyes and stopped fighting. She stopped fighting to live and she stopped fighting to break Lorin's hold. It was all irrelevant because they were both going to drown anyway. And then she was aware of another voice screaming above the storm. It was Rena, screaming encouragement to Lorin. She had seen the boat sink and waded out from the shore into chest-deep water to try and reach them. Her voice spurred Lorin to one last, final effort as a wave pushed him forward, and then the old woman's hands were clutching at them. She caught Lorin's arm and dragged them both close to her breast.

Somehow the old nurse had pulled them both into the shore, and there Zela lay, sobbing and choking in her arms. The old woman wept. Lorin lay sprawled on the sand, gasping for breath, his strength gone, his body exhausted. Then in anguish he pushed himself up and stared out onto the rain-lashed wildness of the lake. Their brothers and the boat had vanished. Lorin called their names in heart-broken despair and staggered back toward the lake. He would have thrown himself into its water and gone back for them if Rena had not left Zela on the sand and run to stop him at the water's edge. They struggled before Lorin collapsed again and Rena had to drag him clear of the lake for the second time. Zela could only watch and weep, and weep and weep...

ଓ

There were tears on her cheek now as she relived those awful moments. Her words died away and she became silent. Kananda put his arm around her shoulders but said nothing. He sensed that there was more.

"Lorin saved me," she continued at last. "But our brothers perished. After that there was only Lorin, and because I owed him my life, I worshipped him all the more. We were closer than any other brother and sister could be."

Kananda nodded in understanding, thinking of his own

affection for Maryam.

"When he was old enough, Lorin joined the Alphan Space Corps," Zela said quietly. "He became a first class pilot and a natural leader in everything. He was their star and champion in every kind of sport and skill. He rose faster through the officer ranks than any man before him. He was a member of the expedition that established the first base on our largest moon. And later he commanded the first manned expedition to the fourth planet. It was a dead planet, a red and hostile world of no practical value, but it was a vital stepping stone to this planet which you call Earth."

She stopped again. Telling how her younger brothers had died had been hard, the memory almost too painful to bear. But this was harder still, the memory pure anguish and undying rage, and when she next continued her voice was bleak and bitter, with the cutting edge of steel.

"Our first expedition to the fourth planet clashed there with a Gheddan expedition. Both sides had raced for the prestige of putting the first man on the red planet, and the race was a tie. Lorin was killed there, in a sword duel with the Sword Lord who commanded the Gheddan spaceship. Sword-play was the one skill which Lorin had not thought it important to master. He accepted a challenge because he was the kind of man who could do nothing else, but his death was ritualized murder."

She turned grim eyes upon Kananda. "From that day forward I vowed that I would take Lorin's place in the Space Corps. And from that day forward I have trained and practised with the sword. One day I shall meet with my brother's murderer and it will be my greatest pleasure to slay him with his own chosen weapon of honour and by his own chosen code. It is both my prayer and my destiny—something I sense with every fibre of my being—that one day I shall face and kill the Gheddan Sword Lord named Raven."

Chapter Seven

The lush green lawns between the palace and the limpid waters of the Mahanadi were filled with feasting tables, with altar and cooking fires, and a vast, colourful throng of nobles, warriors, priests and ladies. The women wore their most gorgeous saris in swirls of patterned silks, while their men were almost as resplendent in bright tunics, trousers and turbans. All of them dripped gold and jewelry in intricate chains and necklaces and pendants, all dazzling with precious stones. The royal princes sat like brilliant peacocks at the central table where Kara-Rashna's gold-and-ivory throne had been carried out of the audience hall and placed at the head of the table by a dozen slaves. The princes sat on the monarch's left, while Raven and four of his crew lounged nonchalantly on his right.

The sweet scents of roasting meat, burning sandalwood and incense drifted in the air. A priest recited the Vedas in a low, monotonous voice beside one of the altar fires, although no one seemed to listen. Other priests in their white robes dispensed flower garlands and soft prayers. The fierce heat of the afternoon had passed, but the evening was still warm. Sitars and flutes played trembling background music and there were subdued murmurs of conversation. There were pigs, deer, pheasant and an ox roasted whole, a variety of spiced eggs, grilled fish, platters of hot rice and bread, bowls of honey and small mountains of vegetable and fruit.

However, it was not the rich abundance of food and wine which slowed the hub-bub of talk that was normal on such occasions. The banquet and festivities had been ordered by Kara-Rashna to provide fit and royal welcome for the strangers from the stars. Every noble house of Karakhor was represented here—none had dared to ignore the invitation—but the visitors were greeted with as much apprehension as honour. The sardonic amusement with which they viewed the proceedings had not earned them any affection, and the general atmosphere of nervousness was growing.

Only Maryam seemed blind to it. She sat between her father and Raven, glowing with more radiance and beauty than any other woman present and smilingly indicating to the Sword Lord the select morsels and delicacies she thought he would enjoy the most. The queen Padmini, Kara-Rashna's first wife and Maryam's mother, sat at the monarch's other side, and twice she risked raising her eyes to signal her cautious disapproval to her daughter, but Maryam pretended not to notice. Kara-Rashna looked most uncomfortable and toyed fretfully with his food. His brothers felt that, although they could not communicate with their guests, it would still be impolite to exclude them by talking between themselves, and so they remained mainly silent and ill at ease. Only the Gheddans talked carelessly and ate with hearty appetites.

There was almost a sense of relief when enough food and wine had been consumed for it to be deemed proper for the entertainment to begin. A small orchestra formed and began to play and a group of slave dancing girls began to perform. They danced slowly at first, their supple movements graceful and teasing. Then gradually they moved faster, bare thighs flashing beneath their swirling skirts, hips undulating, and their almost bare breasts vibrating erotically with their exertions. Now even the Gheddans were silent, watching for the first time with interest and without a sneer.

Raven reclined on his chair, a goblet of wine in one hand and the fingers of the other resting lazily in a fruit bowl. He watched with his eyes but his mind was far away, comparing the scene before him with similar occasions on Ghedda. There in the rock-bound stronghold that his male ancestors had ruled for ten generations, the food had been as filling and the wine as plentiful, but the surroundings more spartan. The massive stone walls had been built to withstand siege in the days before air and space travel. The tables in the long eating hall were bare wood, knife-scarred and wine-stained, and there was no white lace and silken cloths. On Ghedda there was no incense, no altars and no priests. There were none of the pathetic rituals and pointless sacrifices that these people seemed to find so necessary. Religion was a dead relic of the distant and decadent past. There were no gods on Ghedda. There, man was supreme, and if he was strong enough and skilled enough, then nothing ruled over his own strength and his sword. Also there were few dancing girls, to be found only in cheap bars and drink dens. There was bloodshed enough in a Gheddan stronghold without inciting the swordsmen and masters to more with the cavorting of half-nude females.

At this stage of a Gheddan feast, the sword duels would begin. With other weapons, a duel could end in injury or first blood, but with the sword it was always to the death.

Raven thought back to his own duels with satisfaction. Few males on Ghedda were without sword scars. All of his crew had their fair share. Even Thorn, with the skills and the rank of swordmaster, bore the scar on his wrist with pride. But Raven had never been touched by an opponent's blade. His pale blue body was perfect and unblemished beneath his white uniform.

He remembered the day that Gaunt, his father, had died. The old tyrant had fallen drunk down three flights of stone stairs, cracking open his bald skull and spilling half his brains, but still he had taken five more days to finally expire. The stronghold had waited, almost in silence, but not the silence of respect. Instead it was a silence of grim anticipation, as though even the shadows watched and waited. Then at last Raven's mother had walked slowly out into the courtyard where the fighting men were assembled, wearing the red robes of grief. Under the cowled hood, her face was daubed with grey ashes, but her eyes were dry and there were no tear streaks. In a hollow and emotionless voice she announced that her husband was dead. All that had been Gaunt had ceased to exist. There was only the corpse to be disposed of.

There was another pause of silence, but not of mourning. The waiting was over, the first long phase of tension had snapped, but the second phase quickly tightened. The disposal of the corpse could wait, for immediately there were more serious matters to be settled. Volkar, Raven's eldest brother, did not spare a single glance for their mother. Instead he drew a deep breath to prepare himself and then walked into the centre of the duelling ground. He was one of the largest warriors in the stronghold, a battle-scarred giant in a laced black leather tunic and breeches, with bronze breast plates and arm guards. His helmet was a fearsome bronze hawk's head. He drew his sword and the long blade flashed in the harsh mid-winter sun. He looked around the stone-faced assembly and declared grimly, "I, Volkar, claim mastery of this stronghold."

As the first son of Gaunt, it was his right to make the first claim, but not to go unchallenged. Raven glanced toward Taynor, his second eldest brother. Taynor matched Volkar for size and weight and ferocity of appearance, but he made no move. Volkar was an accomplished swordsman with eighteen kills. Taynor had only twelve to his credit and was biding his time. Raven smiled a bleak smile of understanding. There were two more sons of Gaunt, Bhorg and Scarl, third and fourth in line above Raven, but they too made no move. Raven shrugged and moved out to face Volkar. Calmly, he drew his own sword.

They were brothers, but there could be no quarter between them and they both knew it. Because they were brothers and the sons of Gaunt, they were destined to be rivals and mortal enemies. At the end of this day, only one of them could live.

Volkar laughed briefly as they faced each other, but his contempt was for Taynor and the others. His careful gaze shaded beneath the sharp beak of his helmet, never left Raven's.

"So, I must fight the boy before I can fight the men," he jeered.

"You will never fight again," Raven answered. And there was both certainty and finality in his voice.

Volkar scowled and spoke no more.

They were an ill-matched pair: Raven still a slender youth of nineteen, Volkar massive and bear-like and twelve years his senior. Raven wore black-laced leather similar to his brother, with a minimum of armour. His helmet and arm guards were of plain but highly polished steel. The thin sunlight flashed from his helm and arms as well as from his blade as they slowly circled each other, causing Volkar to curse and squint his eyes.

The elder began to twirl his blade slowly, cutting circles in the air. Raven matched the intricate movements and the swords whirled faster as they built up to the moment of impact. Then, with a bull roar, Volkar sprang.

Raven defended against the initial attack, moving fast and light on his feet as Volkar blundered to and fro in his efforts to strike a death blow. In a savage symphony of steel, the long blades clashed and echoed as the two men fought their way around the courtyard. On all sides, the watchers alternately pushed forward or drew back as the duel moved closer or away from them. At some points they cheered or jeered, but mostly they were silent. It would be unwise to have jeered at the victor and, for the moment, the outcome was uncertain.

Volkar was tiring, cursing with rage and frustration, and slowly Raven shifted from defence to attack. Sparks flew from the hammering crescendo of sword clashes and Volkar fell back. Raven was not fooled. Suddenly Volkar made a cart-wheeling dive sideways, his left hand scooping up a handful of dirt to hurl at Raven's eyes. Raven was already spinning neatly away. The dirt hit him in the back of the neck. A split second later, Raven faced his brother again. Each of them had used that split second to draw a hunting knife from his boot sheath. Volkar cursed. Raven laughed.

They menaced each other, breathing heavily. Then Raven made a half turn and calmly threw the knife away. It was a left hand throw, but practised and accurate. On the far side of the courtyard was a target that the men used for sport, and the hunting knife stuck dead centre. A cheer went up, for the sword was the weapon of honour, and this contest could not be settled with a knife thrust. Volkar scowled and threw his own knife. It thudded home an inch further out from centre than Raven's. Volkar cursed and charged again.

The sword blades crashed again and again and Volkar's fury gave him a momentary advantage. Against Raven's measured cut and thrust, Volkar was swinging madly, hacking and chopping with all his strength while Raven nimbly ducked or blocked every blow. Volkar made one final, stupendous effort, a mighty stroke that might have shattered Raven's blade and split him from neck to crotch if it had landed. But Raven was not there. His movement was too fast and before Volkar could recover his balance, Raven had lunged forward again with the death thrust.

Volkar froze, his eyes wide and staring as his gaze locked on Raven's. His bulk was fixed and held up by Raven's sword. Without a word, Raven used his boot to push Volkar off his blade and the big man collapsed dead on the ground.

While Raven stood for a moment to regain his breath, two of the spectators dragged Volkar to one side. Then the silence returned, tense and still expectant.

Raven squared his shoulders and then raised his eyes and sword to the assembly. He echoed the fatal words of the brother he had just killed. "I, Raven, claim mastery of this stronghold."

Now all eyes turned upon Taynor. The second son of Gaunt had already lost face by allowing the first challenge to pass, but here was his chance to take the stronghold and avoid disgrace. Raven had already fought one duel and should be tired. Taynor was fresh and at full strength. All in one swift movement, Taynor drew his sword and rushed headlong into the attack.

Like Volkar before him, Taynor calculated that his superior weight and sheer fury would crush his younger brother down. But Raven had faith in his own skill and speed. He gave ground in defence as before, but there was no fear in him to instill panic. He still had total control of his own movements and the combination of quick feet and lightning blade again turned the tide of attack. Taynor found himself on the defensive, floundering before Raven's attack. Raven was tired but adrenaline-powered. He had never felt better in a fight and was almost reluctant to finish it. Then Taynor slashed at Raven's neck with his sword, missed and left himself wide open. Raven returned the compliment with a back-hand cut that did not miss and his sword edge sliced home deep just below the edge of Taynor's helmet. Taynor was cut, spinning to the earth, where he lay with his life-blood forming a thick red pool around his shocked face.

It was over so quickly that the watchers were stunned. They had expected to see Volkar kill Raven and then to watch Taynor kill a weakened Volkar. This turn of events had them all gasping but then they began to cheer. The noise was deafening and Raven waited for it to subside.

When the echoes faded, Raven was still standing in the centre of the duelling ground with his bloodied sword still in his hand. They expected him to walk away, for after two duels the code allowed him to rest for twenty-four hours before issuing his challenge again. But Raven was in no mood to rest. His blood was hot and singing and the sword felt like a natural extension to his arm. He smiled slowly as he looked around the respectful circle of faces, and his eyes rested on his brother Bhorg. He said again, "I, Raven, claim mastery of this stronghold."

Bhorg swallowed hard. He was a tall man, his face deeply scarred from his sixth duel which he had barely survived. He was an able fighter but he knew when he was outmatched. Almost imperceptibly, he shook his head.

Raven looked to Scarl. The fourth son of Gaunt also declined the challenge.

Raven's gaze moved from face to face, resting briefly on each man in the circle. No one moved.

Finally Raven reversed his sword, stabbing the point into the earth at his feet and holding the blade just below the hilt. "Then kiss the sword," he commanded.

Bhorg came forward slowly. He knelt and his tight-lipped mouth briefly brushed the hilt of Raven's sword. It was enough and he rose again and walked away. Scarl came next, and then one by one, every fighting man in the stronghold made the brief gesture of allegiance. From now on they were honour-bound to fight for Raven and never against him. When the last man had kissed the sword, Raven was the undisputed master of what had been Gaunt's stronghold. If Raven had sons then he would have forced them to kiss the sword, just as he and his brothers had been obliged to kiss the sword of Gaunt as soon as they were old enough to know the meaning of the act. It was for that reason only that he had been obliged to suffer the old tyrant while Gaunt was still alive. Now he was obliged to suffer no one.

Raven cleaned and sheathed his sword, then collected and sheathed his boot knife. Only then did he mount the steps to enter the castle. His mother was no longer there. Whether she had watched either of the two duels before she had turned away he did not know, but it was not important. There was nothing here that was important now.

The bodies of Gaunt and his two sons were removed and hurled over the convenient lip of a thousand-foot cliff. There the bones were picked clean by scavenger birds on the rocks below. There was no ceremony for death was oblivion. On Ghedda, the only power was in life, strength, and the sword. When life ended, there was nothing.

Raven remained for another year to consolidate his position. After two months, he fought another duel. On attaining the age of eighteen each youth in the stronghold faced a choice; to show allegiance to his Sword Lord, or to challenge. One youngster who believed he had perfected a new trick of swordplay chose to challenge. Raven despatched him neatly within two minutes.

A few more weeks passed and Raven fought another duel. The Law of the Sword was simple in that all differences between men were settled by the sword, either by drawing first blood or by death, depending on the severity of the difference. However, a man could choose whether to fight for himself, to pay a champion to fight for him, or petition his Sword Lord. In most strongholds, a sense of rough justice prevailed whereby the

Sword Lord himself would defend a deserving case. In this instance, the wife of one of the older men had been raped by one of the young hot-heads. Raven had accepted the old man's petition and killed the young offender. It was not only justice but a means of keeping order. No stronghold could exist for long in anarchy.

There were no more duels, the men of the stronghold having learned that there was no future if they risked having to face Raven's blade. Bhorg and Scarl both accepted their positions as his administrative lieutenants for neither of them had ever hoped to rule, and finally Raven decided that he could safely leave the stronghold under their joint control. His brothers were honour-bound to hold the castle on his behalf, and any who tried to supplant them would know that they would have to face Raven on his return.

He had to wait impatiently for spring, for during the long months of winter the vast northern mountains of Ghedda were icebound and snowbound, buffeted by sleet-filled winds and roaring storms, and almost impassable. At last the weather cleared and he was able to leave, riding a sturdy mountain horse and heading south through the first of a series of high mountain passes. He did not look back.

It took him five months to cross the vast continent, through mountains, forest, swamp and desert. And in his passage he killed five more men who foolishly considered a mere northern Sword Lord something to be trifled with. He also slew a variety of wild beasts that crossed his path. Occasionally he took shelter in a village or stronghold, but most nights he slept out in the open, close to his horse for warmth, and with one hand on his sword. On these nights he would lay awake for a long time before sleeping and gaze up at the glittering canopy of the heavens. There, he knew, was his future.

Burning inside him there was an ambition and a sense of

destiny that could never be fulfilled in the medieval world of a northern stronghold. Raven yearned for power and glory, and most of all for the stars. They were a magnet to his mind, an enticement to his very being. His visions carried him up into the dazzling patterns of the constellations and into the great star streams of the galaxies.

And it was all there to be taken. In a land where might was right, martial and military traditions were the only traditions. The sword was still the only weapon of honour, but now there were new weapons of greater power and new paths to greater glory. Gaunt's stronghold was a forgotten backwater in the vastness of the mountains, but to the south was the new Gheddan Empire that had begun the conquest of space and was forging its way to the stars.

His destination was the City Of Swords. It was built upon the shore of a great bay where the Sword Lords of the coast had first united to pitch their camps and build their ships to attempt the conquest and plunder of Alpha three hundred years before. Now it had grown into a city of steel, still ruled by the Council of the original twelve Sword Lords. There were twelve gates to the city, each one surmounted by a fifty foot steel sword. And in the centre of the city, in the parade ground of the Space Corps Centre, was the giant sword, a towering one-hundred-and fifty foot edifice of steel, the symbol of the Gheddan Empire and the only sword to which Raven would ever bow allegiance. He would bow because he was determined to widen his world, to become part of the greatest military power that had ever been known. And most of all because he wanted to lead that journey to the stars.

ᘓ

Raven's memories faded as the succulent scent of a roast pigeon breast touched his nostrils. The meat was held on a golden fork close to his lips and he became aware of Maryam smiling at him anxiously. He had made that first journey to the City Of Swords fifteen years before, but this fascinating Hindu princess was tempting him here and now. He permitted her to feed him and smiled his thanks. Maryam looked relieved and blissful in return.

The orchestra was playing faster and faster. The dancing girls were whirling into the high point of their performance, their lithe young bodies glistening with the sweat of their exertions. Swordmaster Thorn watched them with seemingly his full attention, and yet he was aware of his commander's behaviour. When they had been presented to Kara-Rashna at the beginning of the evening, Thorn's counsel had been that they should simply lazer-blast the old king and that Raven should take his throne. But Raven had answered that there was no need and that their earlier demonstration of their ship's fire-power already had the city suitably subdued. Now Thorn had it worked out that the young woman fawning over Raven was probably the old king's daughter and he wondered if Raven had been influenced by that fact.

Thorn's opinions on the matter were mixed. The girl was ripe and pleasing enough and it had been a long time since any of them had enjoyed a woman. Space flight forced an unnatural abstinence on a man and Thorn was already beginning to wonder how these third planet women would perform sexually. But if Raven wanted the girl, then he should simply take her. That would be more fitting for a Sword Lord. There was no need for concessions.

Thorn watched Maryam smiling at Raven, whispering something in her alien language, trying to communicate. Raven was smiling in return, understanding her eye and body signals even though the words were meaningless. Thorn made an effort to shift his attention away. It would not be wise to be caught staring too critically. The dancing girls were still spinning to the frenzied beat of the music, their flesh gleaming in the firelight. Thorn watched them for a moment, and then slowly became aware that he too was being watched. He turned his gaze to the next table and looked directly into the wide and wondering eyes of another dusky, Hindu beauty.

Namita blushed hotly and quickly lowered her eyes, her long black lashes fluttering in agitation. Like Maryam, she was convinced that these incredible blue-skinned warriors could only be from the same race as the gods. In all her picture books, *Indra* and *Varuna* were depicted with pale blue skins and giving off an aura of soft golden light. These men had no such aura, so perhaps they were not the high gods. However, they did have the same pale blue skin, and they had used the powers of light to destroy rocks and hills and forest. They came from the heavens and could only be gods. Their presence terrified Namita and yet fascinated her. She had been unable to resist watching their every movement and now she had been noticed. She stared at her plate and did not dare to look up again. She had dared too much already. Her heart hammered in her trembling breast and she almost fainted.

A hand steadied her. Her brothers Rajar and Nirad sat on either side of her and Rajar had missed nothing. Rajar also refrained from looking directly at the strangers, but his face was suddenly thoughtful.

The dancing came to an end with a final crash of cymbals and a swirl of half nude limbs and brief silk skirts. Each of the five dancers finished kneeling before the central table where the five Gheddans were seated, their heads bowed, their arms and palms out-stretched as though in offering. Kara-Rashna leaned forward from his throne and made an expansive gesture with his hand, motioning from the visitors to the kneeling girls and then from the girls back to his guests. The Gheddans realized that the girls were offering themselves and that the king was approving their sacrifice.

There was a burst of laughter, and then, jesting lewdly between themselves, Caid, Garl and Landis went forward to claim three of the girls. Thorn held back, waiting for Raven to make the next move,

Raven looked down at the dancing girl kneeling before him. She was a tempting morsel and he knew he could enjoy her, but she was only a slave. Beside him was a princess, although suddenly a very stiff and tense princess. Maryam sat biting her lip, her eyes clouded with apprehension. Raven turned to smile at her, and then turned toward her father and waved the slave girl away. Now it was the turn of Kara-Rashna and his brothers to look worried and uncertain, but Maryam was smiling again.

Raven knew that he could take her any time he wanted and there was a powerful urge in him to simply pick her up and carry her off to the nearest bedchamber. But he restrained the impulse. After fifteen years, he was no longer the raw northern barbarian who had ridden down from the wild mountains. He had learned the arts of political subtlety and calculation, for he could never have reached his present rank in the Gheddan Space Corps without them. This was only an exploratory mission and he knew that within a few days they would have to leave. Several months would then elapse before a garrison force could return here to hold the city permanently as an outpost of the Gheddan Empire. In the meantime it was best not to over antagonize these people, but to let their present king remain a suitably subdued and docile puppet. It was for this reason that he had allowed Kara-Rashna to live and remain upon his throne, despite Thorn's advice to the contrary. And it was for this reason that he would refrain from taking the old king's daughter too soon and too crudely. He was confident that she would come to his bed of her own free will soon enough.

Thorn was frustrated and angry. If Raven had set a precedent by grabbing Maryam, then Thorn would have had no hesitation in rejecting his own slave girl and laying claim instead to Namita. He had already realized that she too was a daughter of the king and Thorn wanted his own princess. Thorn did not always understand Raven's thinking and actions, but his commander's rank and sword skill permitted him to flout many conventions and even Thorn knew better than to risk his anger. Scowling, Thorn got up to claim his own slave girl, and then as an afterthought, he also grabbed the girl Raven had discarded and brought them both back to his seat.

Caid and Landis hooted with laughter, while Garl made ribald but approving comment. Raven remained relaxed and simply smiled. Thorn fondled the two girls and felt better, but he was still not fully satisfied.

Kara-Rashna hurriedly called male slaves and ordered them to show his guests to their bedchambers. Four of the Gheddans departed promptly with the five slave girls. Raven remained a moment longer, smiling at Maryam, and lightly touching her lips with his finger in a Gheddan promise for the future. Then he was led away alone.

The king and his brothers looked relieved. Queen Padmini was also relieved, but determined to scold her promiscuous daughter fiercely at the first opportunity. The feasting was over, the orchestra departed, and the rest of the guests began to say their goodbyes and disperse.

Namita joined Maryam and the two departed together. Rajar watched them go, his face was expressionless but he was thinking furiously. His half-sister's flagrant behaviour throughout the evening had made no secret of her intentions.

She was making up to the leader of the blue-skinned strangers with the obvious aim of forming a marriage alliance. Such an alliance would clearly be beneficial for Karakhor, for the power of the strangers would be more than enough to protect them from the threat of Maghalla. But such an alliance would not further Rajar's own ambitions.

Rajar concentrated hard, reviewing all that he had observed here tonight. The one they called Thorn was clearly second in this hierarchy of the gods, and if anything happened to the leader then it was reasonable to suppose that Thorn would be the new leader. Thorn had cast lustful glances at his full-sister Namita, and if something could be arranged to remove Raven from the picture, then an alliance between Thorn and Namita was one that Rajar was certain he should be able to manipulate.

Persuading Namita to make a more positive response to Thorn might not be too difficult. It was the idea of removing Raven and the possible consequences that made him shiver inside. However, it could be worth thinking about. The art of palace intrigue was to turn the unwitting into tools and to devise methods that could not be traced back to the instigator. The unseen hand behind the scenes need have no fear.

That was how the principles worked with mortals, but would it be different with the gods.

The young prince trembled and went to his bed with plenty of food for thought.

Chapter Eight

The three great temples to *Varuna*, *Indra* and *Agni* were the natural focal point of Karakhor, and the obvious starting point for any idle exploration of the city. The carved ramparts of red sandstone glowed with polished and intricate beauty in the bright mid-morning sun, and on leaving the palace, Raven strolled casually toward the nearest of these strange monuments to an even stranger faith. He could not understand the devotional psychology that had urged their creation, but the sheer size and dominance of the temples demanded a closer inspection. He was accompanied by Maryam, Namita, and Thorn.

Maryam was at his side because this was where she wanted to be. Her bravado of the previous evening had dwindled with the cold light of dawn and a bout of warning chastisement from her mother, but she was still convinced that fate had ordained that this was to be her place. She had appeared, trembling a little, with the slave girl who had served his morning meal and had made it plain that during his waking hours she intended to be his constant companion and guide. It had been her suggestion, transmitted in smiles and gestures, that he should make a tour of the city.

Namita was there because it would not have been seemly for Maryam to go with the stranger alone. She was a reluctant chaperone, bound by her sense of royal duty, her obedience to the anxious wishes of the queen, Padmini, but most of all by her own love and concern for her sister.

Thorn was there as Raven's second sword, although he doubted that his commander would meet with any danger he could not overcome alone. The people here were too soft and too primitive to be dangerous and were too cowed to be even hostile. At the same time, this was a largely unknown planet and Thorn had his own curiosity and his own sense of duty. The discovery that Namita was also to be a member of their party had been an added incentive to his decision. He had favoured her with a smile but her only reaction had been a look of terror. Now he scowled a little because she had contrived to walk so that Maryam and Raven were between them.

Twenty paces behind them there followed a nervous captain and a small detachment of warriors from the palace guard. They were present under the orders of Warmaster Jahan to observe, to protect their strange guests while in the city, and to protect the city and their princesses from the strangers. For the first two tasks, they were equipped and capable. For the latter, they could only pray that no such need would arise.

Raven stopped in the shadow of the first temple, gazing up at the sculpted bands of men, beasts and gods. There were garlands of stone leaves and vines, lines of marching war elephants and warriors, huntsmen and chariots pursuing game, and then elaborate stone panels showing couples and foursomes in explicit sexual poses and detail. Maryam followed the direction of his gaze and blushed hotly. She had seen these scenes before but the proper thing was to pretend not to have noticed.

However, Raven's gaze moved on. He was not so much impressed by the loving artistry of the multitude of sculptures as by the vast amount of time and human energy that must have been poured into the creation of these apparently useless monuments. The waste was a measurement of the backwardness and mental weakness of the people of this planet.

"What is its purpose?" Thorn asked in bewilderment. "It is neither a war ship nor a fortress. Why would they want to build it?"

Raven shrugged. "It must serve a religious purpose. We know that on Dooma such ideas still flourish on the continent of the Alphans. They still believe in gods, or a god, and raise strange buildings in which to house them."

"What is a god?" Thorn demanded. His education had been a purely practical one of military matters and spaceship navigation."

"A god is a kind of super-being, an invisible power that is supposed to be greater than a man and his sword. There are many of them. At one time, even on Ghedda, every group of people claimed to have one as its guardian." Raven smiled sardonically. "They were even believed to grant their followers some kind of life after death. They were a refuge for those who were afraid of death, and because they were afraid to die they were afraid to live."

"Fool's nonsense," Thorn agreed. "How could men be so stupid?"

"They were not men. They were women and children. On Ghedda it was all a long time ago, before men found the courage to face the truth and take command of their own destiny."

They turned a corner of the building into the sunlight and moved toward the main entrance, which faced onto the central square. There were crowds of people hurrying about their daily business who now began to stop and stare, half in wonderment but more in fear. The two blue-skinned Gheddans ignored the growing number of brown-skinned Hindus and paused again before the temple doorway. On either side, set in porticos carved out of the solid stone, were life-sized statues of human form, but with the heads of a boar and an elephant. Each figure was richly dressed and jeweled, with six arms holding weapons and tools, and representations of the sun and the earth.

Thorn indicated the boar-headed figure with bafflement in his voice. "Is this a god?"

"Perhaps." Raven's knowledge was limited to a lecture he had once attended on Alphan psychology. It had been one of a compulsory series at the City Of Swords Space Centre, given with the aim of understanding the enemy.

Maryam could not understand their words, but she knew they were speaking of the god. "This is Lord Shiva," she tried to explain. "The Lord of the Beasts in his boar incarnation."

Raven and Thorn looked at her without comprehension. Thorn shrugged. Raven smiled.

"We shall look inside," Raven decided. He moved to enter the doorway.

None of them had yet noticed the fearful priest standing in the deep shadows inside the temple. Now he came quickly forward. He was a young man, shaven-headed and wearing only the simple white robe of his calling. His face was almost as pale as his robe and his slim hands fluttered in bird-like agitation across his breast as he tried to wave them away. The interior of the shrine was holy and forbidden to all but known believers.

Thorn and Raven stopped. The young priest bravely spread his arms wide to bar their way, a clear indication that they should not enter. Thorn looked at him in astonishment and then laughed and drew the hand lazer from his hip. He raised the weapon and aimed at the white-robed breast. Maryam and

Namita recoiled with gasps of horror, turning their heads and covering their faces with their hands. Then Raven's hand closed firmly over Thorn's wrist and pushed the lazer down and away.

"Destroying a fool will prove nothing," Raven said calmly. "But if we destroy one of their god images, then we will instill a real respect."

He drew his own lazer as he spoke, aimed, and exploded the boar's head from the nearest statue. The young priest and the princess Namita both collapsed in a dead faint.

Raven holstered his lazer, stepped over the inert priest, and entered the temple.

Thorn paused for a moment to look around the shocked faces of the people clustered in the square, and then at the drained white face of Maryam who was fighting to prevent herself from swooning. Raven's words and actions made tactical sense, but again Thorn wondered whether Raven might have been partly influenced by the weaker motive of sparing the earth woman the greater distress of seeing the priest killed. Finally he dismissed the idea and followed his leader.

The young guard captain came forward to steady Maryam. It was all he dared to do, for his own heart was beating fast and his throat was too dry to issue orders. Maryam pushed his hand from her arm and bade him to tend to Namita. She stared up at the temple and now she knew who her chosen champion represented.

The door was guarded by the Lord of the Beasts, but the temple itself was dedicated to the worship of the Lord *Varuna*, the high god of the blue sky. Only one god was equal in power to *Varuna*, and that was *Indra*, the mighty god of war. She looked to *Indra's* temple on the opposite side of the square, as high and as splendid as the temple to *Varuna*. Only *Indra* would dare to destroy the Lord of the Beasts and desecrate the temple of

Varuna. Therefore it could only be that the blue-skinned ones were messengers from *Indra*. Perhaps their leader, was an incarnation of *Indra* Himself!

ଔ

Zela was violently awakened as a coarse hand crushed against her mouth. She had fallen asleep in the small wooded glade where they had stopped to snatch a short night's rest, and her last memory had been a gentle one of the brilliant canopy of stars spread high above her. She had identified the nearer speck of light that was Dooma and her fading thoughts had been of her home planet, together with a brief prayer to the God Behind All Gods, the spiritual essence of all creation.

Now the stars were blotted out, and the dark side of creation loomed over her in the form of a man whose only thought was to kill her. She saw a cruel face with fierce, dark eyes, and recognized the black turban and laced black waistcoat of a Maghallan soldier. She smelled the rank sweat and bloodlust on him and saw the glint of steel as his dagger swept down toward her breast.

She would have died, but another blade was faster. A sword slashed the wrist wielding the dagger aside and then Kananda kicked the Maghallan away from her. The man rolled into bushes and darkness, screaming as he clutched the severed stump of his wrist.

The camp was in uproar. The two guards Kananda had posted lay sprawled in the grass with slit throats, and from all sides the Maghallan soldiers were rushing forward through the surrounding trees.

"Stand! Stand!" Kananda roared the alarm. "Stand for Karakhor!"

He suited his action to the words by standing astride Zela as she still lay half shocked, his sword in one hand and a dagger in the other as he fought back the first wave of the Maghallan attack. His companions rose quickly, grabbing for their weapons, but half of them were too slow and too weary. The Maghallans had cut down four more of the Karakhorans before they could begin to defend themselves.

They were heavily out-numbered, taken by surprise, and within another minute they would all have been butchered. Zela's blood ran cold but her mind ran fast and she drew her hand lazer as she still lay sprawled on the ground. After retrieving the body of Ramesh, she had fitted a new fuel pack and the weapon was fully re-charged. She fired forward, through Kananda's spread legs, and then rolled quickly onto her elbows and stomach to fire left, right, and directly behind. She aimed only to miss their still-surviving companions, but the ranks of the Maghallans were so thick that each energy bolt killed or scorched at least two or three of the enemy. The Maghallan onslaught became a rout, and as they turned and fled, the lower branches of the trees behind them burst into flames.

Zela struggled shakily to her feet. "The horses," she gasped, and gestured to where their tethered mounts were plunging and rearing in their terrified attempts to escape from the crackling heat.

Kananda understood and shouted more orders to the rest of the group. They ran for their mounts and grabbed for the reins before the animals could bolt. With swords they cut them free and backed them away from the fire then quickly they swung up into the saddles. Hamir and Kasim together heaved up the still unconscious body of Ramesh onto a spare horse and quickly roped it into place before finding their own mounts. Zela fired another lazer blast at the re-grouping Maghallans, but the beam was noticeably weaker and only one man fell.

"Ride," Kananda commanded.

They were seven. Four of them instantly spurred their horses and charged out of the glade. Kasim was the fifth. He looked back in anguish to their fallen companions, but there was no time and no way in which any who might still be alive could be helped. Kanada struck the flank of Kasim's mount with the flat of his sword, and then scooping up the reins of the horse to which the body of his brother was now lashed, he followed with Zela at his side. Zela had holstered her lazer and her sword was now in her right hand as she carved their path.

The horses needed no further urging as they raced away from the smoke and sparks. A flurry of spears and arrows followed them but most were deflected by the branches of the forest and the rest were poorly aimed. The shouts of rage and pain faded behind them, but in the echoes Kananda faintly heard the commands of a Maghallan officer ordering a mounted pursuit.

They let the horses run in blind panic, crouching low to avoid being swept from their backs. The first pale rays of dawn were filtering through the broken gloom, slowly forcing back the shadows, and mercifully the undergrowth here was not too densely tangled and the trees were tall and not too thickly crowded. The riders gathered a painful assortment of cuts and bruises in their headlong flight, but none of them were thrown from the saddle. They emerged at last onto a plain of tall grass, and here they reined back and paused to let the panting horses recover their wind. They also needed to unwind their own frayed nerves.

"Where did they come from?" Kasim demanded, his voice both angry and anguished. "We must have been well ahead of any pursuit from Sardar's camp.

"I too thought we were safe," Kananda said wearily. "Perhaps the monkey tribes were able to supply trackers who can track faster than we expected. But I did not see Sardar there, so perhaps we had the misfortune to cross the path of another Maghallan force."

"But we set guards." Kasim was still at a loss to understand.

"Our guards were killed by stealth. They were tired—as we all are— perhaps they were not as alert as they should have been." Kananda was too heartsick to debate the matter any further. He looked to Zela and said gratefully, "Again we have to thank you for saving our lives. Your lightning bolts got us out of Sardar's camp, and now they have saved us again."

Zela had drawn her lazer and ejected the spent fuel pack. She took another from her belt and showed it to them briefly before pressing it into place. "I have only two more of these," she warned them. "I am using them up much faster than I anticipated. When they are dead, there can be no more lightning bolts. We shall have only our swords."

"Then we must move on," Kananda said. "The Maghallans have a strong leader. I heard him trying to organize a pursuit."

No one argued and they started the horses at a steady trot. Ahead of them was largely open terrain, with scattered tumbles of piled rock and patches of scrub trees breaking up the grassland. It made for fast progress, but there was no real cover. This was good hunting country for a predator, and so they avoided the rock piles where a leopard or tiger might lie in the shade. The sun was climbing steadily overhead, its power beating down on them from the burnished blue of the sky. The horses, and then their riders, began to sweat.

They were still just within sight of the treeline when faint cries caused them to look back. The Maghallan force had emerged from the forest, some fifty strong, all of them mounted.

Kananda cursed for he knew the Maghallans rode a different breed of horse to their own. The Maghallan horses were smaller but more sturdy, reared on the fringes of the Great Thar Desert where they had adapted to crossing long distances without water. The Karakhoran horses had been bred in the Ganges plains. In a short race they would beat a Maghallan horse every time, but over long distances the Maghallan breed had the greater endurance and stamina. Before the end of the day, Kananda knew, the Maghallans would run them down.

☙

The chase lasted through the fierce heat of midday until at last the Kharakoran horses were flagging, their nostrils flaring as they snorted painfully, their great chests heaving, and their flanks lathered and slippery with sweat. The yells and shrieks of the pursuing Maghallans became gradually louder and closer, filling with triumph and exultation, and the first wildly fired arrows began to fall just short of the fleeing riders.

Zela looked back over her shoulder, through the spray of dirt and grass blades churned by their own pounding hooves, and saw the Maghallan riders spread out in a gaining line behind them. She drew her lazer and fired at the nearest rider. It was difficult to aim from the swaying back of her struggling mare and the scorching beam did nothing more than set a patch of grass ablaze. The rider she had missed swerved in panic to collide with one of his fellows, but the pursuit was checked for only a moment before it resumed at full tilt.

Zela tasted her first moment of fear as she realized that she had placed too much faith in a single hand lazer. It was not enough to terrify their pursuers completely. Another arrow passed by her shoulder and she began to wish that she had listened to Blair.

Kananda also knew that their situation was desperate. He looked ahead and pointed out one of the larger outcrops of rocks. "We will take refuge there," he shouted hoarsely. "It is better to stand and die than to be pulled down from behind, or to die like cowards with arrows in our backs."

No one disputed his command. They whipped their horses to one final effort and raced for the hill of rocks. As they reached it, they reined in hard and sprang down from their saddles, whirling to face their enemies with drawn swords.

The Maghallans were on top of them in seconds, but as they closed the gap, they made the mistake of pulling into a tight packed force. Zela was again able to use her hand lazer to good effect and three fast shots cut down the first three riders by blasting their mounts from under them. The rest came to a confused stop in a melee of rearing and fallen horses. The shrieks of men and animals made a fearsome din, and only one of the Maghallan riders was quick enough to dismount and challenge the small group of Karakhorans as they stood with their backs to the rocks. He was too rash for his own good and Kananda dispatched him in an instant with a deft parry and thrust of his sword. He paused to cut the rope holding Ramesh to the back of the spare horse, and Kasim and Hamir again took the limp form of the young prince between them. Then, taking advantage of the confusion, they all turned quickly to scramble up into the rocks, aiming for the strongest defensive position at the top of the hill.

They were halfway there when the first flight of arrows followed them. The warrior on Kananda's right gave a strangled cry and pitched forward with an arrow through his upper arm. Kananda picked him up and half dragged and half carried him to the top of the hill. Behind him, Zela turned and fired two more energy bolts to kill another of their enemies and cause the rest to take cover. The respite gave them all a chance to reach the comparative safety of the hill-top where they crouched behind a wall of boulders with their enemies fifty feet below them. Kasim and three of the warriors still had their bows and quivers full of arrows, and Zela grimly fitted the last fuel pack into her lazer. They could repel a few attacks but soon they would be fighting sword to sword.

"At least we will sell our lives dearly," Kananda declared grimly.

"Perhaps," Zela answered. "But if we can hold out for long enough we may still have a chance." She was taking another device from her belt pack as she spoke and continued in explanation. "I think we may now be close enough for me to communicate with my ship."

☙

Raven had completed his casual exploration of the city, finding little of military interest, and had returned to his chamber in the palace. He was better acclimatized to the savage winters of Northern Ghedda and found the midday heat of this sickly and spice-smelling city to be uncomfortable and oppressive. He took off his chain mail and his uniform tunic to wash his face and arms in the basin of cool water that had been provided, and was amused when a Hindu slave girl, averting her eyes, dried him gently with a soft towel.

He took off his belt with his sword and lazer and lay back on the bed. He was ready to rest and he needed time to think over his next moves before he discussed them with Thorn and the others. He had to decide how long he should remain here and whether he should make a closer inspection of the other cities of the subcontinent or other parts of the planet. He doubted whether any other Earth humans could be any further advanced technologically than the people of this city, but his mission was to be sure. Another part of his mission was to search for any traces of Alphan exploration, to deny Earth to Alpha, and to secure anything of value for Ghedda. Those were his primary instructions from the Imperial War Command.

He lay with his hands clasped behind his head and was aware that the slave girl was still hovering on the edge of his field of vision. He guessed that she was fascinated by the naked torso of his blue body, and her furtive scrutiny helped to remind him that it was a long time since he had pleasured himself with a woman. Again he wondered why he had refrained from the opportunity that had been offered last night. He could have had the slave girl, or he could have taken Maryam—he had at least learned her name—for there was no power here that could have stopped him. He had wanted Maryam, and never before had he hesitated in taking any woman he had wanted. But there had been times when taking a woman had also meant accepting a challenge to the sword. This was an unknown world, its codes and customs also unknown and so rationality had decreed a degree more caution that he would have shown on Ghedda.

He had been overcautious, he knew that now. This morning's inspection had shown that these people possessed nothing more advanced than their simple bows and arrows. He looked to the slave girl, noting that she was young with firm breasts and a slim waist. Her manner was half fearful but her interest in him was undisguised. He felt his manhood begin to harden and turned onto one shoulder to study her more critically.

A Gheddan woman would have been bolder or she would have withdrawn. On his home planet, when a woman wanted a man she let it be known. If she didn't she kept out of his sight.

The latter course would not necessarily save her from his attentions, but it was the best chance she might have. This girl could do neither. She did not have the courage to come closer, or the sense to go away. If he took her, he felt that she would be a disappointment, and yet he had a powerful need.

Before he could make up his mind, there was an interruption. Maryam entered with a tray bearing fruit and wine. She spoke a curt word of dismissal to the slave girl, who promptly fled.

Raven watched as Maryam carefully poured the wine. She wore a sari of red silk and a gold lace shawl. One shoulder and part of her waist were bare, and suddenly he wanted to see much more of that warm brown flesh. He smiled, the lazy smile of a man who had suddenly made his decision and was fully confident of his ability to carry it out.

Maryam's hand trembled and a splash of the sweet golden wine spilled onto the tray. She had been instantly aware of the sexual tension that hovered invisible in the room, and they had been the cause of her brief flare of anger toward the slave girl. She had been intuitively jealous, but now she in her turn was afraid for the tensions were still there and were growing stronger.

She handed him the glass, willing herself not to spill any more. She was afraid to fully meet his gaze but in avoiding them her gaze was drawn like the slave girl before her to take in the hard muscles of his beautiful blue body. She too was half fearful, half attracted, and fully fascinated. She felt her heart beat faster. Almost beyond her control, her gaze flickered further down the length of his body, resting on the now definite thrust beneath the chain mail armour at his groin. The crescendo of her heartbeats almost became an explosion.

Raven put down his glass and casually unfastened the last

of his constricting armour. He threw it aside, and with a firm hand on each of her shoulders, he drew her down onto the bed where he lay. She came wide-eyed and wide-lipped, but unresisting. The cry of protest that struggled to be born within her throat was smothered and suppressed by a confusion of different reasons. She believed that he was a god and that therefore she was honoured, and that it was his right to take her and her duty to submit. She was also afraid of his power and she did not want her uncles and her brothers to all die on her behalf. She knew that one cry for help would be enough to bring Jahan and a dozen others rushing to her rescue, but she also knew that they could only die in vain.

Stirred in with her belief and her fears were her own pulsing desires, flooding through her in a hot cascade of violent feelings and emotions. Shocking visions of those explicit amorous couples, locked together in stone on the temple walls, tumbled hotly in her mind. She knew what was expected of her and she wanted all of it with all her being. All the restraint and decorum of her royal upbringing was being washed away in the heat of these fateful moments. He was a god, and so nothing could possibly be wrong.

Raven's mouth was hot and fierce on her own moaning lips, and then on her throat, and then, oh ecstasy, on her bared and heaving breasts. Her shawl had disappeared and his practiced hands were deftly unwrapping her sari. To be loved by a god was a priceless gift, beyond the dared hope of any mortal woman, and yet he was about to love her—or at least to take her. The distinction and the doubt caused a flutter of anguish in her mind, to be followed by another thought of such brazen magnitude that she was shocked by her own impious audacity: she would make him love her by loving him with all the woman's arts of which she knew or could imagine.

Raven had expected submission and to slake his own

physical needs, but nothing more. Thus, to suddenly find the girl taking an active and eager part in their lovemaking was an added pleasure, and after his initial caresses, he relaxed and allowed her to set the pace. Always a connoisseur, he was intrigued by new techniques and a new planet seemed a likely place to offer new surprises.

He was definitely not disappointed, and when finally they reached the erotic peak of mutual fulfillment, they both cried out aloud. From Raven, it was a laughing shout of lustful triumph, and from Maryam, a rapturous cry of exquisite pain and joy.

Behind the closed door of the next chamber, Thorn listened to the faint but umistakable sounds, his face sullen and brooding as he sprawled back on his own bed. The two slave girls he had used the night before were still with him and one of them dutifully tried to arouse him. Thorn pushed her angrily away. He had found both slave girls tame and boring. A dozen of them together could not add up to one good Gheddan woman.

He heard and recognized Raven's climatic shout and felt pure envy. He knew that Raven was with Maryam and obviously the highborn women on this planet had more fire and spirit than the dullards who had been offered to himself and the others.

Thorn would have liked to try Maryam for himself, but she was to remain inviolate for as long as she retained Raven's interest. However, there was another highborn one. His lascivious thoughts centred on Namita. She was younger, not quite so ripe for plucking, but Thorn enjoyed despoiling virgins and it was just possible that she might be as lively as her sister.

ଓ

While Raven and Maryam made love, and while Kananda and Zela fought desperately for their lives, the distraught rulers of Karakhor met hastily in secret council. It was a measure of Kara-Rashna's fear and uncertainty that he did not dare to call them together in the high vaulted audience hall, which had too many approaching corridors and access points. Instead they gathered in one of the smaller anterooms in the royal apartments. The king made do with an ordinary cushioned chair in place of his ornate throne. In a half circle before him stood Jahan, his brothers Sanjay and Devan, his sons Rajar and Nirad, and the titular heads of the three great houses of Gandhar, Tilak and Bulsar. There was no one else present. The priests were in such total disarray after the desecration of one of their temples that they were worse than useless. The warriors who guarded the closed and locked door did so from the outside.

"If they are messengers from the gods, then why should they attack a temple to the gods?" Kara-Rashna asked the question in confusion. It seemed to him that his mind was growing feeble in its efforts to wrestle with these startling new events, and that like his body, it was failing him when he needed it most.

"They cut the head from *Shiva* at the temple of *Varuna*," Sanjay reminded them. "Perhaps this means that these strangers come from *Indra*. Or perhaps there is an even greater god than either *Indra* or *Varuna*—a god as yet undreamed of with power as yet unimagined."

"A greater god than *Indra*." The king's mind reeled. "How can this be?"

"We are not priests," Devan said slowly. "We cannot answer such questions. Not even the priests can answer them."

"But what does it mean? What must we do?"

Devan shrugged. "I would say that we must face the things that we know as they are. We have as our guests a group of very powerful strangers. Perhaps they are gods—perhaps they are not. All we know is that they are here. They came in a temple from the sky and they possess a power that can melt rock, burn whole forests, and cut the heads from our known gods."

"Then we must not anger them."

"No, brother, but we must consider more. We know also that we face an inevitable war with the forces of Maghalla. With these strangers as our allies, our cause is secure. We must befriend them and secure their aid to defeat Maghalla."

Sanjay frowned, the expression making his face seem even leaner and sharper. Where Devan saw the issues as clear-cut, Sanjay saw deeper into their complexities.

"This course could be dangerous," he argued. "If the blue-skinned ones are messengers from *Indra* or some mightier god, then their violation of *Varuna's* temple could bring down the vengeance of more messengers from *Varuna*. If we seek their aid in our battle against Maghalla, then it might be that we will find ourselves involved in an even more terrible war between the gods. Such a war would destroy Karakhor more swiftly and with more finality than any conflict with Maghalla."

The noble heads of Gandhar, Tilak and Bulsar made varying signals of agreement. They would fight if it became necessary, but they were all older men. The fire of youth no longer burned in their blood and so they counselled caution.

Kara-Rashna closed his fist and chewed on his knuckles, something he only did when extremely agitated. He felt that he was receiving good advice from both his brothers, and yet their reasoning conflicted. He finally looked, as always, to his warmaster general.

"Jahan, without Kaseem I have no priest who is wise enough to guess at the ways or intention of the gods, but you have always known what is best in matters of war. What say you? Should we look upon the blue-skinned ones as potential allies against Maghalla? Or should we stay neutral and pray that they will depart without involving us in some greater tragedy?"

It was Jahan's turn to frown. For once in his life he lacked the background information that his carefully created espionage network had always been able to provide. He had been pondering deeply as he listened to the debate between the princes, but now he was thrown back onto nothing more than his own instincts

"Whether they are gods or not, I cannot say. I only know that I cannot wholly trust them until we know what they are and from where they have come and with what intentions. So my counsel is that we watch and wait until we do have some knowledge of these things. Only then can we decide whether we should court their favours."

"If they are not gods, then what are they?" Gandhar asked helplessly. "Surely they are not mortal men?"

"Whether they are mortal or not, again I cannot say. But last night four of the blue-skinned ones took slave girls to their beds. The slaves reported back directly to me this morning. All the strangers used them exactly as ordinary men would use them, perhaps more crudely and more roughly but in the same way. The strangers all eat, drink and sleep, the same as ordinary men."

"But they have such fearful power." The head of the House of Tilak shivered as he spoke.

"But the power does not seem to come from the blue-skinned ones themselves," Jahan said slowly. "At first the power came from their strange temple. Less than an hour ago, I closely questioned the guard captain I posted to accompany the strangers on their visit to the city. The one who cut the head from the statue of *Shiva* used some kind of weapon. The guard captain was very sure. The power did not come from the visitor's eyes or from his fingertips. It came from this weapon which he wears at his waist."

There was silence while they considered these observations, then Sanjay made his own contribution.

"They also wear swords which appear to be similar to our own. So perhaps there are times when their weapons have no power and they must use swords."

Jahan nodded. "It would be very useful to know how well they would fight if they possessed only swords. Are they really gods, or is it just the power weapons that make them appear to be gods?"

'They came from the heavens," Gandhar reminded them. "We saw them descend. Our talk could be blasphemy."

Kara-Rashna groaned and chewed on his knuckles again. "If only our old friend Kaseem was here! Why must my high priest be absent when we need him most?"

"Perhaps we should send more runners to Kananda," Devan suggested. "To urge the hunting party to return with all speed. The matter of Prince Ramesh killing a tiger seems of lesser importance now."

"Yes, yes." The king's agreement was immediate. It was the desire closest to his heart. "Send our fastest runners at once. Kananda and Kaseem must return without any further delay."

Jahan nodded his approval and reserved his doubts. Despite the deep respect he held for Kaseem, he did not expect that on this occasion the high priest would be of any more use than all the other priests. In times of crisis, he had noticed that the priests rarely did more than they did in peace times, which was to consult their holy books, make sacrifices and pray. The only difference being that they did it all more fervently. However, the delay suited him, for at least it would give him more time to observe their uninvited visitors and hopefully to gather more information.

The meeting broke up with nothing positive decided or achieved and most of the participants left as uncertain and fearful as when they had arrived. Through it all, the two younger princes, the sons of Kara-Rashna, had listened silently. For once Nirad had realized that in this discussion he was greatly out of his depth and so he had curbed his normally imprudent tongue. His brother Rajar had been more intent on listening and learning.

Jahan's question—how would the strangers fight if they had only swords?—echoed through Rajar's mind. The idea that perhaps the strangers could be separated from the source of their power was both a comfort and a goad to his calculated scheming.

Chapter Nine

For three days, Kaseem fretted and worried about the fate of his young princes. He knew that, despite his youth, Kananda had been well trained in the use of weapons and the command of men. The old warmaster Jahan had seen to that. But Kananda's force was small and still vulnerable. Ramesh and his group were even more so. They were just children in Kaseem's eyes. Like newborn deer, a ready prey for any predator, even the lowest jackal. His anxiety grew when they did not quickly return together and he was haunted by his fears of what might have befallen them.

He took some comfort from the fact that Kananda had the support of Zela and her lightning-bolt weapon. However, Zela's absence meant that the only woman left in the camp was Laurya, the cause of the other anguished turmoil of his thoughts and emotions. The voluptuous Alphan was totally unlike any of the dusky-skinned, dark-haired Hindu women of India and yet he could not rid himself of the disturbing certainty that he had seen her somewhere before. He dared not look into her eyes, although he felt a desperate desire to do so. It was as though they held all the secrets of her soul, secrets which he knew he must unlock, and yet he was terrified of what he might find.

He avoided her as much as possible and yet he could not

help but be constantly aware of her presence. Gujar and the young lords competed with each other to offer her small services, which she accepted with endless good grace and easy smiles. She and the Alphan, Kyle, were clearly lovers and so secure in their love that neither felt any real threat from her new admirers. Kaseem watched covertly from a distance and realized that he felt jealous.

It was a ridiculous notion. He was an old man, old enough to be her grandfather, and he was the High Priest of Karakhor. He had forsaken the lures of the flesh many years before. His manhood was a wrinkled thing of no further interest to him and no possible attraction to any woman. And yet he was envious of Gujar and the young lords whenever they won the smallest of Laurya's smiles. To see her hand-in-hand with Kyle was even worse, and when the two Alphans left the glade together, as they often did to be alone, he felt an almost violent urge to chase after them and knock the young man away with his staff.

He did not understand these crazy frustrations and feelings and tried to ignore them. His refuge was prayer and ritual, sitting cross-legged for many hours and struggling to concentrate on his recitations of the Vedas.

By the fourth day he knew that something more was necessary. He made his needs known to Gujar, who promptly sent one of his warriors off into the forest. The man returned two hours later with a live jungle cock he had captured in a snare. Kaseem took the bird gently, carrying it by its bound feet which had been lashed with a short cord, and set off along the bank of the stream, moving away from the camp and leaving the others to continue amusing themselves in their own various ways. He walked until he was well out of sight of that awesome temple of black steel. Although he was not sure whether it was the dark powers in that towering spear of the gods, or the thought of those gold-lashed, green eyes of the unsettling

Alphan woman that disturbed him most.

He found the perfect spot to suit his purpose: a slow bend where the stream ran shallow and there was a small beach of white sand. Birdsong warbled in the branches all around him, and a small group of white-tailed monkeys gibbered in protest at his intrusion before abandoning the fruit they were gathering and disappearing into the deep forest.

Kaseem laid down his small shoulder bag and the bound cock and spent the next few minutes gathering dry sticks and grass. When he had collected enough materials, he built his sacrificial fire, adding to it a few pieces of sandalwood from his bag. With a knife and flint he struck a spark and crouched puffing over the twists of yellowed grass until he had bright flames shooting up through the pile of sticks.

While the fire burned stronger, he took off his robe and, in only his loincloth, he waded knee-deep into the stream. There he bathed to purify himself, praying all the while and still praying as he returned to the fire. He knelt before the flames, positioning himself so that he could breathe in the rising smoke.

The trussed bird watched him with one beady, remorseful eye, as though it knew what came next. The old priest did the job mercifully, a quick, practised cut with the knife across the bird's throat as he lifted it high by the feet. The fowl barely had time to squawk and then its bright red blood was dripping steadily into the flames. After a few minutes, Kaseem laid the bird in the heart of the fire. There was the stink of burning feathers, which made him squint his eyes and flare his nostrils, but soon it was replaced by the sweeter smell of the roasting meat. From his bag, Kaseem added handfuls of powdered incense to sweeten the smoke even further and inhaled deeply as he prayed over the flames.

His prayers were first to *Agni*, begging the fire god to carry his message to the realms of the great gods, *Indra* and *Varuna*. And then to the great gods themselves, pleading for news of his lost princes, begging for a vision of where they might be. He prayed with his eyes closed, ignoring the slowly growing pains in his cramped knees and his stiff-hunched shoulders. Occasionally he opened his eyes, staring briefly past his clasped hands for a sign in the heart of the flames, but time after time there was nothing.

Time itself became like a dream as the coiling smoke stung his eyes and drugged his senses. He had the gift of far-sight. Visions had come to him before, but never completely at his command, and he was never sure of how he had achieved them. He only knew it could happen, and so he concentrated and prayed with a fervour he had never reached before.

He felt his consciousness slipping away, as though he were falling into a vast black abyss in the very bowels of the deep earth. The darkness whirled around him, split by vivid images of Kananda and Ramesh and of the carved stone faces of the gods in the temple precincts he had left behind. Then the faces of his princes were both washed away with blood and his heart turned to ice as terror flowed through his reeling mind. The forms of *Indra* and *Varuna* became blue and alive, smiling wickedly and waving a multitude of arms. It was as though the sacrificial flames burned in his head and in his soul and the dead jungle fowl was alive again and pecking at his eyes.

He tried to force his mind back, to visualize again the faces of Ramesh and Kananda. Their features blurred and wavered in his mind, fluid like images seen through rippled water. Both faces were fading and he tried to hold onto just one, the face of Ramesh. It was still too much and the familiar features were melting away—to be replaced by a pair of golden lashed, deep green eyes. He almost screamed his frustration. And suddenly a tumult of erotic images flooded his fainting brain. They were visions of himself and Laurya, impossibly and lasciviously entwined, lost in the heights of love and lust. In his present purified state, the very thoughts were sacrilege and the conflict of emotions made his head feel as though it might explode in lost agony. His body collapsed into a shapeless sprawl beside the stream, half in and half out of the unfelt water, and his mind soared free and upward.

☙

He hung suspended in a strange, weightless limbo of darkness, and slowly, infinitely slowly, his tortured nervous system stabilized and became calm. All the pains and stresses of his over taut body faded and vanished, almost as though he had become bodiless. He opened his eyes then and saw that he was indeed detached from the frail old body that he knew. He saw it crumpled far below him and for an instant believed that he was dead. Perhaps he had suffered a heart attack, or choked and suffocated in the sacrificial smoke, or perhaps his brain had truly burst.

The forest and sky around him seemed normal, vividly green and blue, except that instead of gazing up into the branches from below, he was gazing down through the treetops from above. His body lying between the softly gurgling stream and the white-smoking fire seemed to be shrinking away as he rose higher and yet he did not feel the cold touch that he would have expected from death. He felt vibrant and free and more alive than he had felt for a very long time. This experience was both frightening and exhilarating and he knew that it was something much more than the brief visions he had glimpsed in his previous smoke-drugged trances.

He looked down at himself and saw a young body that was his and yet was not his. It was the body he remembered from thirty years before, firm-muscled and supple, when he had been in his prime. He wore a brief leather vest, laced leather leggings, and the sword of a warrior. But he was not a warrior of Karakhor. The apparel was both strange and vaguely familiar.

He allowed his gaze to range wider over the canopy of the forest. He was high enough now to see the great steel nose of the Alphan Tri-Thruster where it pierced the trees. He was on a level with its needle. He moved closer until he could look down and see his companions, the Alphans standing out clearly from the Hindus in their bright silver suits. He decided that this was not a vision but reality, even though the whole experience was totally unreal and bewildering. Somehow he also knew that he was not dead.

He began to experiment, moving himself tentatively from one part of the sky to another. He was like a chick learning to fly, except that he had no wings and he was not conscious of any movement of his limbs. It was as though he just willed himself to move from one place to another and without any effort it simply happened.

For several minutes, he was lost in the wonder of these new experiences and the mystery of what was happening to him. Then abruptly he remembered why he was here, the driving purpose that had pushed him to the limits in attaining the trance state that would lead him to his far-sight and his visions. Somehow he had succeeded more brilliantly and clearly than ever before and he must not now waste the opportunity. His task was to locate Kananda and Ramesh.

Kananda had headed almost due south, following the cold trail of his younger brother, and Kaseem turned also in that direction. His new young body seemed to float with ease, gathering momentum as he willed it until he was travelling at two or three times the speed of the fastest chariot. He knew he could move faster, but if the terrain below him became too blurred then he might miss the vital signs for which he was searching. Like an eagle he swooped and circled, always moving swiftly southward.

He left the stream, the jungle ridge and the next valley where they had flushed the sabretooth far behind. The high waves of treetops gave way to open plains of yellowed grassland and outcrops of piled bare rock. He saw deer of every variety, grazing or moving slowly in search of greener grass or water. A black panther crouched at a water hole, drinking deeply before lying down for the heat of the day. A small dust cloud near the far edge of the horizon marked the progress of a wandering herd of wild elephant. A single tiger slept in the deep shade of a massive boulder. The land was alive with animals which would have fled without him ever catching a glimpse of them if he had been on foot. Around him, hawks and vultures flew at ease, totally unaware of his passing presence. It was a wondrous revelation which, even in the urgency of his mission, touched his soul. He had never before realized how much diversity of animal and bird life his world contained.

He changed direction frequently, veering left or right or doubling back on his track whenever a hint of movement caught his eye. Always the cause proved to be a natural inhabitant of this rich world of predator and prey. There was no sign of Kananda or Ramesh or of their passing. It was as though both groups had vanished or had never existed here.

He realized that he had already travelled as far as a group on horseback would have reached in two days of hard riding, and he began to fear that he had missed them. If Ramesh had turned east or west on reaching the plains, then the sharp-eyed Hamir would have found the fresh track at ground level and Kananda would have followed. The fact that the trail had led south when Kananda left the camp by the stream meant nothing. The trail could have turned and led anywhere.

Kaseem paused and hovered, suddenly apprehensive. He did not know which way to turn or whether to go on. Even with this new found extension of his far-sight, he was searching blindly and he did not know how long the experience might last. At any moment the trance might end and he could find himself back in that weak old body, exhausted and drained and having learned nothing. He might not have any time to waste and yet it seemed that he was wasting his time and failing his princes.

Slowly he searched the far horizons, letting his gaze linger on every puff of dust and movement. Nothing indicated anything more than a small animal. He had already checked three groups of elephant in the hope that they might be horsemen only to be frustrated and disappointed, but now there was not even a dust cloud of that size. South and west were empty of clues and he turned his gaze to the east. A storm was building up in that direction, purple-black thunderclouds formed and were rolling toward him. Beneath them, the plain ended and there was a treeline barrier of jungle.

Ramesh would have stayed on the plains to hunt, Kaseem decided, so there was no point in searching any further east. He was about to switch his attention back to the south and west when a small fluttering of black specks registered on the edge of his vision. He had almost missed them against the roiling black masses of the advancing clouds. He turned hopefully, yet fearfully, toward them.

Within a few seconds, he had definitely identified the black specks as circling vultures. The kill below them could have been a gazelle or a rabbit or anything brought down by one of the big cats or some other predator. But somehow he knew for certain that it was not, even before he was close enough to see that the half-picked bones were those of men. The bloodied skeletons that had been slashed free of their clinging meat and tissue by the cruel beaks of the carrion birds were only slight. They were not the heavier bodies of Kananda and his warriors. They were striplings, not much more than boys, and Kaseem knew that he had found what remained of the group led by Ramesh.

Kaseem roared his rage and his fury. There was no gentle priest within him now, just a soul filled with grief and violent lust for vengeance. The sword that had hung at his hip was suddenly in his hand and, with a shock, he knew that it was familiar and that he knew how to use it. He was no longer a priest. His soul was that of a warrior.

The first fat drops of rain fell upon the bloodied grass and the dark clouds were now directly overhead. Kaseem had dropped low to confirm his fears and even he could read the wide trail left by the perpetrators as they had headed back to the depths of their forest. He soared upward again, like an untouched arrow through the hammering rain, and sped toward the tree line.

The storm lashed down in all its fury. Great bolts of lightning split the black skies in jagged white flashes. Kaseem the priest would have read the wrath of *Indra* in the tumult of the elements, but he was no longer Kaseem the priest. He no longer knew who he was. He no longer cared about or believed in the power of the gods and the sword was a living extension to his arm.

The swirls of smoke from the many cooking fires led him to the great open space in the forest where the monkey tribes had gathered, and he saw instantly the large tent with the Black Leopard banner. Below him, there were hundreds of the near-naked monkey men and almost as many soldiers in leather and steel. The encampment bristled with spear blades and sword blades and the bows of the archers. Maghalla was here in force, and the Black Leopard could only mean that Sardar himself was present.

Kaseem surveyed the milling scene and, for the first time, the thought of caution nudged at his mind. He was suddenly not sure whether he was visible or vulnerable to the enemy below and he prudently lifted himself out of arrow range. The sword in his hand seemed suddenly less potent against the great mass of weapons that could be marshalled against him.

Again, he did not know what to do next. He was too late to help Ramesh and his friends, for they were already a vulture's banquet. The scene below indicated that Sardar had made an alliance with the monkey tribes and that was information which must be passed back to Karakhor. However, he still did not know what had happened to Kananda, and the need to avenge Ramesh was a hot fire within him. Like a leaf in the storm that crashed around him, he was caught up in conflicting whirls of doubt and confusion.

He saw that most of the men below him were cowering and sheltering from the rain. Like the animals on the plains and the raptors in the skies, they seemed unaware of his presence. So far there had been no indication that any living thing had noted his passage and he began to feel more secure. He could choose to watch and observe or to move on and search further. It did not seem that there were any other real options open to him.

The storm raged around him. Although he seemed to be in the very heart of its lightning and thunder, he was untouched and unharmed, protected by his own subtle aureola of diffused light which the elements could not penetrate. The storm was of that other dimension which he had left behind. He could hear it and see it, yet it was not of his present world. He tried to understand this strange fact, trying to focus his mind on the subtle differences of the two dimensions. And suddenly he was aware that there was something up here with him that was not part of the storm—something that also existed on the same plane of his current being.

Kaseem whirled full circle and instinctively let himself fall as he did so. A double-bladed axe head whirled where his throat had been a split second before and he felt its wind whipping his hair. His sword came up to block the axe blade on its reversed downward chop and the clash of steel upon steel rang unexpectedly loud in his ears. The sound startled him as much as the unexpected attack, but he had the wits to keep moving and somersaulted to his left. He came erect again in a defensive crouch, the sword blade held at an angle across his body, and stared at the two nightmare figures that faced him.

One had the squat, powerful body of a man, but with the head of a snarling leopard. He wore silver-coloured armour and carried the wicked double-bladed axe that had almost severed Kaseem's head from his shoulders a moment before. The leopard's eyes blazed and the peeled-back lips revealed slavering jaws. The second creature was also human in basic form, but with the head and powerful hooked beak of an eagle. It carried a knotted wooden staff with a heavy, squared bronze cap on one end.

The eyes of both creatures were again strangely familiar and Kaseem realized that he knew them both. The leopard head and the black leopard banner over the tent below made the connecting link. Kaseem's mind flashed back to that dreadful day when Maryam had almost been married and he knew that he was looking again into the eyes of Sardar.

With one connection made, the other was almost as easy. On that day, the High Priest of Maghalla had carried a wooden staff with a bronze head. Kaseem recalled the name—Nazik—and when he looked into the eagle eyes, he was again certain. In this dimension, they preferred the exotic images before him, but their eyes were unchanged.

Suddenly many things became clear. Sardar's rapid rise to power and the ease with which he dominated the lesser tribes around him were now all too easy to explain. Even if the two dimensions could not interact, one was still an open window to the other. Old Jahan's laboriously constructed intelligence network paled into insignificance by comparison.

The thoughts flashed through his mind, but it was as though he had spoken aloud. Sardar chuckled and said harshly, "You are right, of course. And you are Kaseem, the High Priest of Karakhor, a foolish old man in a young warrior's body. Your eyes betray you too."

Kaseem realized that Sardar was talking to distract him and flicked his gaze to Nazik. The eagle beak opened and the man shrieked at him and in the same instant, the staff in the creature's hand became a full-length cobra, the hooded head striking viciously forward and spitting venom toward him. Was this the real danger or another distraction? Kaseem was uncertain but he skipped back in midair and again he nearly died.

"Kharga!" The warning voice snapped in his mind and again he ducked and turned.

A third creature was behind him, a man-sized blue baboon with a mottled red face and fearsome teeth. It clutched a massive wooden club in both hands and the long hairy arms gave it a wide, murderous swing. He saw bloodstains and scraps of hair and brains stuck to the sharp steel spikes that were hammered into the thick timber as it whirled within inches of his eyes.

Screaming blasphemies, Sardar and Nazik hurled themselves at him in a concerted attack. Caught between three opponents, Kaseem could only fight in desperate defence and would not have lasted more than a few minutes if a fourth unexpected figure had not hurtled into the fray. This time the surprise was to Sardar and his allies and this was no monster. Instead, a beautiful and naked woman burst upon them from above with only a sword and arm shield.

Kaseem saw the flash of angry green eyes. The colour of a forest pool or a sunbird's wing, he was still not sure. But her nakedness was more effective than any image of hell or horror. Glimpses of her perfect nude limbs, the ripe full breasts and the golden cleft between her magnificent thighs were all the distractions she needed. As the leopard and the eagle both fractionally dropped their guard and gaped, she swept through them with all the speed of a hurricane. One accurate kick landed between the startled eyes of Sardar, and then her sword was slicing down and cleaving into the neck of the shocked baboon. As the creature screamed and tumbled forward, Kaseem saw a fine silver thread which seemed to trail from the back of its neck and drop toward the ground. Laurya severed the thread with the second swing of her sword and in a flash of dark blue light the creature vanished.

Kasseem would have joined her in an immediate attack on their enemies, but the heavens cracked with thunder and a sheet of lightning split the skies between the two opposing pairs. Laurya spun in midair and dropped like a stone, catching Kaseem's arm with her free hand and pulling him into a direct dive into the treetops. Bewildered by the fast-changing speed of events, Kaseem gave up any attempt to resist and allowed her to lead him in headlong flight. If they had crashed into one of the huge trunks, Kaseem had no idea whether it would have brought them to a senseless full stop or whether they would have simply passed through. All he knew was that Laurya chose to weave through them, using the green-black canopy and the torrential thunderstorm to mask their escape.

Several times she zigzagged, turning sharp left or right to

throw off any possible pursuit. His own sense of direction was confused, but he had the feeling that she had dived deeper into the jungle before doubling back on her tracks. He felt frustrated and helpless, like a child holding her hand, for he was still not sure of his own capabilities, or hers, in this bizarre new situation. His one overpowering emotion was that of ecstatic triumph now that he had found her, or to be precise, now that she had found him.

They came suddenly to the edge of the forest and she stopped, pulling him down into a crouch beside her. For a moment she was silent as she stared up into the storm-wracked skies. The rain still created an almost solid curtain and even in the white-streaked lightning flashes there was nothing to be seen.

"We should have fought them," Kaseem said at last. "We could have killed them."

Laurya turned her face toward him and smiled faintly. "Dear foolish Kharga, they almost killed you!"

Kharga, that name again. Kaseem blinked and struggled to focus his mind. He was Kharga—had been Kharga—and she was—

"Liane!" The floodgates of memories opened. There had been so many incarnations when they had been lovers, on Alpha, on Ghedda, and on Earth. Through centuries they had been eternal soul mates and the past lives they had not shared together were the ones that were not worth remembering.

The lights of laughter danced in her green eyes and she leaned forward and kissed him. Her lips were soft and sweet, the promise of a million delights. But when he moved to embrace her, she drew back.

"Kharga, we have no time. We are in great danger here. And there is a desperate need for us to return."

"Danger!" He looked at the sword in his hand and smiled his contempt for anything that might attempt to come between them now.

She shook her head sadly. "Kharga, in this life you are still a child on the astral plane. You have forgotten how to screen your thoughts. Until now, you could not even recognize me. When you found the bodies of those you sought, you howled your anguish and made your presence known. That is how your enemies found you so quickly and fortunately how I found you also."

Kaseem stared at her, unable to deny that he was out of his depth. The new abilities he had suddenly discovered within himself, he now realized, could be dwarfed by those who were more familiar with this dimension.

"Nazik," he said slowly. "The high priest of Maghalla—"

Laurya nodded in affirmation. "The eagle man you call Nazik is obviously a very powerful presence here on the astral plane. That trick of turning his staff into a striking serpent requires a frightening level of mind and will control. That is why I pulled you out of there quickly. Even though I destroyed one of their number, we were still no match for them."

"We cannot be destroyed." He spoke with a false certainty, for although he could now remember flashes of many past lives, he was not really sure.

Laurya half turned so that he could see the beginning of the silver cord that emerged from the nape of her neck, and he vividly remembered her cutting a similar cord just behind the cloven neck of the baboon creature seconds before it had vanished. He remembered then: the cords were the invisible link between their physical and their astral bodies. If the silver cord could be severed, then both bodies would die. Even here on the astral plane, they were not immortal. Now that his mind was opened, many things were slowly coming back into his awareness.

Laurya smiled at him again. “When we return to the astral with each new life span, it takes time to recall all that we know. And sometimes we never remember. That is why you are not yet ready to challenge your friend Nazik or his ally with the leopard head. Also, there is another reason why we must return swiftly to our physical bodies.”

Kaseem remembered his original mission and asked quickly, “Kananda?”

She nodded. “And Commander Zela. I saw them while scouting for you. They need help but we cannot give it to them. Somehow we must alert Blair and the others on the physical plane.”

They moved out from the concealing edge of the forest and made one last searching scan of the rain-lashed skies before they felt safe to thrust upward and speed back toward the north. Kaseem had a million more questions to ask, but had recognized the urgency in her last words. The plains blurred below them and they came out of the storm into bright blue skies. They were moving too fast now to pick out any individual animals or landmarks below, and it was only when the grasslands ended at the first jungle ridge that he was sure that they were on the right course.

Laurya led them over the tall spire of the Tri-Thruster command ship and dropped down over the small upstream beach where the sacrificial fire was now a smouldering pocket of grey ash. Kaseem saw his own priest’s body exactly as he had left it and nearby a golden-haired, silver suited body that lay as though more peacefully asleep.

It was too soon. He felt Laurya’s hand slipping out of his own and he did not want this reunion to end. He tried to hold onto her fingers, but they were gone and there seemed no way to halt his headlong downward rush toward the stream. The sunlight faded and the blue sky and green branches became a black tunnel. A scream of rejection rose in his throat, but then his mind was swamped by darkness and it seemed as though he was sucked down into a lost whirlpool of pain and despair.

☙

Above the jungle encampment to the south, the storm still raged, and the sheeting downpour of rain hammered heavily on the large tent where the Black Leopard banner of Sardar was humbled and plastered to its mast. Inside the tent, Sardar sat cross-legged on silken cushions, scowling into the heart of a small fire. His hunched, hairy body was naked except for a loincloth, and his face was a dark and thunderous mirror of the elements outside.

Opposite him sat Nazik, now attired in his red and grey priest's robe, with the long, brass-capped wooden staff of his office resting across his lap. The high priest's face was faintly reminiscent of the eagle visage he preferred on the astral plane: his nose was a long thin curve of bone with a minimum of flesh and his dark brown eyes had a fierce yellowish sheen at the edges of his pupils.

They were alone in the tent except for the corpse that lay huddled against one of the black leather walls, almost out of reach of the flickering firelight. The corpse had the red-dyed hair of the red monkey clan, and around its neck was a necklace of monkey skulls. Beside it lay a woven straw mask painted with the face of a blue baboon, together with its other badge of office, the witch doctor's staff with its embellishment of more bones, claws and small animal skulls.

Sardar finally spared the corpse a glance, and then hawked and spat into the fire. He looked up to Nazik. "What now? Will the Red Clan still follow us with both their old chief and their medicine man dead?"

Nazik shrugged. "Enough of them saw the Karakhoran prince kill their old chief. And now his brother rules and wants vengeance. Also, they have a powerful greed for the rape and loot we have promised when we take Karakhor. The Black Clan is our firm ally which means the Red Clan will not let them ride to grab all of that loot alone. Have no fears, my friend, the Red Clan is still ours. Malik was a crude but useful ally. We do not need him now."

"Perhaps not." Sardar was still troubled, "But what of our new enemies on the astral plane? This is something we did not expect."

Nazik's eyes narrowed and he pursed the thick cruel lips below the hooked nose. It was a sign that his thoughts were not pleasant. "The old priest of Karakhor has much to learn," he said slowly. "He was a blind bull wallowing in a mud hole. But the woman could be dangerous. That trick of flying naked—for a second even I was tempted by her honey pot! If I ever catch her, she will regret flaunting that little enticement in my face. Or perhaps she will enjoy it!" He laughed suddenly, but the sound was harsh and malicious.

Sardar scowled again. He was in no mood for even the blackest of humour. "If we meet again, I will tear her to shreds," he promised. And he flexed his thick, hairy fingers as though they were still leopard's claws. "I will rip her open from the honey pot upwards. She will give birth to her own entrails. Then I will snip her silver cord."

"An admirable ambition," Nazik agreed. "But perhaps first we should do something about our late friend." He nodded toward the corpse of the Red Clan witch doctor. “It might not be a good political move for him to be found dead in your tent.”

Sardar considered the implications and then stood and crossed to the drawn flaps that closed the tent. Loosening the lashing, he snarled at one of the two miserably drenched and rain-chilled guards who stood outside. “Fetch Tuluq,” he commanded. “I have a task for him.”

He returned to the fire and squatted again. For a few moments Sardar and Nazik discussed the prospects of the coming war with Karakhor. They had the monkey tribes of the forest and the Kingdom of Kanju already aligned to their banners. They had no evidence yet that Karakhor had gathered any allies, and so the question was simple. Should they wait to swell more kingdoms to the ranks of their own forces, or should they move quickly before their enemies also gained in strength? Sardar still burned with the insult of his rejection, but they both knew that the coming slaughter would be mainly about conquest and domination as such events always were.

While they talked, the tent flaps rustled and Tuluq pushed in. The oldest son of Sardar was taller than his father and had inherited the subhuman ugliness of his sire. Rain dripped from his bare muscled arms and from his tunic and leggings to form a puddle around his booted feet. He carried a sword at his hip and a pair of razor sharp knives crossed at his chest. He grinned with good news.

“A rider has arrived from one of our search parties,” he informed them. “They have caught up with the Prince of Karakhor. Half of the enemy is dead and our riders are in close pursuit of the rest. Soon we will have all their heads.”

Sardar sat up, almost cheerful. He beamed benevolently at his son, and then at Nizak. “We have lost a key player but so have they. It seems the battle honours are even.”

His high priest also found a smile. "But we still have to dispose of this. He indicated the unfortunate Malik.

Sardar nodded and gave orders to Tuluq, one of the few men whom he knew he could reasonably trust, at least for the time being.

"Take this out quickly, while the storm still keeps the monkey clans hiding from the rain. It will look better if he is found in his own hut. There is no mark on him so let them think that he died of a heart attack or some over indulgence of his own vices."

Tuluq stared curiously at the corpse for a moment. Then he stooped, heaved, and slung it over one shoulder. If he had any questions, he did not bother to ask them.

☙

Kaseem returned to consciousness feeling as though both his body and mind had been thoroughly beaten, like a bundle of old clothes that a washer-woman had thrashed against the rocks at the riverside. He groaned as he opened his eyes and saw a blurred silver figure and then a pair of anxious deep green eyes. Laurya was sitting on her haunches with his shoulders cradled in her lap and his head leaning against the soft swell of her bosom.

He remembered and a smile creased his features. He reached for her hand and covered it with his own and saw the swift rush of sadness that swept over her shadowed face. He realized then that his hand was again the wrinkled, blue-veined hand of an old man. He turned his head and saw his reflection in the stream and it was the same, deep-lined, gap-toothed old man's face that he had worn for so many years.

"I am so sorry," Laurya said softly. "In this rebirth we are not meant to be together. We were born on different planets. Our paths should not have crossed. Kyle is my lover in this life. He is a good man. We are happy together."

Kaseem felt a deep sense of shock and loss. His eyes filled helplessly with tears.

"I saw you leave with the live bird," she explained quietly. "I was curious and Gujar needed no urging to tell me exactly what you intended. He told me that in the trance state over the sacrificial fire you could experience dreams and visions. If you had flashes of what you called far-sight, then I knew they could only be glimpses of the astral. Somehow you were partially breaking through to the psychic plane but obviously you did not realize exactly what was happening. That can be dangerous, so I followed you."

Kaseem nodded dumbly, knowing now that she was right. His present Earth life had led him into the priesthood in his search for spiritual understanding. And it was as though he had followed the right road to the right crossroads and then knocked on the wrong door. When he had attempted to see visions or signs in the sacred flames, he had in fact been touching on an unnecessarily complicated approach to astral travel. It was as though he had been struggling up a steep and tortuous path on a mountain when there was a direct and easy means of elevation that he had simply failed to see.

"You knew me," he said. "Although I did not know you."

"I saw into your eyes, but you would not search into mine. I thought that was for the best and allowed you to avoid me." She paused and sighed. "Perhaps it would have been best if I had not followed you."

"No," he said sharply, for then he would never have known who he was, and who he had been. He gripped her hand tightly but that again only made him aware that she had the slim hand

and the lithe, supple body of a woman who was forty, perhaps fifty years younger than him. His own desiccated skin bag of old bones could never be a partner to her youth and beauty in this present physical world.

She pushed herself upright and helped him to stand up beside her. He tottered unsteadily, like a drunken man or one still affected by a fever. She kissed his cheek briefly, her sweet, moist lips brushing the old parchment skin.

"We still have duties in this life," she reminded him.

She began to run, back along the stream bank to where her spaceship and their companions were still invisible behind the trees. Kaseem remembered Kananda, and on unsteady legs and with a wildly beating heart, he stumbled after her.

Chapter Ten

They were four: Kananda, Zela, Kasim, and Hamir, the head huntsman, who by sturdy determination and an almost animal instinct for survival, had managed to outlive all of the trained warriors. They bled from a dozen minor wounds where they had been grazed by arrows or nicked by sword blades and yet miraculously, six hours after taking their stand on the hilltop, they were still alive. But Kasim had fired his last arrow and Zela had fired her last lazer bolt. They stood now in a defensive square, back to back, facing outward, awaiting the final Maghallan onslaught.

Their three companions lay dead at their feet but the Maghallans had paid dearly. More than a score of the enemy sprawled lifeless on the blood-splashed slopes of the hill and as many more nursed painful or crippling wounds. The carrion birds circled high over head, their ghastly presence a grim portent as they waited for it to be finished, for the victors to depart so that their own feast could begin.

The Maghallans had given up using their bows. They had killed three, but so many of their shafts had landed harmlessly among the rocks on the hilltop, only to be returned with swift and deadly accuracy by Kasim, that they had learned the folly of supplying him with arrows. Kasim's fame as an archer would become legend after this day, if any of them lived to tell of his skill and valour.

Their throats were dry with thirst. They had fought all through the blistering midday heat and their tongues were beginning to swell in their throats. There was no shade on the hilltop and the sun was still hot enough to suck the last of the moisture from their dehydrating bodies.

Come, Kananda thought bleakly, *come while we still have enough strength to wield our swords and take more of you with us on our journey into death.* And he offered another brief prayer to *Indra*, no longer for life and salvation, but simply for more blood to spill down his own sword before he died.

Zela's head was swimming in a red haze brought on by fatigue and heat and she too prepared to die. She had succeeded in contacting her ship, but the communication had been brief and Cadel's voice had been faint and broken. She knew that her own signal must have been even more so and its location difficult to pin-point. Her crew would not find her in time. Her despair became diffused with anger. She still believed that there was a God Behind All Gods, but she could no longer ask Him to save her. She only demanded to know why he would permit her to die when she had so much to do and so much to live for. It was a question that the philosophers had never been able to answer.

Why? Why live? Why fight? Why die? Why anything? Was there a deeper meaning behind all things, as her father taught? Or could it be that the Gheddans were right and there was nothing beyond the here and now? A fearful doubt cavorted with the questions in her mind and she felt dizziness sweeping over her. Was dying a journey into knowledge and another plane of existence, or simply an end, an obliteration, a nothing? Soon she would know, or not know, as the case might be.

There was a silence, a stillness, a deceptive lull before the storm. Some thirty Maghallan warriors crouched on all sides of the steep pile of cracked boulders, most of them more than half way up to the summit. It was a difficult climb and on the summit the defenders had rolled the loose boulders into an encircling rampart. During the early stages of the battle, the Karakhorans had crouched behind their ramparts, making themselves almost invisible targets. But now they stood boldly, heads and shoulders in full view.

The Maghallan commander was a hard, sword-scarred man, his face hollow-cheeked and hollow-eyed like a dark, living skull. He held his position because he was the most savage of his men. He was tempted to order another volley of spears and arrows to be hurled upward and yet he refrained. He had formed a grudging respect for the four who had held his force at bay for so long and he knew from the bejeweled helmet and insignia that their leader was a Karakhoran prince. He would permit them to die fighting and their prince would die on his own bright blade. He stood upright and voiced a command. And with screaming, blood-curdling battle cries his men followed scrambling at his heels as he charged for the hilltop.

“At last,” Kananda breathed, almost joyously. His eye was on the skull-faced man whom he had identified as the Maghallan chieftain, and his fighting soul soared in eagerness. He would have sprung forward to meet the man, but his military training forbade him to break the defensive square. Like a coiled cobra, he waited.

Two Maghallan warriors sprang together over the stone barrier on Kananda’s right flank. Zela was there, blocking their attack in a succession of ringing sword clashes. One man was flung back, his cheek bones and jaw cleft by her cutting blade. The other sagged gasping to his knees as he was impaled below the breastbone. Two more rushed the left flank where Hamir defended. Kananda half turned to deal with one of them, making a slicing backhand stroke behind the Maghallan's guard that severed his sword arm above the elbow. He left the huntsman to deal with the other. Behind him, he heard Kasim defending his back with desperate swordplay. Then the Maghallan chieftain was leaping into the tight, rock-bound arena to face him.

In aiding Hamir, Kananda had lost the first initiative. The skull-faced man hacked wickedly for his throat and Kananda brought his own sword back only just in time to deflect the blow. The Maghallan roared his fury, a sound echoed from all sides by his attacking fellows, but Kananda and his three companions conserved their energy to fight all the better in tight-lipped silence. The skull-faced man was no master of his blade, but he fought with a homicidal mania that gave no quarter.

Kananda held his ground, turned the Maghallan blade, and as their bodies met in solid, sweating impact, he smashed his elbow into the Maghallan's nose, breaking the bone and causing a spout of blood to spill from the screaming face. The skull-faced man fell back, but in the split-second before Kananda would have killed him, another was in his place. And then another. As fast as they fell, there were others, until his blade arced in a bright rainbow of splattering gore.

Hamir cried in pain and sagged to his knees, clutching at the Maghallan spear that had pierced his belly. Kananda wheeled to cut the spearman down, and the fighting square reformed as a triangle with the fallen man in the middle. Still the Maghallans came on. Kasim hewed mightily, left and right, severing limbs and laying open heads and breasts and faces. Zela spun lightly on her feet, her blade flying faster and with more deadly accuracy than any of them.

Even so, the sheer weight of numbers would have borne them down. But then, from far away, the shrill sound of a battle horn echoed across the grassy plain. The first notes failed to penetrate through the battle clamour of screams and groans and sword blows, but then the Maghallans at the rear of the conflict began to take notice. A score of chariots were thundering toward the besieged rock pile from the east.

The Maghallan attack faltered, and some of the warriors began to hurry back down the hill to take up defensive positions or to reach their tethered horses. The rest rallied again as the skull-faced chieftain screeched at them to finish this fight before they faced the next.

The Maghallan commander had briefly withdrawn to nurse his shattered nose, but now he was back with a vengeance, his face a red mask of blood and his heart black with rage. Six of his warriors joined him, and Kananda and Zela faced them together while Kasim protected their backs. Again their swords whirled and sang in showers of bright red rain.

The leading chariot flew the bright green pennant of the young lord Gujar and was the first to skid to a halt at the foot of the hill. The neighing horses reared and trampled two of the fleeing Maghallan warriors before they could get away, and then Gujar leapt down and was leading a dozen fresh fighting men on foot as they fell upon the disorganized Maghallans from behind. The remaining Karakhorans fired a deadly covering rain of arrows from their chariots over the heads of Gujar and his force as they advanced. With the rescue mission were two of the Alphans, distinctive in their bright silver spacesuits, striking death and terror into the enemy ranks with searing energy bolts from their hand lazers.

Gujar stormed the hill at a run, cutting down all who tried to bar his way, and at his side, never a pace behind, with a sword in one hand and a lazer in the other, was Blair. The tall Alphan was as reckless with his life as the young lord and they reached the crest of the hill together. They arrived just in time to see Zela dispatch the second to last man of the enemy. Kananda thrust his sword through the frustrated heart of the skull-faced chieftain a moment later.

"Kananda!" Gujar cried. "Praise *Indra*! You are alive!"

"Gujar!" Kananda answered. "I have never been happier to see you."

They sheathed their swords, laughed aloud, and clasped arms violently in the eternal gesture of friendship. Kananda offered his free arm to Kasim, and Kasim and Gujar completed the arm-locked triangle. They had been boyhood friends and now they were comrades-in-arms and brothers in the hot blood of battle. The emotion and the love between them were electric.

Slowly the elation and the blood-lust cooled. Kananda broke the circle and checked the body of Ramesh who still lay unconscious, protected and ignored and half buried under the corpses of their fallen comrades. He said grimly, "I am alive and so barely is Ramesh, but so many of our friends are dead."

He knelt by the fallen huntsman, lifting the man's head and shoulders to find that he was still breathing, although unconscious and sorely wounded. He looked up again to Gujar. "This one has fought valiantly and loyally. We must find something to stop his bleeding."

There was a silver suit beside him. Kananda recognized Kyle. The Alphan laid down his hand lazer and took his medical kit from his belt pack. He was breathing heavily from his run up the hill and said briefly, "I can help him."

Kananda nodded and entrusted the care of the fallen man to the others. He rose and turned to look for Zela.

He wanted to embrace her with a passion and emotion that soared far above his feelings for Kasim and Gujar and yet he held back. Zela stood with her feet apart, her reddened sword tip touching the ground, still panting from her recent exertions and smiling as she faced Blair.

"Commander." The tall Alphan was formal in deference to her rank, but his anxiety showed through. "Are you harmed?"

"No." Zela shook her head, her long golden hair dancing silkily on her shoulders. "I think I am in one piece."

Blair's gaze roved over the cuts and stains on her suit, the bruise on her jaw and the graze on her temple that denied the reassurance of her smile.

"But you are wounded—"

"Only a few scratches and I am very tired. But there is nothing serious." Her eyes softened and she reached forward and touched his arm. Relief and anguish filtered into her voice. "Oh, Blair—there was a moment when I felt that you would not find me. I should have known better."

"Your message was badly distorted," Blair explained. "You were too far away, but somehow Laurya managed to pinpoint your position. I feared she was guessing but it seems she was not."

"Laurya seems to have gifts that none of us can understand," Zela said thankfully.

"We couldn't use the ship." Blair's voice hinted at his frustration. "Cadel has been doing more maintenance work on the engines and parts of the engage thrusters were dismantled. We were fortunate that Gujar decided to bring up the Karakhoran chariots and the rest of their horses soon after you left. Laurya was able to establish the distance and direction of your signal and we calculated that the chariots would reach you more quickly than the time it would take us to get the ship ready for flight."

Blair's voice continued calm and matter of fact, but Kananda detected the undersurface tension beneath the formal exterior. The Alphan had fought with a rash ferocity that had been totally unsuspected in his previously imperturbable personality and suddenly, with a lover's instinct, Kananda knew that Blair was also in love with Zela.

Here was another unexpected and this time unwelcome surprise. Kananda realized that because Kyle and Laurya had been so open in their love for each other, he had mistakenly assumed that all Alphans made no secret of their feelings. Now, Kananda guessed that for reasons of his own, perhaps because a love affair at the command level might prove detrimental to their mission, Blair had chosen to keep his feelings secret. Or perhaps Blair had not even admitted his inner feelings to himself. Perhaps Zela knew. Perhaps she did not. Kananda was unsure. He only knew he was right about Blair.

When the huntsman's wound had been sealed and they had gathered up their scattered horses, they began the return journey. This time Ramesh and Hamir traveled more comfortably in two of the chariots. For Kananda it was a silent, thoughtful ride, and his thoughts were divided, jealous and disturbed. He knew that his immediate duty must be to return to Karakhor, to confirm Sardar's alliance with the monkey tribes and to warn the city and his father.

But he did not want to part from Zela, especially now that he knew he had a rival. His heart was torn between duty and love, and the pain was worse than dying.

☙

In the kaleidoscope of life's rich patterns that pulsated continuously in the vibrant city of Karakhor, every single stage of its population's life cycle could be witnessed on almost every day. Working and bargaining, playing and loving went on as busily as usual, despite the overlay of apprehension that followed the arrival of the Gheddan spaceship. At every sunset, the funeral pyres glowed on the burning ghats on the lower reaches of the Mahanadi River just below the city, and day and night squalling infants continued to make their traumatic entrance into the world. Weddings were equally a daily occurrence, and on festival and holy days there would be a spate of them. Today was one of the many feast days of *Agni*, god of the sacred sacrificial flames that acted as messengers between men and the gods, and so it was not difficult for Maryam to find a temple where a marriage ceremony was taking place.

This was something she particularly wanted Raven to see, but she had chosen the location with care. She did not dare to offend him by leading him to another shrine of *Varuna*, and she could not be sure which side *Agni* might have taken if there was conflict between the gods. So the temple had to be dedicated to *Indra*. It was a smaller temple of more ancient design but exquisitely crafted, with curves and turrets flowing upward in sculpted tiers to a crowning lotus of stone. It was situated on a platform overlooking the river and the wedding pavilion had been erected in bright red and gold silks on the greensward beside it.

Maryam had timed their arrival to coincide with the moment of betrothal for she did not want Raven to arrive too soon and become bored before the crucial rites were performed. It would ruin all her plans if he chose to leave before the full implications of the ceremony became clear.

The sacred fires were lit upon the altar and censers of burning incense added their curls of fragrant smoke to the scented air. Garlands of golden marigolds vied with the rich and colourful finery of the guests, and a profusion of gemstones flashed and sparkled in pendants, rings and necklaces. On a white lace tablecloth, gold and silver bowls and salvers were piled high with fruit and sweetmeats and savoury food, waiting for the feast to begin. A white-robed priest sang the sacred mantras and the bride, almost invisible beneath her splendid bridal gown, golden shawl and veil and more draped flower garlands, was led forward by her father to the altar.

Maryam held tight to Raven's arm, holding him back so they could observe without becoming the focus of attention. She did not know the bride—the girl was a daughter of one of the lesser houses of Karakhor— but a wedding day belonged to the bride and groom and to them alone. Maryam did not want to spoil it by stealing any of their limelight.

The groom was already there, a slender, nervous youth in spotless white shirt, turban and trousers. While the priest read blessings over them, the proud, bewhiskered father carefully placed the hand of his daughter into the hand of the groom, at the same time promising that she would be unto death his faithful wife. The young man spoke his own vows and the girl gravely nodded her assent. The priest threw a handful of powder onto the flames which flashed upward. The father withdrew. Hand-in-hand, the bride and groom followed the chanting priest to walk three times around the sacred fire. With each circuit, the priest threw more powder into the burning brazier and the bright essence of *Agni* flew skyward to announce that two were now blessed as one.

Congratulations and a profusion of flower petals showered down on the happy couple. Their hands were firmly clasped now. The groom was smiling broadly and the bride's eyes shone brightly above her masking veil. An orchestra began to play at the back of the pavilion, the music fluting and tinkling lightly and sweetly above the excited babble of the guests.

Maryam had seen enough. The revels would go on late into the night but the ritual was over. They had not been invited and it would be impolite to stay, but she hoped that Raven had understood the meaning of what they had witnessed. She led him away and they walked through a short avenue of red and purple bougainvillea to the edge of the river.

They were alone and she put her arms around his neck and passionately kissed his mouth. Then, by means of signs and a play-acting charade of themselves going through the same motions as the young couple they had just watched, she made plain her hopes and desires. She had feared that he would be angry, but instead he was amused and, mistaking his smile for joy and acceptance, she hugged him to her and kissed him again and again.

Raven enjoyed her attentions. He could and would take her as and when he wanted, but a warm and loving woman always gave more satisfaction than one that was cold, hostile or frightened. Also, he had no doubts about what she wanted, although a Gheddan marriage would have been a much more robust affair. On the home continent of his world a man simply called his stronghold together, placed his left hand firmly upon the shoulder of his chosen woman, drew his sword with his right hand and proclaimed that she was his wife. If the woman's father and brothers approved, they cheered and offered him beer and wine. If they did not, they drew swords and challenged. The suitor calculated his acceptability or his sword prowess in advance and took his chances.

To go through this hand-in-hand nonsense of free giving, chanting priest, burning powders and cascades of flower petals, would be for Raven both meaningless and non-binding. But he was shrewd enough to see the political value of going along with her wishes. This pompous and insipid ritual would clearly have profound meaning for Maryam and for the city's rulers and its people. Political alliance marriages were not unknown in Gheddan history and he could see how such a gesture could help to stabilize the situation here while his ship returned to

Ghedda.

And so, to Maryam's overpowering delight, her awesome hopes were fully realized. The blue-skinned god enfolded her in his strong arms, purposefully returned her enraptured kisses and nodded his glorious blue-curled head to signify his agreement.

She almost swooned on the spot, except that this was a moment to be forever cherished, an emotional excitement too wonderful to be missed by the departure of her senses. She held fast to her god and wished that he would consume her with all the fires of his passion.

Some time later, when her senses calmed, she realized that she still had to obtain the consent of her father.

ଓ

She found Kara-Rashna and Jahan in private conference, two worried grey heads talking close together in low voices. One bearded face was pale and pain-filled, the other grim and thwarted by the consistent absence of any hard intelligence on the problems that confronted them. They were in one of her father's private apartments and she, in her excitement and impetuosity, barely paused to brush away the startled protests of the armed guards at the door. The king and his general both looked up, astonished, as she burst in. Their private talks were normally sacrosanct.

"Daughter—" The king's voice faltered.

"Maryam!" Jahan rose swiftly to his feet. His hand moved automatically to the hilt of his sword. "What is wrong?"

"Nothing is wrong," Maryam cried happily. She gave him a fleeting kiss and a hug and then the same to her father. "Uncle!

Father. I have marvelous news!"

The king brightened. "Kananda has returned?" he asked hopefully.

"Not yet." Maryam paused for breath, suddenly uncertain of how to tell them. She loved them both and she knew they loved her, but now she could not guess how they might react. They waited, baffled and expectant.

"The God," she blurted at last. "The High One—Raven—He has chosen me. He has shown his desire to make me his bride!"

It was their turn to be speechless. The king's jaw dropped open helplessly. Jahan's eyes opened wide and for several seconds he could not even blink. They stared at her, then at each other. Then they looked at her again, shocked and unbelieving.

"How do you know?" Jahan finally recovered his voice and part of his wits. "Has he spoken to you in our language?"

"No, but this afternoon we watched a marriage ceremony taking place at the temple by the river. Raven—the God—then made signs to indicate that he wished for the two of us to go through the same ceremony."

"Raven? That is his name?"

"He has made me understand his name and he knows mine. Beyond that our different languages still make things difficult."

"Our priests know of no god named Raven," Jahan said doubtfully.

"*Indra* uses many names." Maryam was impatient. "And the priests do not know everything."

"Even so, it is strange that this god cannot communicate in our language."

"He communicates with signs and by means of his power.

Is this not the way with all gods?"

"You took him to the temple by the river?" Kara-Rashna asked the question searchingly. He knew the willful ways of his daughter and he was aware of her growing confidence in her subtle woman's skills.

"We saw a marriage ceremony." Maryam was not going to confess herself so easily. "Raven made it clear that he wishes for us to be joined as man and wife—as God and Bride."

"If this is so, then where is he now?" Jahan pressed the question. "He should know that it is the business of a man, or even a god, to come in person to proclaim his intent to the father of his proposed bride."

"This is truly so." The old king was even more concerned with the total lack of protocol in these bewildering events. "It is not done for young women to speak of arranging their own marriages."

This was delicate ground, which was why Maryam had chosen to tread it alone. She was not sure whether Raven would even have troubled to seek the permission of her father. She desperately did not want either of them to be offended by the other in any discussion or argument. And even more desperately, she did not want her parents to know that he had already loved her and become the despoiler of her sacred virginity. In her own mind, and in the eyes of the gods, she knew that now she could never belong fully to any other man. For her secret to be protected, for her own love to be fulfilled, for the security of the city and for the honour of all Karakhor, she knew that whatever their objections, this marriage had to take place.

She hesitated, and then argued forcefully. "But, father, the ways of the gods are not the ways of mortal men. We cannot expect them to arrange things in an ordinary way. Could a god ask for a bride? And perhaps be refused? It is unthinkable. But Raven has made his wishes known. We cannot refuse him."

"We have refused Sardar and Maghalla," Jahan reminded her, his glare suddenly ferocious. "Even though it may mean war between Karakhor and the rest of the known mortal world. If it needs to be, then we will defy the gods as well."

"But, Uncle, if I wed with Raven, it will protect Karakhor from Sardar and Maghalla and from any other threat of war. This marriage will fulfil my duty to all our people. Karakhor will be allied with the gods. We shall become the greatest empire the world has ever known."

The appeal failed. For Jahan was not a power-builder, but just a brilliant old soldier with undaunted devotion and pride. "You do not have to marry anyone," he told her. "Neither king nor god. Unless it is your heart's desire, Karakhor will not permit it. Your father and I will not permit it. The virtue of our royal princess is beyond any price on Earth or in heaven.

It was a splendid speech, and inside her breast Maryam felt her soul burn with shame, for her virtue had already flown. But he had given her the key to his consent and she knew she had won. She said bravely, "But, Uncle! Father! This is my heart's desire. I want this marriage for myself as much as for Karakhor. This is my life, my destiny. It is ordained by the gods themselves. I am filled with joy and happiness. I only want that you should share my joy and be happy with me."

Her plea was anguished and her hopes were radiant in her eyes. Jahan believed her and he knew when his own argument had been turned back against him. He had no words left to challenge her and he looked defensively to the king.

Kara-Rashna was not having a good day. His body pained him, his head ached and his mind was a struggling battlefield of awesome questions that were beyond his powers of comprehension. He did not know what he wanted to say or what decision he should make. He needed more advice on these portentous matters and he clearly saw that Jahan was also well out of his depth.

He said slowly, “If this marriage is to take place, then only one man is sufficiently holy to perform the rites. Of all our Brahmins, our High Priest Kaseem will be the only one acceptable to the gods. And as we must await his return in any case, then perhaps we should await his advice.”

Maryam showed her disappointment. She wanted an immediate wedding, not an excuse for a postponed decision.

However, Jahan was a master tactician and quick to see an opportunity for delay. He put a fond hand on her shoulder and said cheerfully, “When Kaseem returns, then Kananda will return also. Surely you would not want such a magnificent event as your wedding to take place without your favourite brother being present?”

It was Maryam’s turn to have her mind and emotions abruptly divided. In her excitement, she had temporarily forgotten Kananda, but suddenly she knew that Jahan was right. She could barely wait for her union with Raven to be made sacred and complete. Yet if Kananda were absent, her cup of happiness would be less than overflowing. He had always been more than a brother. He had been her friend, confidant and ally. Her love for him was almost as overpowering as her love for Raven, although it was adoration on a different plane. She did want him to be at her wedding. She wanted Kananda to see her joined to Raven and she wanted him to approve. She desperately wanted her faultless brother and her god-lover to be friends.

Kara-Rashna saw that Jahan had scored a winning point and he made the effort to restore some apparent mastery in his own household. "We will await the return of Kaseem," he said firmly, "And of our son, Kananda. We cannot celebrate such an important alliance without the presence of our High Priest and First Prince."

ɞ

The king's belief that his non-public conversations were private was mistaken. The young princes had always been free to roam and play in the palace maze of rooms and corridors, and long ago Rajar had found the perfect place for eavesdropping. He had been playing hide and seek with Nirad and Namita and had concealed himself in a cupboard in one of the smaller rooms above the king's apartments. There, by pure chance, he had discovered that by pressing one ear to a gap between the floor tiles, he could clearly hear all that was said in the room below. It was a secret that he had kept to himself and a knowledge that he used more and more frequently as he became older and more ambitious.

Now he hurried with what he had learned, first to collect Nirad, and then to call upon their sister. "Maryam plans to marry the one called Raven," he told them bluntly. He was angry and barely constrained. "We know that when our father dies, Kananda will be king and with his sister's alliance to support him, there will be no sharing of power at all with our mother's bloodline. We shall all be mere vassals. If we hope to adjust this balance of power back toward our own favour, then we need to act now!"

"How do you know all this?" Nirad wanted to know.

"That does not matter. Just believe me. It is true."

"But what can we do? How can we act?"

"Our sister must act for us—as Maryam acts for Kananda."

Rajar looked to Namita. “We have seen how the one called Thorn looks upon you. He desires you. If Raven will marry Maryam, then perhaps Thorn will join with you. Our bloodline will have its own alliance with the power of the strangers. Then Kananda and Maryam will have to accept our due voice in all the matters of state.”

Namita recoiled, her face drained of colour. “But the one called Thorn is cold. He looks cruel.”

“Marriage is about politics.” Rajar shrugged as he spoke. “If you wait for Kara-Rashna to arrange your marriage, it will probably be to some ugly old king, just as Maryam was almost married to Sardar of Maghalla. At least this way you can serve us all.”

“But how—?”

“All you have to do is smile at him. Show a woman’s willingness. He will do the rest.”

“But I do not like him. I do not want to be joined to this man.”

“Bahdra has a king who is seventy years old. He dribbles constantly and smells like an incontinent goat, but he is always ready to accept another young bride. With Kanju alligned to Maghalla, Karakhor may seek an alliance with Bahdra. Kara-Rashna might well choose to marry you to this old king.”

“Our father would not do this to me. He reprieved Maryam from Sardar.”

“Kara-Rashna does not love you as much as he loves Maryam. He does not love Nirad and myself as much as he loves Kananda.” Rajar gripped her shoulders fiercely, barely holding back the urge to shake her. “Do this for us, Namita,” he implored her. “Just smile at the one called Thorn. I have plans that will work if only you encourage him a little.”

“What sort of plans?”

"You will see, all in good time. But surely anything would be better than to wait to be married to an old goat like the king of Bahdra. Smile at Thorn, little sister. Just be pleasant."

Chapter Eleven

After Blair and Gujar had left on their rescue mission, Kaseem had prayed almost hourly for their safe return with Kananda and all of those who rode with them. His spirit flight had left him exhausted with all his beliefs badly shaken, but just as he had always believed that there were gods above this world, he now believed that it was still possible that those gods could exist somewhere above the astral plane. Also, his priestly ministrations were still expected of him and in this physical world he had no other role.

It was only the attempt to break his physical bonds and seek his far- sight that had called for a live sacrifice and privacy. For his normal daily routines, he had lovingly built a small altar in a lush glade close beside the main camp where he kept the sacrificial fire continually burning bright. At sunset and at dawn, he had ritually faced the setting or rising sun as he solemnly offered the gifts of small cuts of animal meat that the hunters brought to him as the gods' due portion of their endeavours. He had barely eaten or slept over the past four days and again all his consciousness was directed to the vital task of enlisting the aid of *Indra*, *Varuna* and *Agni* to support and protect his absent companions. The return to his ritual routine was his only comfort.

Laurya had discreetly retired into the background after

convincing Blair that she was able to pinpoint the location of the faint and distorted message that had come through from Zela during their absence. Blair had been dubious but desperate, and since the tall Alphan's departure with Gujar and the chariots, Kaseem had remained on his knees before his altar, reciting endless mantras of supplication. When the chariots at last returned, he was on the point of collapse and unable to rise. His stiffened legs were crossed beneath him and temporarily useless. Two warriors came to lift him gently and reverently and carried him to face Kananda.

Kananda, Kasim and Zela were also on the edge of exhaustion. They had been forced to hand over their mounts and finish the ride as passengers in three of the chariots. The day was ending and the twilight fading when, with huge relief, they saw again the peaceful campfires by the valley stream, the welcoming faces of their friends, and the black, needle spires of the Alphan spaceship.

The old priest wept tears of joy when he saw that his prince was alive. They embraced and the two warriors stepped back a pace while Kananda held the old man in his arms. When they parted, the warriors supported Kaseem again and he blinked his tears away as he looked around him. He had been babbling praises to *Indra* in thanks for Kananda's safe return, but now he saw that of the two parties that had been missing for so long, only two others were alive and unwounded. He recognized the bloodied form of Ramesh that lay in the back of one of the chariots. His first thought was that he was looking at a corpse and a piercing wail of pure anguish was torn from his breast.

Now he wept again, more profusely than before, and these were tears of torment and pain. He tore at his white robe and beat his fists upon his shriveled breast. He pounded at his forehead and temples with the heel of his palm until Kananda feared that he would knock himself senseless and moved to restrain him.

"Holy One," Kananda almost shouted at him. "Do not torture yourself. Ramesh is alive. He is sorely wounded. But he is alive!"

Kaseem paused in his wailing and self-punishment and Kananda led him closer to the chariot. Gripping the priest's wrist, Kananda held the wrinkled palm against his brother's white temple. "He is still warm," Kananda said softly. "He has survived his wounds and our flight to safety. With care and gentle treatment, I think he may now recover."

The pale flesh under his hand was not icy, Kaseem realized. Ramesh still clung to life, even though his eyes were closed and he would clearly need much time and care to recover.

"I have still failed him." The old priest would not wholly give up his bitter lamentations. "I failed my princes. I failed my duty. I failed your father. It was my place to watch over you, to counsel and advise you. My miserable wisdom was meant to be your protection. I did not watch you enough. I did not advise you correctly. The gods are angry with me. My prayers were useless—"

"Kaseem, Holy One, beloved by the gods and of my father—" Kananda wept with him, his arm around the old man's frail shoulders. "The fault is not yours. If there is any fault, it is mine. I have twice failed in my duty. I could not catch up with my brother in time. And I could not prevent the forces of Maghalla from slaughtering more than two score of his companions and mine. Surely I am the one who has found disfavour with the gods."

Kaseem could not be comforted. The fervent intensity of his prayers and devotions over the past four days and then the rigours of the astral flight had taken a heavy toll on his strength and spirit. Now it seemed that almost all of his efforts had been in vain.

"The gods have deserted me," he insisted wretchedly. "They reject this sinful Brahmin as unworthy and unclean. I must have performed my sacrifices incorrectly. I must have recited the Vedic verses wrongly. I must have bad *karma*, for which I must suffer as the gods abandon me."

"No," Kananda groaned. "It is my *karma* that is sinful. It is because of me that Karakhor must now suffer the full onslaught of both Maghalla and the monkey tribes."

"What is this *karma*?"

Zela asked the question partly because she was puzzled and did not know what they were talking about and partly in an effort to break them out of their mutual exchange of self-blame and self-pity. For a moment they were too distressed to respond, and then it was Gujar who answered.

"The law of *karma* is the prime law of creation. It is the law which balances all the good and bad deeds of our previous lives and thus determines our place and status in our next incarnation."

This was a new concept and Zela was no better informed. "What is incarnation?" she asked blankly.

The young lord's brow furrowed as he sought for a clearer explanation, but he was saved by Kaseem, who was not yet ready to be fully usurped from his privileged role. The old priest ceased beating himself, struggled to rally his thoughts and mournfully expounded on the subject.

"It is known that men and all other beings are primarily spirit," he said tonelessly, for he was still sure of that much. "We die, but we are endlessly reborn. Each birth is an incarnation of the soul in its next body. What governs each rebirth, its time, place and duration is *karma*. It is both the sum of our past and the whole of our future. It is our destiny, written by our own actions from the beginning of all things."

Kananda nodded gravely. "No man can escape his destiny, but I did not know that mine was so black. My spirit must have committed great evil for the gods to punish me so grievously. For Ramesh to be so gravely wounded. For so many others to have died. And for the royal House of Karakhor to lose face and dignity before the monkey tribes and Maghalla, my sins must indeed have been terrible. So terrible that now all of Karakhor must face destruction and disaster."

"Past sins! Future destiny! Souls reborn into new bodies!" Zela lifted her hands in helpless amazement. "Surely you cannot believe in such things?"

Kaseem was scandalized by such blasphemy. He clasped his hands in horror to his ears. "*Samsara* is the ever-lasting stream of consciousness," he told her angrily. "It is the stream of life—of existence itself. And *karma* is the law of *Samsara*. Not even the gods are above the law."

Zela saw from the shocked faces gathered around her that she had been tactless and so she was prepared to let the matter rest. But Kananda was now looking at her with eyes that were filled with infinite sadness.

"Zela," he said softly. "Do you not realize that your people also have their own *karma*? You told me how your earlier generations have created weapons of fire and power so monstrous that they can destroy your entire world. And now those weapons have passed into the hands of your Gheddan enemies who will turn them against you. By creating those weapons, your race has sown the seeds of its own destruction. That is the law of *karma*. The actions from our past forever haunt us and determine what will happen in our future. There is no escape."

The evening was warm and a nearby campfire cast its flame

shadows over them, but suddenly Zela was cold. For a moment, it was as though a gust of air from the coldest ice world on the far rim of the solar system had briefly caressed her spine. And for that moment, she believed him.

Her home planet did face imminent catastrophe. The Gheddan Empire was sufficiently insane to launch all of its vast thermonuclear and lazer capability in the suicidal folly of a first strike. Every Alphan adult had faced up to the fact that it was only a matter of time.

Zela shivered and turned wearily away.

☙

They were awakened soon after dawn. Kananda felt the urgent hand upon his shoulder and reached instinctively for his sword, but it was only the hand of Gujar.

"Runners have arrived," the young lord informed him, "from your father."

Kananda felt as though he had barely had time to close his eyes. His body felt as heavy as stone. With an effort, he roused himself and followed Gujar out of the tent to where two lean and long-legged youths, garbed only in sandals and loincloths, were waiting.

"Speak," he commanded them. "What news do you bring from Kara-Rashna?"

"Sire, the news is not good." The spokesman hung his head as though he was responsible. "Our Lord Jahan has discovered that Maghalla is now aligned with Kanju. A Kanju prince has been married to Princess Seeva, a daughter of Sardar. Lord Jahan and your royal father both feel that this alliance may make Maghalla bolder and thus endanger yourself and Prince

Ramesh. Thus it is Kara-Rashna's wish that you conclude your tiger hunt quickly and return with all speed to Karakhor."

"Your warning comes too late," Kananda said bitterly. "We have lost many of our young lords and warriors and Prince Ramesh still hovers on the edge of death."

The camp was now wide awake, the warriors gathering round to listen. Kaseem emerged from his tent, wringing his wrinkled hands together, his face anxious. Zela and two of her crew were walking curiously toward them.

"Maghalla, the monkey tribes and now Kanju—all arrayed against Karakhor." Kaseem was ready to weep again. "Truly the gods have forsaken us."

"Then we must stand alone," Kananda said grimly. "With or without the gods, Karakhor will fight. Gujar, give the orders to break camp. We return to the city as soon and as fast as we are able."

Gujar nodded, but the runners were still hovering tentatively and so he waited.

"Is there more?" Kananda asked.

"There are strangers in the city." The youth who was spokesman half turned and pointed to the Alphan Tri-Thruster standing further up the valley. "They came in a steel temple as tall as this one. They came in fire and thunder and their powers are in fire. Many people in the city say that they are from the gods."

Zela was close enough to overhear. She stepped forward and said quickly, "Describe these people. Do they look like myself and my friends?"

The youth gaped at her, taking in the silver suit and golden hair. Then he shook his head. He remembered to look back to his prince.

"Sire, the strangers in the city have blue faces. The hair upon their heads is of darker blue. They wear white clothing with pieces of golden chain armour."

"Gheddans," Zela said through compressed lips. She turned to Blair who was beside her. "The Gheddan Empire has sent a ship to follow us."

"How many of these strangers are there?" Blair asked the runner.

The youth looked awkwardly to Kananda. He did not know the correct protocol here. Kananda indicated that he should answer.

"They are five."

"Look at our temple," Zela suggested. "Tell us how this other temple is different."

The runner stared at the spaceship, biting his lip, struggling to compare the impossible reality with the miraculous memory. "The centre spire was as tall but not so slender on the other temple," he decided at last. "The smaller spires were much closer to the central spire, and there were four, not two."

"A Class Five Solar Cruiser," Blair said with conviction. "Its lazer power is slightly more formidable than ours, and its pulse bombs are heavier. But we have the edge on speed, range and manoeuvreability."

"So we believe," Zela said cautiously. "The two have never met in hot combat."

"A Class Five carries a crew of six," Laurya pointed out. She had come up beside them with Kyle.

"Only five would show themselves." Blair was certain. "The sixth would stay on board at all times to man the lazer banks."

Kananda was losing track of this conversation. He pushed

between them, facing Zela and said grimly, "Explain to me. What does all this mean?"

She put her hand on his arm, and although her touch was soft and concerned, her face was set hard.

"It means, Kananda, that the threat from your earthly enemies is now a minor one. It is still imperative to reach your city of Karakhor as quickly as possible—but now some of us must come with you and we must get there before Gheddan treachery can take over the city."

"This time I will come," Blair added firmly.

Kananda half turned, giving him a searching, uncertain look, but then Kyle intruded with a warning.

"Commander, have you considered that this might be a trap—a means to divide some of us from our ship?"

Zela frowned. She looked to the Hindu messenger who stood bewildered beside them, and then to Laurya. The young Alphan woman raised an almost imperceptible golden eyebrow in enquiry and Zela nodded. Laurya stepped forward and took the hands of the startled runner gently in her own. Kananda shot Zela a questioning glance.

"It is all right," Zela calmed him. "Laurya seems to have a highly developed sense of instinct. I would guess that is how she was able to be so sure of our position when my radio communication only half got through. By making touch contact with another, she can also sense and tune in to the vibrations, tensions and feelings in the other's body. She cannot read minds, but she is very accurate in detecting hidden feelings and reading emotions. She is almost a human lie detector."

Kaseem had appeared to stand on the edge of the silent group of Hindus that simply watched and listened. His eyes were fixed on Laurya and he began to realize that there was much more about her present incarnation that he did not know.

Laurya was smiling at the young messenger. She closed her eyes, her brow furrowed lightly and a full minute passed. Then she broke her concentration, opened her eyes, smiled again and gently released the young man's hands.

"I think that the only instructions he has received are those from his king. The rest of his news comes from his own observations. I cannot be wholly sure, because he is naturally afraid of our strangeness. But there are no deep panic fears and no signs of guilt or hidden secrets. I can only be sure that he is not knowingly deceiving us."

"Then we go to Karakhor," Zela decided.

Laurya's face was expressionless. She touched Zela's hand and said, "Be careful, commander. Let reason rule your anger."

Zela felt a moment of discomfort. This rare sensitivity in her communications officer was often a valuable asset, but was also an occasional embarrassment. She nodded briefly and then turned away. Kananda fell into step beside her.

As they moved out of hearing, Laurya turned with a final word for Blair. Her hands touched his for a moment as she said softly, almost sadly, "And you too be careful. Let caution rule your heart."

଼

The day passed. Dusk closed around Karakhor, the shadows thickening into night. The random patterns of the stars were crystals of white fire embedded in black velvet. Torch and camp fires glowed smokily and moonlight bathed the city. It was a warm night with no breeze, too warm for Gheddan comfort.

Garl and Landis had rejoined Taron and Caid on the ship.

There were regular checks and maintenance work that had to be done between interplanetary flights. Only Thorn remained in the city with Raven and Thorn was bored. Raven was spending most of his time with Maryam, and Thorn had been left much to his own devices. He had eaten and drunk as much as any man could and he had made sexual use of his two slave girls. But the wine here was too weak to get a man really roaring drunk and the slave girls too timid to give him any real sport and satisfaction.

There was no sound from the next chamber, and for the moment, he had no idea of where Raven and Maryam might be. He remembered the sounds of their lovemaking. There was at least a little promise in the highborn women of this city and that seemed to be all that this pathetic planet had to offer. He stirred himself and kicked one of the slave girls off his bed in disgust.

His thoughts drifted to Namita. The other highborn one had passed him twice during the day, each time accompanied by the puffed-up, self important and grandiose little man-imitations whom he guessed were her brothers. Each time, she had smiled at him, but it had been such a pale and ghastly little smile that he had decided the creature must be sick. His interest had decreased rather than strengthened, but now, in the crushing boredom of the empty night, he began to speculate again on how she might perform in bed.

He made up his mind abruptly. The girl could not be any less inspiring than the two he had already experienced, and there was nothing else to amuse him in this dead rat-hole. He kicked the other slave girl off his bed and swung his feet to the floor. He was a Gheddan Swordmaster, accustomed to taking anything that he wanted, even if he only half wanted it. He buckled his weapon belt with his sword and lazer about his waist and went out of the chamber. The two slave girls lay terrified on the floor behind him and dared not move until he had gone.

The time he had spent in the city, like Raven's, had not been without purpose. Together they had made note of the city's defences and the strength and morale of its warriors. Like Raven, Thorn was not impressed. The city walls and the river could only protect it from the most primitive form of land assault and all resistance would collapse at the first flash of a lazer. One minimum-yield pulse bomb would obliterate it within seconds. However, the survey had been completed as a matter of trained routine and had included noting the residence and sleeping quarters of all the key figures in the opposing military and power structure. Thorn knew where the king, his general and all his brothers could be found and assassinated at night. He had also noted the private apartments of the two princesses.

He marched carelessly down the high-vaulted corridors, lit by moonlight shining through the stone-latticed windows or by torchlight where the shadows were thick. He passed several doorways where sentries stiffened fearfully, their knuckles whitening on the shafts of their spears, but he disdainfully ignored them. He came at last to the double doorway where earlier in the evening he had seen Namita take leave of her brothers and disappear inside.

A single warrior guarded the door. Thorn faced the man squarely and motioned him to move aside. The guard went pale. Sweat beaded his forehead, but he knew his duty and he was loyal. His hands trembled as he shifted his feet and his spear into a more threatening stance. He spoke a hoarse denial.

Thorn shrugged his shoulders, stepped back a pace and drew his lazer.

The guard's nerve broke. He had heard of these white fire weapons that destroyed even the gods, and among his companions, the tales had grown more lurid with every telling. Before the weapon could be leveled, he had lowered his spear and fled.

Thorn's roar of laughter echoed, loud and cheerful, along the corridors. Then he pushed open the double doors and went inside. He was in a room furnished with rich carpets and drapes, a cushioned couch and chairs. It was empty except for a startled slave girl crouching beside an inner door. She had obviously been sleeping there, but now her eyes were wide and bewildered.

Thorn crossed the room and kicked the slave girl out of the way. He was getting good at kicking slave girls and his booted foot connected neatly with her plump buttocks, tumbling her in precisely the direction he intended her to go. He laughed again and went into the inner room.

As he expected, it was a bedroom. Moonlight filtered through an arched window and showed a large bed with white silk sheets beneath a shrouding canopy of white muslim. Thorn tore the flimsy curtaining aside as Namita sat bolt upright among her pillows. She wore a brief nightdress that hid nothing of her slim beauty. Her face, even without its veils and jewelry, was still young and lovely. Her dark eyes were petrified.

Thorn reached forward and casually ripped open the nebulous material of her nightdress, revealing curved young breasts with dark brown nipples. Namita screamed.

Thorn grinned happily and began to unfasten his tunic.

☙

Raven had also found the night air in his bedchamber too warm and too close for comfort and so he had strolled down to the riverbank in the hope of finding a cool breeze. He walked alone. Maryam had again made love with him earlier in the evening, but for some reason he could not fathom, she had preferred to return afterward to her own apartments. It was not important and he did not want her always under his feet anyway. He needed time to think and so he had let her go.

His thoughts, however, were mainly about Maryam. Her ideas of sexual sporting were far removed from the wild abandon of a Gheddan woman, but there was an eagerness and novelty about her approaches that he found wholly satisfying. Her willingness was more than a raw desperation to please him. It was somehow warmer and more personal, both more vulnerable and more valuable than anything he had ever known. Despite himself, he was warming toward her. Sex was an animal act, a mutual pleasure, and yet he sensed that for her it was something more profound and that somehow she was giving him more of herself than any Gheddan woman ever would, or could.

She had made him understand that the marriage ceremony she wanted would have to wait for a few days. He did not understand why. Probably she was bound by some law of her menfolk. He could break it, but there was no need. It would be several days before his ship was ready for its next space flight. He could not escape the delay so there was no hurry.

He stopped at the river's edge, the dark water swirling softly at his feet, gazing at the distant silhouette of the Solar Cruiser that stood stark and dominant against the star bright sky. If necessary, the ship could return with a crew of three, which meant that he could safely leave two or three behind. He had already decided that the ship would make three more Earth orbits, a final search for Alphans or for any advanced Earth civilization which might have passed this one. Then it would head for home. It would carry his recommendation for two fighting ships and a troop carrier with fifty men to be stationed here as a permanent garrison.

The three man crew would have to include one of the engineers, one of the lazer gunners, and either Thorn or himself in command. Who should go and who should stay? That was the final decision he had yet to make. He was tempted to give command of the ship to Thorn and to remain with Maryam. Their marriage would place him in the stronger position to maintain control. That might be important, for without the ship, there would be no power to recharge the fuel packs for their lazers and so there could be some risk if the earthmen ever realized that their fire-power was not unlimited. Unlike Thorn, Raven was not prepared to dismiss the people here as total cowards. They were temporarily demoralized and held in check, but he had noted flickers of defiance. Some, like the old man with the purple turban, needed careful watching.

There was logic in remaining here himself, but on the other hand half a year would pass before the garrison force would reach Earth and perhaps a whole year before he could hope to make his own return to Dooma. In a year, many things could happen in the City Of Swords. There were constant power struggles, sword challenges, and shifts in the empire command structure. He needed to be there to protect his own interests and to forge his own opportunities. It was also too long since he had visited his own stronghold. He had no fears that Bhorg or Scarl would betray him, but there were neighbouring Sword Lords who might grow bold and ambitious from his continued absence.

He made his decision. If anyone remained it would be Thorn, with Landis and perhaps Taron. His own time was too valuable to waste cooling his heels where there was no action.

He turned away from the river, breathing the soft breeze deeply before plunging back into the city with its night-smoke and incense and its unguessable combination of foul and fascinating odours. His pace was unhurried and his thoughts were still far away on Dooma.

He had followed the curve of the river for some way below the palace and now he followed his instinct in search of a more direct way back. He entered a narrow alleyway which he thought would lead him toward one of the main avenues which all converged on the central square behind the palace. The lanes were empty between the close-pressed houses, the doors all closed and bolted. They were lit by torches on the balconies above his head where the sounds of voices and laughter and sometimes music filtered out from the open upper windows. In places, the starlight was blotted out altogether, leaving only the smoky flicker of the torches. There were puddles and squashed things underfoot which he preferred not to think about.

There was a movement to his left. He whirled with his hand on his sword. A scavenging dog slunk past him cringing with downcast eyes and he laughed at his own reaction. He pushed on into the twisting maze.

He passed an even narrower side alley and did not even feel the nimble fingers that reached up to pluck at his weapon belt from behind. But the belt leather was thick and stiff, resisting the thin, razor-sharp blade that sliced through it, and he felt its pull against his stomach as it came away. Again his hand flashed with a lightning instinct to his sword. The belt was ripped away from his waist, his holstered hand lazer and the sword sheath disappearing with it. But the sword blade slipped free of the sheath and the hilt was held fast in his practised hand.

He spun round in time to see the child thief still crouching at his feet. He stayed the sword. One dirt encrusted infant face peering horrified out of a bundle of rags was hardly worth the bother of cleaning the blade. The boy shrieked, flung the weapon belt hard to one side and then scuttled off frantically down the alley.

Raven did not give chase, for suddenly the night offered better sport. Two men, as ragged and dirt streaked as the child, had dropped neatly down from the balcony in front of him. One of them crouched, with a drawn short sword in one hand and a long dagger in the other. His lean face was a ravaged mask in the dim glow of the nearest torch, pitted and scarred by some unknown skin-eating disease. His companion was a hunchback who whirled a rope weighted with a spiked iron ball.

A soft thud from behind warned him that a third assassin had dropped down from one of the balconies to block his retreat.

Even as he heard the sound, Raven was spinning on the ball of his right foot and the heel of his left, bringing his back against the wall, crouching and drawing a knife from his left boot with his left hand. A steel discus whizzed past his head, flung with such force that it smashed through one of the wooden struts supporting the nearest balcony. If Raven had not moved, it would have decapitated him from behind.

The thrower was a broad, squat man, hulking almost shapeless in the gloom. He cursed softly, but his eyes glittered and he too drew a short sword from the rags at his waist.

Raven flicked a glance in search of his weapon belt and his lazer. It had landed beyond the two men on his right. Until he had dealt with his attackers, it might as well have been on another planet. Their gazes were watching his. They seemed to understand his thoughts and laughed. Without the lazer, he was reduced to their level of sword and knife, and they were three against one. This was their chosen ground, assassination was their profession. They were more than confident.

The two swordsmen attacked together, rushing him from both sides. With his longer blade, he could keep the diseased face at bay, but there was no room to turn in the narrow alley. He was trapped too tightly to make full use of his superior sword skill, and here the short swords favoured by his opponents were the more useful weapons. He knew he had to reduce the odds quickly.

He blocked the squat man's sword with his knife and kicked savagely sideways at the man's groin. The man swore and backed off. Raven flung himself at the man with the diseased face, the sudden, furious clash of their sword blades violating the still night. Sparks flew like bright fireflies and the startled man gave ground, his attack faltering into defence. Block, parry, feint, thrust and kill—the ritual sang in Raven's mind and he almost brought it to completion. As he thrust, something caught at his right ankle and hooked his leg from under him. Cursing, he tumbled down onto his left knee and elbow, sliding on something revolting in the gutter.

The squat man had a second weapon that Raven had not been aware of, a simple hooked stick like a shortened shepherd's crook. He gave it another fierce wrench, dragging Raven face down and then lunged for the fallen body with his sword. Raven was rolling out of the way but it was his chain mail that saved him, deflecting the sword thrust that would have killed him. The squat man followed through too violently, falling heavily on his intended victim. Raven turned the knife in his left hand, slamming the blade upward as the squat man crashed on top of him, driving the blade deep behind the breastbone. The man screamed once and Raven felt the heart's blood pumping over his fist.

Raven continued to roll in a flailing embrace with the dying man, spinning into the man with the diseased face and forcing him to stumble backwards. The second man hacked desperately at the entwined bodies at his feet, but succeeded only in half severing the arm of his now dead companion. Raven thrust the corpse away from him, still using it as a battering ram to defend himself and succeeded in regaining his feet. He had cut the odds to two, but he had lost his knife which he had been unable to wrench free.

He was breathing heavily and he knew that so far he had been lucky. The way behind him was now clear and he was tempted to back up, to hope for a small square or courtyard where there might be room for some real swordplay. But the men in front of him were enraged by the death of their friend and were too experienced to give any quarter.

The man with the diseased face stepped back but only to give room for his friend to act. The hunchback stepped forward. The rope whirled in his hands and Raven tilted his head sideways as the iron ball shot straight for his face. It sped past his cheek, but then the hunchback flicked his wrist and the ball was spinning back on itself, winding the rope twice around Raven's neck. If the spiked ball had smashed into his face it would have finished him, but instead on its final twist it slammed into his right shoulder, the spikes penetrating and embedding in his chain mail waistcoat.

Raven felt the sharp pain and the warm blood seeping down his chest. Then the hunchback yanked on the rope, trying to bring him staggering forward onto the other man's sword.

The rope was strangling him. Raven knew that if he tried to pull back, it would choke him to death. The blood was already pounding in his temples as he gasped for air. It was as though a red cloud had enveloped his brain. He knew his life expectancy could now be counted in seconds.

He refused to fight the rope and instead allowed himself to be catapulted forward. Again the swords rang and crashed as he engaged the man with the ravaged face. The hunchback had danced back out of the way to get another heaving pull on the rope. Raven couldn't think. He couldn't breathe. He fought with Gheddan instinct and the stubborn Gheddan refusal to face oblivion.

His sword arm hewed with a ritual will of its own. Block, parry, feint, thrust—but his opponent had learned, the thrust was parried in turn and the dagger in the assassin's left hand was striking for Raven's heart. Raven hooked the blade away with his left arm, the point slicing through his tunic sleeve and the skin over his bicep. For a second, they were chest to chest, arms apart, and Raven used the last of his failing strength to headbutt the ravaged face before him.

The swordsman fell away, blood streaming from his shattered nose. Raven's head was yanked sideways in the same moment. The hunchback had taken up the tension on the rope and was hauling him hand over hand up the alleyway. Raven swung his sword in a gleaming arc. The blade seemed to move in extreme slow motion. Raven was blacking out and he no longer knew what he was doing. In a red dream, the sword blade faltered at the top of its curve, and then fell limply. The cutting edge struck the taut rope, severed it, and the hunchback went flying backwards.

With his left hand, Raven clawed at the strangling coils round his neck, his desperate fingers gouging deep into his own flesh as he pulled the rope loose. He gulped air, gagged and gulped again. His chest heaved. The red mist partially cleared in his brain, his reeling senses fighting to focus.

The hunchback was on his feet, screaming obscenities. He was surprisingly nimble for such a grotesque shape and he had produced another short sword from his own ragged robes. He charged full tilt at Raven.

The Sword Lord met the headlong attacks and again, the long blade keeping the shorter one at bay. Raven gulped down more air. The adrenaline flowed. He felt strength returning to his body and arm. Slowly and terribly, his lips peeled back to bare his teeth and at last he smiled.

The hunchback had no more tricks. Death stared him in the face. Again he screamed in frustrated rage. Then the long blade swept the short one aside and flung it against the alley wall. The hunchback froze, perhaps he prayed. His eyes tilted up in final horror to watch the long blade fall, and then it smashed through flesh and bone as it split open his skull.

Raven turned. The man with the diseased face still slumped with his back to the wall, still dazed and only half conscious. Raven deftly ran his sword through his body.

There was silence. Raven withdrew his sword and stood back, panting. His senses were still alert but the night held no more threat. The very air seemed hushed and fearfully listening. Cautiously, Raven moved to pick up his severed weapon belt, hanging it lightly over his sound shoulder. The hand lazer bumped solidly against his chest, but he let it hang in the holster. There was no longer any need for it.

With grudging respect, he examined the three dead assassins. They had been good, as excelled in their trade as any he might have met in the back alleyways of Ghedda. They had clever techniques and they had worked well as a team. Such men, he knew, did not select victims at random and never worked unpaid.

He did not expect to find any clue as to who might have paid them, but as he turned them over he found, to his mild surprise, that each man wore a leather armband with three short ribbons of fine green silk. He had seen that identifying mark before, on the warriors of the House of Gandhar.

Chapter Twelve

Thorn had thrown his tunic aside and was removing his weapon belt. Namita had recoiled on her pillows, clutching her sheets around her and was still screaming hysterically. Thorn's grin slowly dissolved into a scowl. He had not wanted quite so much fuss. He could deal with any interruption—if anyone dared to interfere—but it would be an embarrassment to be interrupted. He told her curtly to be quiet and moved around the bed to smack her hard across the mouth with the back of his hand.

Namita was a royal princess. Apart from the gentle chastisement of her mother and her aunts, no one had ever dared to strike her before. The violence and effrontery of Thorn's blow shocked her into a frozen silence. Suddenly she dared not even whimper.

Thorn grinned again and took off his weapon belt. He hung it carefully at the head of the bed where his sword and lazer would be within instant reach. Before he could remove the golden chain mail of his codpiece, Raven's voice came sharply and clearly from his belt communicator in the pouch behind the lazer holster.

"Thorn. I am on the far side of the main square of this miserable city—about one hundred paces along the central avenue. Join me here. There has been treachery and we have work to do. Acknowledge."

Thorn stopped in mid-movement. His face darkened with anger and frustration. He mouthed a vile string of obscenities that would have flushed Namita crimson if she could have understood them.

"Thorn!" There was a cutting edge to Raven's voice, a dark impatience. "Respond."

May the fangs of a Silurian lizard chew on your balls, Thorn thought bitterly, but this was one interruption he could neither defy nor ignore. With the thought still in mind, he reached for the communicator and flipped the speak-switch.

"Thorn, commander. I acknowledge."

There could be no delay. Even if Raven had not been a Sword Lord of superior skill, he was still the Mission Commander and representative of the empire and that one-hundred-foot high steel blade in the City Of Swords to which Thorn had sworn his own sword and his allegiance.

Still cursing, Thorn buckled his weapon belt back into place, snatched up his tunic and body armour and hurried out of the room.

☙

Namita was still sobbing wretchedly when the door crashed open again a few minutes later. Jahan burst in with a dozen warriors at his heels, still in his nightshirt and without his turban, but with his ruby-hilted sword grasped firmly in his right hand. The face of the old warmaster was thunderous and he came ready to fight and die, but he could only stand baffled when he saw that she was alone.

"Where is he?" he cried angrily and blended in with his rage was the awful fear that he was too late.

Namita could not answer. She only wept more loudly.

"Where is the defiler?" Jahan roared. "By *Indra* and all the gods, for this I will kill him."

He turned on his heel, ready to storm out in search of Thorn. Namita realized what was happening and a new panic filled her fearful breast. She struggled up on her pillows and desperately called him back.

"No, Uncle! Do not follow him. He will kill you with his white fire."

"Then I will die." Jahan's fury was unstoppable. "But I will not stand by when you have been dishonoured."

He pushed through his warriors, scattering them from his path, but then found the doorway blocked by the king's two senior wives who had donned their night robes to hurry to the scene of commotion. Padmini, the mother of Kananda and Maryam, laid a restraining hand upon his arm. Kamali, the mother of Namita, Rajar and Nirad, hastened to the side of her daughter. Both queens were pale and trembling.

"Wait, Jahan," Padmini begged him. "At least let us find out what has happened."

Jahan hesitated, torn between the different pulls of duty. A command from the queen carried only slightly less weight than the command of Kara-Rashna himself. He found himself ushered tactfully but firmly out of the doorway and into the outer chamber where his warriors still crowded.

"Truest and most loyal friend of ourselves and our husband, please wait," Padmini pleaded with him again, and then she too disappeared quickly into the bedchamber, closing the door behind her.

Jahan could only stand fuming, frustrated by the delay.

The minutes passed. The princes Devan and Sanjay arrived together with drawn swords and more warriors from their respective palace guards. Then the king appeared, distraught and confused, half supported by his guard, but bravely clutching his sword. Jahan reported what he knew, which was no more than he had been told by the young warrior whom Thorn had chased away from Namita's door.

They debated the outrage with hot tempers rising, and were upon the point of marching in a mass upon the chambers occupied by the Gheddans, when the door to the inner bedchamber opened and the First Queen emerged. All voices and movement stopped as they faced her anxiously.

"Princess Namita has not been dishonoured." Padmini gave them that vital reassurance first in an effort to calm them and restore some sensible order. "The one called Thorn was here, but a voice spoke to him in his own language from the little box they carry on their belts, and he hurried away." She chose not to tell them that their princess had been struck across the face or that Thorn had started to remove his clothing. These things were best left unsaid if she was to prevent them from destroying themselves. "Princess Namita is distressed," she admitted. And then repeated with emphasis, "But she has not been dishonoured!"

"Even so," Jahan growled, "for any man to enter her bedchamber is punishable only by death."

The royal princes nodded grim agreement. Even if their niece had not been bodily violated, the honour of them all was still besmirched and would remain so until Thorn had paid the price.

"How can you kill a god?" Padmini cried in anguish, addressing the question directly to her husband. "You all know their power. How can you stand against the white fire of the gods?"

"If we do not stand, then how can we prevent this god from returning to complete what he so clearly intended?" Kara-Rashna asked helplessly. "How can we protect our daughters?"

"Kamali and I have discussed this." Padmini risked her husband's disapproval. "With your permission, sire, Kamali will take Namita secretly to one of the noble houses. There she will be safe and can be kept hidden until these strangers depart."

"What if the gods have the vision or other means to find her?" Devan asked slowly.

"Or if the strangers do not depart?" Sanjay added with equal doubt.

"We can only pray that they will not find her and that they will depart." The queen clasped her hands together and bowed her head as she spoke.

"Pray!" Jahan drew himself up to an unsurpassable height of apoplexy, forgetting that he was garbed only in his nightshirt. His knuckles were white around the raised hilt of his sword. "Pray, and hide our women while we are afraid to act. It is better to die first."

The princes nodded their grim confirmation and looked to their older brother. The will of Kara-Rashna would decide.

The ailing king drew himself up and raised his own sword. He opened his mouth to speak, but then a vast, hollow, booming sound rolled throughout the palace. It came again and again and all ears recognized it.

The sound was the beating of the great gong in the king's audience hall, which was only used to summon the city's rulers to a meeting of great emergency.

CB

Raven had returned to the palace with one of the dead assassins draped across his unwounded shoulder. Behind him marched Thorn, stolidly carrying the corpses of the other two. Raven had already made up his mind how he would act and he carried his burden straight to the king's audience hall. Torches burned in brackets attached to the high central pillars but the hall was empty and unguarded.

Raven went inside and deposited the dead man at the foot of the splendid, elephant-tusked throne. The head lolled back over the edge of the raised dais and the wide-open, rolled back eyes stared at him blankly from the ravaged face. Thorn allowed the bodies of the hunchback and the third man to slide down from his aching shoulders so that they all sprawled in a piled heap. Blood stained the white uniforms and gold body armour of the two Gheddans. More blood began to seep from the freshly killed bundle of limbs to run between the brilliant green and blue mosaic tiles that covered the entire floor of the great hall.

Behind the throne, suspended between two only slightly smaller tusks gilded with red and gold, hung the great gong. Raven had seen it used and had noticed its purpose. Now he walked up to it and took down the large, leather-padded drumstick that hung beside it. With both hands wielding the hammer, he struck the centre of the gong with all his strength. Its deep, resonant boom filled the vaulted hallway, echoed through the palace corridors and carried out into the still night air to awaken and alarm the whole city of Karakhor.

The magnificent dome above the dais that supported both the throne and the gong acted as a huge amplifier for the dreadful sound. There was no corner of the city, alleyway, cellar or dungeon, that its repeated reverberations did not reach. Like a knell of doom, it shattered the rest of princes and peasants, warriors and priests, merchants and artisans. Raven continued to pound at the gong until his arms ached, and by then the summons had brought its first responders.

The young princes Nirad and Rajar had heard the earlier disturbance in the women's quarters but had delayed to dress themselves properly before seeking to investigate. They had been on their way when the first gong beat sounded, and after staring at each other in frightened stupefaction for a few minutes, they had reluctantly turned their faltering steps toward the audience hall. They entered warily, almost on tiptoes, but Raven's hearing was sharp. He turned and faced them.

"You!" He indicated Rajar. "Come here and continue this."

They did not understand the words, but the gesture and the offered hammer carried his meaning. Rajar came closer to take the padded drumstick with tentative fingers. The young prince was white-faced and sweating.

Raven drew his sword from the weapon belt that was still slung over his shoulder. "Strike!" he commanded and unceremoniously jabbed the sharp point at Rajar's flinching ribs.

Hastily, Rajar took up the task of beating mightily upon the gong.

Raven seated himself in Kara-Rashna's throne and watched. When he heard the sound of more footsteps approaching the hall, he transferred his sword to his left hand and drew his hand lazer with his right. Thorn stood solidly to one side of the throne, feet apart and ready for anything. He too held his sword in one hand and a lazer in the other.

They entered in a group, the king, his general, and his brothers. All of them, by mutual agreement, had taken the time to complete their formal dress. They could not ignore the urgent summons that filled the night, but they were too proud to attend in the disarray of their night clothes. All were sashed and jeweled and turbaned. Behind them was a gathering crowd of priests, slaves and warriors, but these stayed wisely outside the vast double entrance doors.

"Rajar!" The king was suddenly furious as he saw his son at the gong. Even the lowest night soil child should have known that the great assembly gong could only be sounded on the order of the king and then only when the king was already present and seated to receive an audience.

The luckless prince stopped his efforts and looked up with an anxious face.

"Continue!" Raven barked.

The command was in another language but Rajar understood. He cast an appealing glance at his father and uncles and then resumed his frantic beating as energetically as before.

There the tableau froze for more long minutes: Raven languishing indolently on the king's throne, Thorn standing and threatening, and the rulers of the city huddled in a tight, confused and angry knot. The two hand lazers held them at bay, while the monotonous booming of the great gong continued to deafen them all.

At first Jahan could only stand and stare balefully at the sardonic figure of Thorn. Here was the vile, blue-skinned creature he sought, the one who had dared to defile his princess, whose actions had dishonoured them all and who was now showing a mighty contempt that brought shame to all Karakhor. Jahan could barely control himself. His honour, his pride, his great senses of duty and loyalty, all demanded in one almost overpowering scream inside his head that he should defy death and charge forward to attack this sky-monster with his sword.

What held the warmaster general back was not the fear of his own death—that was an indifferent price to pay—but the fact that Kara-Rashna and his two brothers were in the same direct line of fire. All that Jahan had seen and heard indicated that one bolt of white lightning from the weapon in Thorn's hand would destroy them all. The old warrior would happily fling himself into hell to restore all that had been lost, but to carry with him almost the entire royal House of Karakhor was a decision he could not make.

The others were staring at the pile of bodies at Raven's feet, and now even Kara-Rashna's kingly fury had been replaced by confusion and uncertainty. Events were moving too fast for all of them, but they sensed that there was more here at stake than ruffled dignity and palace protocol. After his initial protest to his son, the king was too stunned to speak. His bodily weakness swept over him again and Devan and Sanjay had to support him on either side. The princes too were shocked into silence.

In any case, any words they might have uttered would not have been heard while the great gong continued to boom. Raven showed no hurry to commence whatever he had in mind and gave Rajar no sign to stop. The young prince hardly dared to look for such a sign and devoted himself to his task. The gong beats were remorseless and began to seem unending. But one by one the heads of the other great noble houses of Karakhor were hurrying to the palace to join the assembly.

The fat lord of Bulsar stumbled into the room. On his silk waistcoat was embroidered the blue raven that was his banner emblem, and a raven in blue gemstones fastened his blue turban. However, his whiskers were uncombed and his sword belt was askew. He stopped beside his king and princes and gaped.

Tilak came next, puffing and gasping, having run all the

way from his own house. He had forgotten his sash and sword belt. His waistcoat was only partly buttoned and the black turban on his head was at an unseemly angle. Raven's cold eyes noted the black orchid emblem that Tilak wore but he made no move.

The back end of the audience hall and the corridors outside were now packed and crowded, the sons and warrior guards of Bulsar and Tilak having pushed in to join the palace inhabitants. The press of bodies made passage difficult for the last of the ruling elite, and several more minutes passed before he could force his way to the front. There Gandhar's ancient lord took his stand with the rest, his rheumy eyes blinking, his creaking knees almost buckling beneath him.

On his breast Gandhar wore the emblem of a double-bladed axe on green silk. Green was the colour of his turban and the livery of his soldiers. At last Raven leaned forward on the throne and showed interest.

"Enough," Raven commanded.

The Gheddan word had no meaning for the Hindus, but it caused Rajar to hesitate and turn his head. He saw that the blue-skinned god was looking directly at him and correctly guessed that he was to stop beating the gong. He held back the next hammer blow until he was sure and then sank exhausted onto his knees.

The great gong hung still. The last reverberations slowly faded away, receding sound waves of dark foreboding in a nightmare that was not yet ended. Silence seeped over the audience hall and the city, more awesome and terrifying than the noise had been. None dared move or breathe.

Raven rose calmly to his feet. All eyes were fixed upon the grim figure of the Sword Lord. Even Jahan moved his frustrated glare from Thorn.

That the blood-spattered god had been engaged in battle was plain for all to see, and the corpses at his feet testified to his triumphant victory. But now Jahan's eyes began to narrow a little. He began observing small points and filing the information carefully away in his brain. First, there was damage to the golden chain mail, just below the god's left shoulder. Second, there was a neat cut across the fabric of his left sleeve. Could it be that some of the god's own blood mixed with the bloodstains from his enemies? Did the god bleed as a mortal man would?

Raven extended his sword arm, pointing the still red blade directly at the old lord of Gandhar. With a curt motion of the sword, he indicated that the old man should come forward.

Gandhar was bewildered and afraid. He looked beseechingly toward his companions, but none could aid or advise him. Raven repeated the ferocious motion with his sword.

The old man gulped down a deep breath and rallied his failing courage. He was almost at the end of his years. It would soon be time to die anyway. Perhaps it was better to die with a little dignity than to endure dribbling in his dotage. He shuffled forward, held his head high and waited.

Raven laid down his sword on the vacant throne. With his free right hand, he reached down for one of the corpses, and grasping it by the rags at the neck, he hurled it forward to slither to a stop at the feet of the old lord. Angrily he heaved and kicked the remaining two corpses to join it. He picked up his sword again and stabbed the blade first toward those already dead, and then at the one about to die.

"These carrions are yours," he accused.

Gandhar looked blank. The actions and the anger of the strange god were more revealing than his meaningless words, but still the old man was slow to understand. Behind him, the gathered assembly was equally uncomprehending.

Raven stepped forward. He thrust his swordpoint down at the outflung arm of the dead hunchback, pushing between flesh and the leather armband with the three ribbons of green silk. The blade cut through the leather; the point flipped the incriminating insignia upward to where Gandhar could catch it clumsily in his feeble hands. The old man stared at it and understood.

"But these men are not servants of mine," he protested. "They are not even warriors. They are common cutthroats from the gutters of the city."

Jahan risked a step forward, looking closely at the dead men for the first time. The hunched back and the diseased face fitted descriptions he had received from reports on other incidents. He had not been aware that this unwholesome trio was back in the city, but he knew their trade and their reputation. He added his own bold voice of angry dissent.

"These men are paid assassins. They could have been hired by anyone. The ribbons are a false identification. Everyone here knows that these men are not from Gandhar's household."

Raven ignored him. Even if he could have understood the language and the argument, he would have cared nothing for it. What mattered was that someone in this city had launched an attack upon his person, and such daring clearly indicated that another demonstration of Gheddan power was now due. Whether the old man with the matching green colours was the true culprit or not was a matter of lesser relevance. The point would be made, the warning underlined, so the old man was best suited to serve Raven's purpose.

Without emotion, the Sword Lord leveled his hand lazer. There were mutters of anguished protest but no one moved forward. Gandhar blinked at his executioner and then deliberately moved himself two unsteady paces to one side of the hall. His back was now against one of the high stone pillars. His king and his friends were no longer behind him in the direct line of fire. He looked heavenward and began to recite a prayer to *Indra*.

Raven cut short the pathetic babbling with one short blast from his lazer. The white hot beam punched a blackened hole where the double-bladed axe emblem had decorated the left breast and the old lord of Gandhar was flung dead against the pillar.

Jahan erupted with a roar of rage. His hand dropped to his great sword and pulled it half free. Raven turned lightly to face him, the hand lazer leveling again on its next target. Behind Jahan, the king wrenched himself free from the support of his brothers and lunged to catch hold of his friend's sword arm with both hands. In the heat of the moment, Devan and Sanjay both reached for their swords.

For a deathly moment, it seemed as though Karakhor would sacrifice all her rulers but then Thorn made a dramatic move.

"Hold!" the Swordmaster bellowed. His lazer never wavered, but his sword arm moved to point through the arched window to the open sky where the upper ramparts of *Indra's* temple were silhouetted clear and black against the moon and starlight.

They all turned fearfully to watch.

Raven smiled. He stabbed his sword into the dead hunchback to hold it upright, and then took his communicator from his belt.

"Now, Caid," he ordered briefly.

From the Gheddan Solar Cruiser on the far side of the river, a beam of blinding white light lanced forward. It was aimed high above the city, but low enough to slice the topmost spires from the temple of *Indra,* its tallest and most sacred building. In a thunderclap of sound and an explosion of white light, the carven stone pinnacles simply vapourized and disappeared.

The ship's main battle lazer could have been re-targeted to demolish the temples to *Varuna* and *Agni* and then the great dome of the palace itself, all within a matter of split seconds. But nothing further was necessary. The majority of the assembly had dropped on their knees, begging and crying for mercy. The rest were groveling on their faces and bellies.

Only Jahan remained standing, but Kara-Rashna was dragging at his weakened sword arm and forcing his sword back in its sheath. Bitterly, the old general allowed himself to be pulled down onto one knee beside his king. If resistance meant the possible destruction of the entire city, then they had to accept that it would be folly to resist.

The two Gheddans grinned at each other, sheathed their swords, and walked out. The Hindus blocking the exit crawled and squirmed frantically to clear a path and get out of the way. The humiliation and demoralization of this conquered city was satisfactorily complete.

On the raised dais that supported the throne, the young prince Rajar still crouched in mortal terror beside the great gong. He had remained there like a doe hypnotized by a cobra ever since he had been permitted to cease from his labours. He had prayed that his presence was forgotten, prayed that he would no longer be noticed, prayed almost that he might become invisible. His stomach threatened to rise up and choke him with his own vomit, his heart and soul were locked in ice, and he dripped sweat more profusely than all of the appalled and horror-struck assembly put together.

When he had first entered the audience hall with Nirad, Rajar had immediately recognized the faces of the three corpses that had been so callously dumped on the dais and he had almost fainted with fright upon the spot. Each succeeding event had proved a catastrophic shock upon his nervous system and when Gandhar's lord had been executed he had all but died.

Now he was little more than a trembling jelly and he could only thank the gods and his lucky stars that he had been clever enough to divert suspicion from himself by disguising the assassins he had hired.

Chapter Thirteen

To return to Karakhor with the entire hunting party, including the war elephants, the foot warriors, the trackers and the slaves and all the princely baggage, would have taken at least four days. Both Ramesh and Hamir were too sorely wounded to survive any more fast travel. Time was of the essence and so again Kananda handpicked a small but efficient force and they had set out in all the available racing chariots with the hope of reaching the city by the second night.

Kananda's first choice of those who accompanied him was Gujar, for he wanted only the bravest and the best. He also wanted warriors who were fresh and rested and so he had intended that on this occasion Kasim should remain behind. Kasim had already fought beside him to the point of exhaustion and there was only so much that one friend could ask of another. But that valiant and loyal young lord had only been affronted. If Kananda had the strength to ride, then Kasim would ride with him until they both dropped. Kananda heard his friend's words and embraced him. "So be it," he agreed and so Kasim rode again at his side.

To Kananda's intense joy, Zela had also insisted on again joining his party and this time she brought Blair and Kyle with her. She had tried to explain to Kananda that because as yet there had been no formal declaration of war between Alpha and

Ghedda she could not simply zoom out of the blue in her Tri-Thruster and blast the Gheddan spaceship while it was still on the ground. The high state of tension that existed between Alpha and Ghedda had been defined as a cold war, an exchange of vilifying rhetoric, menace and hostility which was still a few steps removed from a total hot war of actual physical and technological combat. The distinction was a difficult one for Kananda to grasp, especially when she admitted that this far from their home civilization the Gheddans would probably not concede the same conventions to her in refraining from a first strike on her ship if they knew of its presence. However, there was no time for any lengthy debate on the issue and so Kananda swallowed his perplexity and was simply glad that she had again chosen to accompany him.

He was not quite so overjoyed with the presence of Blair, but he had to acknowledge that, with Blair and Kyle, they had now trebled their former level of lazer firepower. In fact, they had done even better, for riding in chariots instead of on horseback, the three Alphans had each been able to double the number of spare fuel packs that they carried for their weapons.

Zela had also loaded a backpack battle communicator into her chariot. It had ten times the range of the personal communicators they wore on their belts and would enable her to transmit back to the ship once they had reached the city.

Cadel and Laurya were to maintain the Tri-Thruster in instant flight and battle readiness, with one of them awake at all times to respond to her call. She was just a little bit worried about leaving the ship with a bare minimum crew, but she had decided that she had to accompany Kananda to keep in touch with what was happening. Without up-to-the-minute information from Karakhor, it would be impossible to plan any definite strategy to counter the Gheddan presence. And even with Blair and Kyle beside her, they would still be outnumbered by their enemies. She was counting on surprise, and the fighting spirit of Kananda and his friends, to tip the balance in any hot encounter.

They rode one to each of the light, two-wheeled chariots, each chariot drawn by two swift horses. They were twenty chariots and Kananda led the way with his golden, sun-burst pennant flying bravely in the breeze. Gujar and Kasim drove their chariots close behind him, flying their own defiant banners of green and blue. The three Alphans brought up the rear, lagging at first as they struggled to master their new roles as charioteers. However, they quickly learned the new arts, their impatient steeds needing little more than a free rein.

In a thunder of flying hooves and wheels, the reckless cavalcade dashed furiously through forest and plains on their desperate race to Karakhor.

By nightfall, they had lost two of the chariots. One had broken an axle and had been washed away into deep water at one of the three fast-flowing river crossings. The other had been charged and smashed into splinters by the swinging horn and massive bulk of an angry rhinoceros. The chariots had burst through its peaceful domain, scattering its browsing harem of three contented cows and turning the short-tempered bull instantaneously into an avenging whirlwind of armour-plated destruction.

The unlucky charioteer at the river had at least been spared his life. He had been able to swim clear of the wreckage and his companions had fished him out on the far bank. However, the driver of the second lost chariot had been disemboweled and pulped by the pounding horn of the rhinoceros long before anyone could come back to aid him. It had been over in minutes, and by the time Zela had hauled on her reins to turn her chariot and get into a firing position, the old bull was trotting off into a curtain of thorn bushes with his attendant cows, snorting his contempt over his shoulder. A lazer bolt then would have been wasted when they might well have greater need of it later.

To Kananda, these losses were again portents of ill will from the gods. When the darkness forced them to halt lest they smash the axles of more chariots, he took his bow and arrows and, in the last glimmer of fading light, shot a small deer. He built a fire to burn the animal in sacrifice to *Indra*, although in his heart he felt that the offering and his prayers were not enough.

Zela watched him with deepening concern. There were some aspects of his faith and its fatalism that irritated her and she wished that she knew the way or the words to help him rise above them. In her own world-view, there were no super-human beings who took sides for or against in human conflicts. Instead, the God Behind all Gods was understood as Pure Spirit, and at last perceived to be removed from the endless squabbles of men, although not indifferent to their overall well-being. The spiritual essence of creation maintained the development and balance of the universe. For her, prayer was simply an acknowledgement of what was, and the hope that eventually her own spirit would prove fit to rejoin the eternal Spiritual Stream. For most Alphans who still prayed, prayer was no longer a pleading for intervention. The God Behind All Gods was not a vain power to be praised and appeased and manipulated.

If there was any meaning to life beyond the immediate physical surface, then to Alphan logic it had to be a spiritual meaning. The physical life of the present, so clearly contingent, uncertain and temporal, ended forever with the moment of physical death. This far, Alpha agreed with Ghedda, but here their philosophies diverged. On Ghedda, all meaning to life, like the physical life itself, was finite. But the philosophers of Alpha taught that the finite life was shared by the infinite and that the meaning to life was concealed in the spiritual development of each individual being.

Herein lay the Alphan answer to the problem of evil, of explaining death, misfortune and disaster in a universe that was believed to be created and maintained by a benevolent, spiritual essence. What happened to each individual being, physically or materially, or in terms of the actual length of the microscopic time-blink that they endured, was all in the eternal scheme of things irrelevant. The crucial thing was not to be comfortable, to be free from pain, worry and fear, but to develop spiritually. Consequently wars, disasters and tragedies, were not the unsolvable problem of evil that previous generations had believed them to be, but were a mere surface ruffle of insignificance, like the wind and storm-tossed waves on a vast, deep ocean. The storms could be terrible indeed in the small boat of physical life caught up in those violent waves, but they had no meaning at all in the endless calm depths of spiritual infinity.

This was the understanding taught by her father, Laton, in the Academy of Knowledge in the City Of Singing Spires, and this was what Zela believed.

ᘛ

They built themselves a circle of small fires to keep out predators and poisonous snakes and, with two warriors posted as guards to be relieved at hourly intervals, the rest lay down to snatch a few hours sleep. Most of them were too weary to talk and Kananda had already made it plain that they would continue with the first glimmers of dawn.

Kananda wished that he could lie close to Zela, but with

Blair and Kyle among the party it no longer seemed permissible. He flung himself upon his back on a patch of soft moss and stared up moodily at the stars. If the other Alphans were not here, he knew that he and Zela would have slept as they had before, with fingers touching. Now he felt that such intimacy might cause her to lose face or be embarrassed before her people.

Zela was also wishing that the hectic pace of their adventures might slow to allow them more time to explore their own tentatively developing relationship. She lay as though asleep, but she was remembering the touch and taste of that one brief kiss on the first night of their search for Ramesh. Since then, they had been through much trial and trauma together, but there was no memory more clear or lingering than the warmth of his lips upon hers.

Zela had known her fair share of young men, most as friends, and only a few intimately. Her beauty attracted them without any conscious effort on her part, despite the determination and dedication it had taken for her to reach her present rank. However, there had been no man who could match up to her idol, her dead elder brother Lorin. Every man she had ever met was automatically measured and judged against that most cherished of memories and all of them had in some way fallen short. One private corner of her mind was forever a shrine to the bravery, the gaiety, the bright intelligence and the handsome, laughing face that was her memory of Lorin.

But now there was Kananda, a barbarian prince from a primitive planet, who was almost everything that Lorin had been. It was true that his deference and devotions to his personal gods seemed to her unbalanced and immature, yet still he fought with a raw and naked courage that accepted no defeat, even when he believed that all his gods were against him. And he possessed the one skill that Lorin had lacked, the one failing that had cost Lorin his life: Kananda was a brilliant swordsman.

Zela wondered if she was falling in love. She was sure of one thing: Kananda was a man she would have been proud to introduce to Lorin. That must mean something. She had never felt like that before. Dreaming of his kiss, she fell asleep.

ଓ

The last pair of messengers sent by Kara-Rashna had been running southward for two days. This was the second night of their journey and at dusk they had stumbled to a foot-sore halt and searched for somewhere to rest. With fears of the monkey tribe savages and Maghallan soldiers in their minds, they had not dared to light a fire in case it attracted more attention than it deterred and so they had simply crawled into a crack in a pile of rocks and prayed to pass the night unseen and unmolested.

There they might have passed the hours of darkness in exhausted sleep, except that a hunting leopard chose to make its kill within their range of hearing. The noise startled them awake and they cowered fearfully together. They carried no weapons which would have slowed them down and so they were defenceless. They could only hide. Finally the writhing and roaring noises ceased. They waited, hoping that the leopard had dragged its kill further away, but they could not be sure. The uncertainty became unbearable and the bravest of the pair inched his way higher into the rocks to survey the moonlit plain around them. He could see no signs of the leopard, but far away in the night he could see the dim flicker of campfires.

He returned to his companion and they discussed the possibilities in low whispers. Fires could only mean men, but were they friends or foes? Perhaps they were neutral travelers, merchants or traders from Bahdra or one of the other southern kingdoms. If they were not hostile, they might at least have news of Kananda's hunting party. Their campfires might also prove a safer place to spend the night.

They finally decided that it was their duty to find out. And convincing themselves that the leopard had secured its meal and therefore would not kill again this night, they left their shelter and hurried at a run toward the far flickers of light. When close, they slowed and approached with caution, but soon they recognized Karakhoran chariots in the gloom, and then, to their elation, the sun-burst pennant of Kananda. They had found their prince and, abandoning stealth, they shouted to the guards to announce that they came with news from Kara-Rashna.

The two men were brought quickly to Zela and Kananda where they made the customary bows and salutations and then told their story. Kananda listened to their excited babbling with a sense of rapidly growing alarm, for only one point was making a total impact.

"You say that my sister Maryam is to be married! Who is this man to whom she is betrothed? What is his name?"

The runner flinched, realizing that his news was not wholly welcome. He said uncertainly, "He is the leader of the blue skinned gods—he is the one called Raven."

"Raven!" Zela echoed the name sharply, her feelings a sudden confusing surge of elation, fear and disbelief. Her hand dropped to her sword and although she did not draw the blade, her knuckles whitened around the hilt. The foul murderer of Lorin was here, on this planet, in the city that was their destination. Her sworn enemy was the leader of the rival Gheddan expedition.

It was too much of a coincidence, too much to hope for.

Perhaps the runner had misunderstood the name. But no—Ghedda had less than a handful of space commanders with interplanetary experience. That her opponent should prove to be Raven was not impossible, it was all too highly probable. Her heart soared in her breast and its violent pounding cried out for vengeance.

"Are you certain—" she demanded of the runner. "Are you sure his name is Raven?"

The runner stared at her silver suit and golden form. She was as strange and unexpected as the blue-skinned ones and the tone of her voice struck a shiver in his soul. He nodded his head and licked his suddenly dry lips.

"Of this I am sure, noble one, the god is called Raven."

Kananda was staring at Zela, his eyes filled with concern and understanding. "Is this the one you seek?" He asked, "The one who slew your brother?"

Zela nodded. "It is the same name. It must be the same man."

"And this monster is to marry my sister! What madness is this? How can my father and uncles permit such a thing? Are they all bewitched?"

No one could answer his outburst and he turned back to the hapless runners. "Answer me. What is truly happening in Karakhor? We have defied Sardar and Maghalla. How can they now sacrifice Princess Maryam to this greater evil?"

"Princess Maryam herself wishes for this marriage." The runner could barely croak the words. "It is she who arranges it. Kara-Rashna not only desires your own return, noble prince, but also the return of the high priest, Kaseem. He seeks Kaseem's holy wisdom in this matter."

"Kaseem is two days' journey behind us," Kananda said impatiently. "But we are only one day's ride from Karakhor."

He turned to face his young lords and the waiting Alphans, and now it was his right hand that closed firmly over the hilt of his sword.

"I swear by *Indra* and all the gods that while I live Maryam will not make this marriage," he cried in ringing tones. "If it is her desire, then it must be because she is not truly aware of the inner nature of this man to whom she is betrothed. She has been blinded by a creature more cruel and merciless than Sardar of Maghalla ever could be. By *Indra*, by *Varuna*, by *Agni,* the sister I love more than my life will never be joined to this man."

Kasim and Gujar took hold of their own swords. "By all the gods, we swear this with you," they bravely proclaimed together.

Have no fear, Kananda—the words were formed in Zela's mind—*for Raven will die upon my sword.* But with Blair and Kyle standing close and listening, she refrained from saying them aloud.

☙

In Karakhor, the day following the brutal execution of Gandhar's lord had been a long and fearful one. No one knew nor could guess at what the strangers might do next. No one yet knew why they were here or what it was that they wanted. The speculation that they were messengers from *Indra,* which had followed their violation of the temple of *Varuna,* was now shattered by the havoc they had wreaked upon the temple of *Indra* in its turn. The mass of the city population was now facing for the first time the apocalyptic thought that there could be an even greater power than the gods they had so revered. No one knew how to pray to these new gods or what sacrifices to make. The holy priests to whom they normally looked to for guidance were mentally paralyzed.

Maryam was as dismayed as anyone, her feelings and emotions tangled and torn as though they had been trampled by a bull elephant. The noise of the preceding nights events had brought her running to Namita's apartments, where she had arrived just as the great gong had begun to boom out its fateful message. She would have gone with her father and uncles to the audience hall except that her mother had stopped her. The two queens needed help to whisk Namita into a safe place of hiding and the best opportunity would be now while the men were busy elsewhere.

So Maryam had immediately become involved in Namita's swift and secret removal from the palace. The House of Tilak could be reached by a roundabout route through the back streets and alleys of the city, and the noble lady of that household was a close friend of Padmini's. The women dressed, cloaking themselves in dark shawls to hide their finery and their faces, and with only two guards, hurried out into the night. When they were only halfway to their destination, the top of *Indra's* temple had abruptly disintegrated in the unholy burst of lightning and thunder, scattering rubble over half the city. Fragments of stone had rained around them, scaring them out of their wits, and they had finished the journey in terrified flight.

Tilak's wife had answered their knock, even though her husband was absent. Namita had been granted sanctuary, but then Maryam found that her mother and aunt intended that she, too, should remain with her half-sister. Maryam had protested vigorously. Raven was not Thorn, she told them. Raven would not harm her and while she had Raven's protection, she had no fear of Thorn. She could not add that what they so desperately feared had already happened between her and Raven and that she had welcomed it and gone to him willingly.

In the end Maryam had won her argument and had returned with Padmini and Kamali to the palace. It was only later that she had learned the full story of what had taken place in the great audience hall. That had been the real shock to her nervous system, spinning her thoughts out of balance and turning her emotions upside down. She could believe that Thorn would attempt to rape her sister but she could not believe that Raven had become a cold-blooded murderer.

She extracted a broken, jumbled and anguished account from her half-brother Nirad and had to rearrange the sequence of events back into order. The young prince had been devastated by what he had witnessed and his chief impressions were of the bravery with which Gandhar had died and the merciless cruelty of the god who had killed him. Everyone had noticed how the old man had stepped forward and to one side so that the white fire would consume him only and spare the king and the others. Such courage should have been rewarded, not despised. And everyone knew that Gandhar was innocent—a true god should also have known that the old man was blameless.

Nirad fumed and wept as he talked. His royal blood was outraged and he was suffering as much pain and humiliation as any of his elders without being able to control it. Gandhar had now to be cremated and it should be done with full funeral rites and absolutions. But no one knew whether they dared to make the arrangements. No one knew whether they dared to show their respects. Such was the deep and overpowering shame to which the blue-skinned ones had reduced the once proud city of Karakhor.

Maryam let the impassioned tirade flow over her, trying to pick out the salient facts. In her own mind, she was trying to redeem the man she hoped to marry and so she singled out the points that were meaningful to his defence. Plainly, Raven had been attacked by three assassins whom he had then killed. Those assassins had been paid to make their attempt by someone in the city. Even if Gandhar was innocent, as everyone seemed to think, the assassins had worn the colour of his household, so Raven had good cause to believe him guilty. Perhaps Raven was justified in meting out the punishment he believed Gandhar deserved.

Maryam felt the need to be alone. She made her excuses to escape from Nirad and retired in confusion to the privacy of her chamber. There, she spent several hours of fruitless agony, trying to straighten out her own thoughts and feelings. It was all too much. Her head began to ache. The heat bothered her. Her room became a prison, too small to contain her restless pacing to and fro, and so she escaped again to the palace gardens by the river. There at least the air was more easily breathable, and the blue sky, the fresh flower blossoms and the limpid blue-green curve of the Mahanadi were all more soothing to her suffering spirit.

Until she walked aimlessly through an archway of trailing bougainvillea and came face to face with Raven.

He wore a clean white uniform and a new weapon belt. His golden chain mail shone brightly in the sun. There was not a mark on him that was visible and he smiled as though nothing at all had happened since they last met.

"Maryam, I have been looking for you. Have you been avoiding me?"

She stared at him, understanding only her own name. The strength drained out of her and she did not know how to respond. Confusion froze in her mind. All her whirling thoughts stopped and her brain was suddenly numb.

Raven laughed, took her nerveless hand and led her down

to the edge of the river. There he sat with her on a stone bench shaded by a large orange tree. He pointed across the water and said calmly, “My spaceship, space—ship.”

Her brain still refused to function. She looked at him blankly.

“Space—ship,” Raven repeated slowly. He pointed again toward his black temple of steel. “Space—ship, space—ship.”

Maryam understood. Yesterday they had begun this game of exchanging words in each others languages, naming objects first with the Gheddan word, and then in Hindu. She swallowed hard to moisten her throat and then said faintly:

“Space—ship, God’s temple.”

“God’s temple?” Raven’s brow furrowed. She had used those words before. And then he remembered their first walk in the city. “God’s temple” was how she had described the carved religious buildings in stone. It struck him suddenly that these people probably believed that he and his crew were their gods, and he began to laugh uproariously.

Maryam could only wait in bewilderment for the name game to continue. She felt as though she was living in some strange dream, or perhaps it was a nightmare. Perhaps the things that were said to have happened in the great audience hall were the nightmare. She felt as though she had become detached from reality.

℘

Earlier in the day, Thorn had gone back to Namita’s apartments and had been furious to find that she was no longer there. The two chambers were empty and there was not even a guard on the door. He had caught a luckless female slave in the corridor outside and had tried to question her, but she could not understand his language and he could not understand hers. Despite her evident terror, it was a hopeless business and after a few minutes he gave up in disgust. He had spent the rest of the morning prowling the palace, becoming quickly aware that everyone from the lowest slave to the king himself was desperately trying to avoid him. At first he had been amused by the sounds of flight and panic that preceded his heavy-footed approach, but slowly he had become angry again. Finding Namita had become an obsession with him and he was determined to find her and have her.

At noon he returned to his own chambers in a particularly vile mood. The two slave girls who had been allotted to tend his needs shrank back against the far wall as he entered. He ignored them and looked to the food and wine that had been set out to please him. There was meat, rice and fruit. He ate hungrily, and then took a large peach and a full wineglass over to the open window. There was a seat beside the window and he sprawled there, eating the fruit, sipping the wine and glowering down into the street below.

It was a narrow street of brightly coloured awnings shading small shops and foodstalls. The rich smells of spices and sweetmeats wafted upward on the languid air. There was the bustling of voices and movement which he assumed was the haggling over prices and the displaying of wares. Thorn watched and listened and contemplated getting drunk. Surely if a man drank enough of this pale virgin's water, there must be some alcoholic effect.

Time passed. Thorn extended his arm several times for his glass to be refilled with wine. He watched the business of the street below without any real interest and yet suddenly his brooding gaze focussed on a young slave girl who was hurrying furtively through the milling throng. The girl wore her veil high and her shawl pulled low and carried a large bundle of what appeared to be fine silk clothing. Thorn leaned forward and stared sharply. He was sure he had seen her before.

As she passed directly below, recognition clicked in Thorn's mind. It was the slave girl whom he had booted away from Namita's door the previous night. His surly face split into a wide grin of triumph. There, sneaking out of the palace and obviously taking clothes to her mistress, was the highborn one's personal slave.

Thorn allowed the girl to get out of sight and hearing and then he deftly swung himself out of the window and dropped down into the street. Ignoring the startled looks and exclamations all around him, he pushed his way through the crowd and began to run after the slave. When he had her in sight again, he dropped back and followed her at a discreet distance.

The slave was moving fast, afraid of her own shadow and too scared to look back. Thorn had no difficulty in keeping pace without being seen. The short pursuit led him through a roundabout route of small streets and alleys to the rear of one of the fine nobleman's houses that faced onto one of the main avenues. Here the slave girl disappeared through a narrow, heavily studded teak door that was set in a high wall.

The door was not bolted behind her. Thorn went through and found himself in an unexpectedly spacious courtyard. A small fountain bubbled in the centre, flowering shrubs were set attractively among the flag-stones and slender columns supported overhanging balconies on either side. The only occupant of the courtyard was a strutting peacock displaying its magnificent tail.

Thorn crossed the courtyard and strode up the short flight of wide steps that led into the main part of the building. He passed down a short corridor and then came into a large central room with more corridors leading off on all sides. On his left, a wide and elegant stairway leading up to a balcony level gave access to more rooms and corridors. Everywhere the house was grandly furnished with drapes, tapestries and cushions, and the floors were either carpeted or tiled.

There was again no sign of the girl he had followed but there were other slaves here and the lady of the house reclining on a velvet sofa. A chorus of shrieks greeted Thorn's sudden entrance and brought the warriors and men of the household running to the scene. They halted in confusion when they saw the identity of their unwelcome visitor.

The frightened glances of several of the women shifted briefly to the top of the staircase. Thorn guessed that his quarry lay in that direction and turned toward it. The fat lord of Tilak appeared hastily at the top of the staircase, spreading his pudgy arms to bar the way. He was shouting hysterically. Thorn drew his lazer and, remembering Gandhar's fate, Tilak abruptly closed his mouth and moved to one side.

There was a rush of feet behind Thorn as the sons of Tilak and the bravest of his warriors surged forward. Thorn spun on his heel, crouching, lazer leveled. Tilak cried out in anguish, ordering his household to move back. They did so and Thorn laughed. He turned again to ascend the staircase, walking past the head of the house and leaving the fat man to weep with shame.

Lazer in hand, he kicked open three doors before he found Namita and her slave girl huddled together in one of the bedchambers. He threw the slave girl out and slammed the door behind her. There was a wooden bar to secure the door and seal it from any outside interference and he dropped the bar into place. Then he holstered his lazer and advanced upon the quaking princess.

Namita began to scream again. Thorn found the sound irritating and to shut her up he stuffed her mouth with one of her own lace handkerchiefs.

He slapped her hands away and tore off her clothing. Then for the second time he unbuckled his belt and dropped his chain mail codpiece and leggings. With both hands gripping her knees he wrenched her legs apart, and at that stage Namita swooned. Thorn completed the rape without any further resistance and when he had finished he decided that the whole experience had not been worth the trouble he had taken. This highborn one had been no more exciting than the other dull women of this planet had been.

He strapped his weapon belt back into place and slowly became aware that the girl was still unusually motionless and silent. She had stopped writhing and fighting the gag. He went back to her and discovered to his mild but unconcerned surprise that she was dead. Namita had choked on the handkerchief and suffocated.

☙

At about the same time, there were urgent whispers of excitement flying about the palace and the news was that a runner had at last arrived from Kananda.

Two couriers had traveled together as was customary, but one of them had suffered a snake bite on the way. The other had been reluctant to allow a beloved cousin to die alone and so the delay had added a further two days to his journey. The news he brought was six days old. It reported only that the two princes and their hunting party had encountered with strange and wonderful golden-skinned gods in silver suits—gods who came in a black temple of steel from the stars.

The news was carried to Maryam on the river bank, where she was still struggling to communicate with Raven. The runner was still with the king and his advisors, but a young captain of the palace guard had gleaned enough to know that he could find favour with his mistress. He ran to inform her, hesitating only briefly when he saw that she was not alone.

Maryam was delighted, bewildered and amazed, her expressions and emotions jumping from one display to another. Any news of Kananda was welcome relief and the story that there were more gods with golden skins was fantastic. She pumped the young guard captain for every detail, but all that she learned further was how little he actually knew.

Raven stood watching and listening. He was intrigued by her excitement. Twice the young guard captain had pointed across the river to the distant Solar Cruiser. Several times there had been mention of the name “Kananda”, which Raven knew had something to do with the delay over their planned marriage ceremony.

He began to ask questions of his own. Maryam tried to answer, pointing to the spaceship and then indicating the southwestern horizon far beyond it. She held up two fingers, tapping one and gesturing back to the spaceship, then the other finger and the horizon beyond.

Abruptly Raven understood.

Somewhere out there was another spaceship.

It could not be another Gheddan ship, which could only mean that it must be from Alpha.

Chapter Fourteen

Raven held war council on his ship where all five of his crew could be present and speak their minds on the decisions to be made. So far their sojourn on this planet had been one of general inactivity and boredom and their expressions brightened at the prospect of blood and battle. The general consensus of opinion was that they should immediately locate and destroy the Alphans and their vessel. Whatever happened here on Earth was beyond the knowledge and intervention of any power on Dooma, which gave them complete freedom to act as they saw fit.

"There is more to consider." Raven did not hold his command solely by virtue of his Gheddan appetite for a fight. "If we are to engage in a ship-to-ship battle, then even in destroying the Alphans we will probably suffer some damage to our own vessel. We may find it necessary to return directly to Ghedda without finishing our business here. We could leave the impression that we have departed in fright at the mere mention of there being other visitors to this planet who have similar powers to ourselves."

Garl shrugged. "Does it matter? The garrison force will soon dispel any such false ideas when it arrives."

"True. But do we need to leave any unfinished business?" Landis guessed at some of what was in Raven's mind and looked back to their commander.

"There is no need," Raven said firmly. "We can see that there are already signs of rebellion in this city which must be crushed before we depart. The attack upon my own person was one such sign. The stronger men of this city, those two brothers of the king and that old war-dog who always stands with them, are all too eager to reach for their swords. They would oppose us if they dared. Until now our lazer power has kept them under control, but if they had Alphan help and Alphan lazer weapons to support them, they could become openly hostile."

"You think there may already be Alphans in the city?"

"I think not. Until Maryam learns more of our language, I cannot question her in detail and I can only grasp the broad outline of what she has tried to tell me. There is an Alphan ship on this planet. It has landed some days travel from here and I think that the crew has made contact with some Earth group who are from, or friendly to, this city. It may be that they are on their way here. It may be that the Alphans know of our presence. These things are possible but are unclear to me."

"So first we crush all possibility of resistance in the city," Landis offered. "Then we seek out and destroy the Alphans."

"We can wipe out the city now." Caid carried the offer one step further. "I have the ship's battle lazers targeted in a maximum destruction pattern of its principle areas."

"No." Raven shook his head. "If there is a possibility that we may have to engage an Alphan ship, then we cannot waste any more of our lazer power on the city. Besides, a pile of rubble is of no value. We want a subject population."

"What of your plan to go through their marriage ceremony with the king's daughter?" Taron asked.

Raven shrugged. "It might have proved useful if the situation had not changed. It would have given me a positive role in their ruling power structure, in terms of their own laws and customs. We could then have left Thorn and one other here to maintain a Gheddan presence in my name until the garrison arrives. Now we have to be more ruthless."

Thorn looked surprised. He had not realized that it had been Raven's intention that he should stay behind. Then he saw that he should have guessed it, for it was obvious that Raven would not delegate his command for the poor pleasures of this puerile planet.

"There is something else." It suddenly occurred to Thorn that this was worth some consideration. "Earlier this afternoon I succeeded in finding the girl they tried to hide from me. She made so much stupid fuss that the only way to give my ears some peace was to stuff her mouth. The silly fool choked and died. This could anger them against us."

It was a careless account, an afterthought added because it might have some bearing on the mood of the city.

Raven realized that Thorn was talking about Namita, Maryam's sister and a princess of the ruling family of Karakhor. He stared coldly at his second-in-command but then he relaxed. Killing the girl was clearly a mistake, but if there was anyone to blame then it was his own fault, for he had not thought to forbid his crew from interfering with the women of the royal family. Thorn was a Gheddan Swordmaster, and in the absence of any direct order from a higher sword, it was only natural for him to take what he wanted.

Raven could see how Namita's death would have worked against his original plans but now it was of no great consequence. Events were moving and the situation was changing fast, which meant that all plans and strategies had to be open and fluid. He looked to his senior engineer.

"Landis, how soon will the ship be ready for flight?"

"The major parts of the maintenance and inspection programme are complete. What remain are minor checks that can be postponed. With Caid to assist me, I can have her ready in a few hours."

"Good enough. We can use the delay to settle matters in the city. Landis, you will stay here with Caid to prepare the ship for immediate launch and battle. Also to maintain a constant all-levels watch for the Alphan ship. The rest will come with me. We will use the gong again that summons all their leaders into the great hall of the king's palace. Last night we only executed one of them as an example. But this time we will kill all of those who show signs of defiance, especially the king, his two brothers, and that growling old war-dog."

Thorn grinned widely. The others showed varying degrees of satisfaction and approval. None of them wanted to challenge any of Raven's decisions.

"We will wipe out all of those who are strong enough to lead a rebellion against us," Raven finished. "That will keep the city crushed and suitably reminded of us until we can return."

"And the Alphans?" Landis asked.

"We shall come back immediately to the ship. As soon as she is ready to launch, we will begin a grid-search to the south west. When we find the Alphan ship, we will lazer-blast it out of existence."

☙

In the dusky twilight, silhouetted against a sky that was the darkening colour of dried blood, the four Gheddans whipped the horses of their borrowed chariots as they raced back into the city. Hooves and wheels clattered and rumbled across the single bridge that spanned the Mahanadi. The warriors guarding the city gates moved forward from their posts but then shrank back again when they saw the stern blue faces of the gods. No one dared to hinder their passage.

At the same moment in time, a mile below the bridge, concealed by the walls of the city and the bend of the river, Kananda and his force entered the smooth flowing water and began to swim across. Zela had warned them that the tall spires of the Gheddan ship had powerful "eyes" that could "see" them over great distances and so they had approached the city with stealth and caution. Their chariots were hidden in the forest and they had kept under cover, skirting the open plain in front of the bridge that was dominated by the Solar Cruiser.

To Kananda, it was galling that he had to enter Karakhor under the cover of darkness, emerging dripping from the river like a thief in the night. But they had to enter unseen and this was the only way. He promised himself grimly that this was another outrage for which he would exact a due price.

He climbed onto the far bank, straightened up and drew his sword. They had picked a deserted boatyard just above the burning ghats. It reeked of rotting fish scales, black pitch and drifting funeral smoke that had the prophetic taint of death. Rats scuttled among piles of refuse. An old beggar opened his eyes under the crumbling boat hulk that was his refuge, but did not dare to move or show himself.

Kasim and Gujar stepped up beside Kananda and they too drew their swords. One by one the other warriors of the small band splashed their way out of the water to stand, sword-ready, waiting for Kananda's command. The three Alphans emerged last from the river. They had taken off their weapon belts and swam more slowly as they struggled to keep their hand lazers and the spare fuel packs high and dry.

When they were all assembled, Kananda made a sign with

his sword and led them swiftly and silently into the heart of the city. The streets behind the boatyards were mainly the areas of the artisans, the metalworkers, wool-dyers, carpenters and weavers. They were by day colourful, overflowing hives of commerce and industry, but by night the wooden doors of the little shops were all barred and bolted. There may have been eyes to see them or ears to hear, but no one interfered or challenged them as they passed through. There were no whispers behind them and Kananda began to sense the hush of cold fear that had settled over the city. He had left Karakhor alive with laughter and movement and now all was unnaturally still, muted and afraid. Again a fierce and passionate anger surged in his breast.

Kananda led them unerringly through the night-dark maze until they emerged from the leather-tanged streets of the harness-makers immediately below the side walls of the palace. The walls were twice the height of a man, constructed of rough-hewn stone, and they moved along the outside until Kananda found a narrow gateway. He tried to push open the heavy, iron-studded door but it was barred on the inside.

Kasim was at his side, as always. The young lord glanced upward at the top of the wall, and then to Gujar who pressed close behind them. "A toss?" He suggested cheerfully.

Gujar smiled and nodded. He braced his back firmly against the wall and then clasped his hands in front of him ready to take Kasim's leaping foot. Kasim sheathed his sword and stepped back to take a short run. Then they all froze as the boom of the great gong shattered the hush of the dread-filled night.

The sound waves of the first stroke rolled away, to be replaced by the second and then the third. As the gong beats continued, the warriors looked at each other with uncertainty on their faces. Zela pushed through and looked to Kananda.

"What does this mean?"

"The great gong calls all the nobles and princes to an audience with the king," Kananda told her briefly. "'But I cannot understand why my father should make such a summons in the dead of night. Something is very wrong here."

"Then we should hurry."

Kananda nodded and signed to Kasim. The young lord took his run and leaped. Gujar caught his sandaled foot and heaved upward with all his strength. Kasim caught the top of the wall, squirmed over it with athletic ease and dropped down on the inside. They heard the rattle of the bar and seconds later the door was opened. They all passed through into a side courtyard, the Karakhorans with ready swords, the Alphans with hand lazers drawn.

Kananda led them into the palace, through kitchens and servants quarters, heading directly toward the king's apartments and the great hall. Urgency gripped him now and he moved at a run, all attempts at stealth and secrecy forgotten. There was something harsh and ominous in the beating of the gong. The blows were too violent and too close together. They were a signal for some nameless savagery, an omen of impending disaster. Instinctively, and as though the gods had at last relented to roar a voice of warning within his mind, Kananda knew that he had to reach the great audience hall with all possible speed.

Fear spurred him on and he ran almost blindly until he reached a point where two corridors converged. There, he collided heavily with another running man, almost impaling the other on his sword as they tumbled over together. Nimble as a cat, Kananda spun onto his feet again, his sword ready to thrust and finish deliberately what had so nearly happened by accident. Then he stayed his hand and checked his followers as he recognized the panic-stricken face and popping eyes of his half brother.

“Rajar ! What is happening? Where are you going?”

The young prince was momentarily incapable of speech. He struggled to his feet and Kasim and Gujar helped him to stand. He hung between them, white-faced and gasping.

“Rajar,” Kananda demanded in exasperation. “Why is the gong sounding?”

Rajar swallowed hard, his throat moving as he sought desperately to gather his scattered wits. He was convinced in his own terrified mind that the gong was sounding for his own sins. The gods had somehow discovered his part in the attempted assassination of their leader and now they were summoning him to meet the same brutal justice that had been dispensed upon the luckless lord of Gandhar. With this fear in mind, he had been fleeing the palace, but these were things he dared not reveal to Kananda.

“Prince Rajar.” Kasim was shaking him gently and repeating Kananda’s question. “Why does the king call an assembly?”

“It is not the command of Kara-Rashna that sounds the gong.” Rajar found his voice at last. “The blue-skinned ones sound the gong. They call the princes and the nobles to their deaths.”

“How? Why?” There was a steel band around Kananda’s heart and he hardly knew how to ask the questions.

“Last night the great gong sounded,” Rajar told them hoarsely. “We all went to the great hall to answer the summons. One of the blue-skinned ones was sounding the gong. Then they killed the lord of Gandhar with their white fire weapons. None of us could prevent it. None of us could avenge him. Now the gong sounds again. I fear it is to kill more of us.”

Gujar had turned deathly pale. He pulled on Rajar's arm, turning the young prince to face him. "My father," he said in stunned disbelief. "They have killed my father?"

Rajar nodded, a cold fist was twisting his entrails and he did not dare look into the son's eyes. "It is so, my friend—you are Lord of the House of Gandhar now."

Tears filled Gujar's eyes. His body trembled and his hand became ice-white around the hilt of his sword.

"They killed my father—why?"

"I—I do not know." The lie almost choked him. He sought frantically to evade any further interrogation on that delicate matter and turned back to Kananda. "There is more—the one called Thorn has raped and murdered our sister Namita."

Kananda stared at him, now the colour was draining from his face and an awful sickness filled his stomach. His heart seemed to stop beating. He said slowly, "Namita—our pure little Namita, so young, so innocent—she is dead?"

Rajar nodded again. "Foully violated—and foully murdered. He choked her to death."

"And the name of this monster?"

"Thorn," Rajar repeated.

"Thorn." Kananda echoed. And the sickness faded in his stomach, to be replaced by a slow swelling wave of righteous and unrestrained fury. His blood flowed hot and his heart began to beat again with the grim, measured thud of a giant war drum.

"Fear not, brave brother." His left hand gripped Rajar's shoulder. "Now you do not have to go alone to the audience hall. You can come with us."

The grip was released and Kananda ran onward. Kasim, Gujar and the three Alphans hurried at his heels. Rajar gaped at the silver-suited strangers and then realized with an awful shock that the rest the warriors were deferentially waiting for him to precede them in Kananda's wake.

Nobody had yet realized that Rajar had been running away and so reluctantly he was forced to join them.

☙

This time it was Garl who was sounding the great gong. Raven reclined on Kara-Rashna's throne as before, his fingers idly caressing the polished ivory arms. Thorn and Taron stood on either side of him, arms folded across their chests, calmly waiting.

For several minutes, it seemed that this time they had misjudged the rulers of Karakhor and that no one was willing to respond. Then Jahan stepped grim-faced into the great hall. The warmaster general wore his best uniform, the tiger emblem snarling from his breast, the fire-red gemstone blazing in his turban and the great ruby-hilted sword at his hip. He stopped, facing the Gheddans, saying nothing, folding his own arms and waiting in turn.

There was a movement in the outer corridor. Raven glimpsed a warrior moving into position behind the doorway. The man carried a bow and arrows. Raven's eyes narrowed. The old war-dog was learning. This time he brought not swordsman but archers, numbers unknown, and keeping just out of sight. The decision to kill this old man was a sound one; he possessed a stubborn fighting spirit which could prove dangerous even on this backward planet.

Kara-Rashna came next, dragging his crippled left leg and assisted by only one young warrior from his guard. He wore his best royal finery, a silk turban that was so heavily encrusted with jewels that it flashed back the flickering torch-light in all directions and sheathed at his hip was his sword.

The princes Sanjay and Devan arrived in almost the same moment to stand on either side of their brother and king, each of them looking only slightly less resplendent.

Jahan spared them a fleeting look that was a heavy combination of disapproval, anguish and pride. He had advised strongly against their presence, insisting that this time he should go alone to discover what new atrocity the blue-skinned ones intended. Kara-Rashna had considered carefully but then rejected his general's advice. If his rule was ended, then let it be so. Let the House of Karakhor fall but he would not let it be known that he was afraid to face his enemy in his own palace. Neither would he allow his old friend to die in his place. Once the king's will was spoken, the princes had steadfastly determined to accompany him.

Jahan had been unable to stop them, although he had hurried ahead to post his best archers in the adjacent corridors. He was not sure that they could do anything against the white firebolts but at least arrows flew further than swords. If he kept them out of sight, they might prove a surprise factor, although he had a sinking feeling that the blue-skinned ones were already aware of them.

Raven made no move, although Thorn and Taron had now drawn their hand-lazers. Garl tired of beating the gong, deciding that it had already been sounded enough and threw down the hammer. He turned to face the four who had answered its summons and he too drew his hand lazer. Still Raven waited.

A few more minutes passed, and then Nirad appeared, pale-faced but bravely taking his place beside his father and his uncles. Jahan looked at the boy and groaned. This one he might have saved with a direct order to hide or quit the palace but he had not realized that the young prince had so much courage. Now it was too late.

Raven waited another minute, and then decided that this small assembly was large enough. Those not brave enough to respond to the gong for the second time would do little enough harm if they were left alive.

He rose to his feet and drew his own hand lazer. He intended no ceremony but simply to give the order to fire. The command almost reached his lips but then there was a movement and a loud, ringing voice of defiance behind him.

"Hold cowards of Ghedda! I am Kananda, First Prince of Karakhor! I challenge the one named Thorn to combat by the sword!"

The men of Karahhor recognized the voice and the Gheddans knew enough of the Alphan tongue to understand the words. All turned sharply to see Kananda step through one of the narrow side doors that were on either side of the hall behind the dais and the throne. He moved through the high, carved columns that supported the great dome and circled to the front of the dais, his sword drawn and gripped firmly in his right hand.

"I seek the one called Thorn," he repeated coldly. "I seek the cowardly murderer of my sister Namita. By your own code—by your own Gheddan law—I challenge him to combat by the sword."

He was one man, a stranger with one blade, standing between four leveled lazers and the men who had been condemned to die. But he had issued a sword challenge and it could not be denied. Suddenly all of Gheddan pride and honour was at stake.

"I am Thorn!"

The Swordmaster holstered his lazer and drew his own long

blade. He moved to the edge of the dais, paused and flickered one brief glance to his commander.

Raven frowned but then nodded. There was no doubt in his mind that Thorn could kill any swordsman that this planet might produce.

"Do it quickly." he ordered. "Do not play with him. We do not have time to waste."

Thorn grinned and stepped down from the platform.

☙

Concealed in the corridor behind the doorway on the opposite side of the hall to which Kananda had entered, Zela was seething with acute frustration. Kananda had chosen to split his small force, taking Kasim and Kyle and half the warriors to one side of the hall and entrusting Gujar with the task of leading her and Blair and the rest to the other side. It made sense to try and trap the Gheddans between a crossfire of lazer beams and so Zela had agreed.

What she had not realized was that Kananda had intended to challenge Thorn. Perhaps the idea had not even occurred to him until after they had parted. She had known in her own mind that she would challenge Raven if the opportunity arose, but theirs had been the longer route and she had arrived bare seconds too late. She had taught Kananda too well on the code of their enemies and he had stolen the opportunity from her.

Now she could only wait and struggle to contain her bitter disappointment. The audience hall could only contain one duel at a time, but perhaps her chance would come after Kananda's battle was decided. Then she could call on Raven to settle her own account for Lorin.

In the meantime, she had to remember that this was not just a personal vendetta. She motioned Blair to take up a position on the opposite side of the corridor so that they had this doorway covered from both sides. Through the doorway, half hidden by columns, she could see the doorway where Kananda had made his entrance on the far side of the hall. There was no movement there but she trusted that Kyle was in position with a lazer in his hand.

Her field of vision through the doorway covered only the back end of the hall, behind the throne and the dais. She could not see what was taking place on and before the dais, but the furious clash of swords told her that the duel had commenced.

☙

Thorn had decided upon a swift, savage onslaught to hack open his opponent's defence and then a neat groin thrust to finish. Kananda wore no body armour and a skewering through the groin was an agonizing way to die. That, Thorn was confident, would teach this upstart challenger the lesson he deserved. He charged with blade whirling and the ferocity of his attack carried Kananda back across the room.

Kananda deliberately gave ground. He knew the Gheddans prided themselves upon their sword skill and he sought to lure his enemy into over-confidence. Thorn's blade crashed against his own in a series of lightning blows which it seemed that Kananda was barely able to match. The Gheddan had superb wrist and arm control and the speed of his sword was like a blur of light. The ring of steel upon steel was echoed in the vast, domed chamber above their heads and was carried outwards over the shocked city. For several terrible minutes, Kananda seemed to reel before Thorn's assault and then his blade was struck aside. Thorn drew back and lunged with all his strength. In that second, Kananda was moving like an uncoiling cobra. His body shifted sideways to let Thorn's sword-point dart harmlessly past the outside of his hip and, like the cobra's strike, his own sword was flashing at Thorn's throat. Thorn knew that he had been tricked and instinctively let his body follow through, diving down onto his knees and rolling his body forward. He avoided death by a hairsbreadth, continued rolling clear and scrambled quickly to his feet.

His tumble had taken him close to Jahan and the two princes. Three hands automatically reached for their swords and three hand-lazers swung to hold them in check.

"Jahan! Uncles!" Kananda called sharply. "Do not interfere. This battle is mine."

Jahan nodded slowly and pushed back his sword. Sanjay and Devan did the same. They understood the principles of gladiatorial combat.

Thorn was breathing heavily now and treating Kananda with caution and a new found respect. They circled each other warily, blades weaving patterns of temptation and challenge.

On the dais, Raven was again frowning slightly. This was going to take a little longer than he had anticipated and he too was sensing the need for caution. There was also a warning thought in his mind. This challenger was Hindu, another prince of this city, but he had issued his challenge in the Alphan tongue. He could only have learned that from an Alphan, which meant that he had Alphan friends. Perhaps they were close.

Garl and Taron were closely watching the sword fight and the small knot of Karakhoran rulers. So Raven half turned to keep watch on the rear of the audience hall where Kananda had made his unexpected entry. He silently willed Thorn to make haste.

Thorn and Kananda sprang together, each attacking the other and this time Kananda gave no ground. They met in a storm of blows and a deafening exchange of steel striking steel. The battle raged too fast for any human eye to count the sword strokes and with a fury that the elements could not surpass. Thorn knew now that he was fighting for his life, while Kananda fought with a lust for vengeance that knew no mercy. Namita had been little more than a child and the thought of her helpless, virginal body being crudely violated by the fiend before him inflamed Kananda to the point of madness. He was no longer planning strategy or false lures, but was simply trusting to the justice of his cause and the gods and striving with every fibre of his being to destroy this demon from another world.

Thorn was tiring. His blade was as sharp but his mind was losing its edge. He was turning Kananda's blows but being forced back, more and more on the defensive. He made a sudden effort to turn the tide, and then stepped back and reached quickly to draw the boot knife that most Gheddans carried. His left hand flipped it upward in a fast, underhand throw. Kananda saw the second blur of steel from the corner of his eye and twisted on one heel, contracting the muscles of his stomach. The knife blade scored a thin red cut across the taut skin. They were both off balance but Kananda recovered first. Thorn was poised for another sword slash, but Kananda risked all on a direct lunge. His blade pierced Thorn's throat just below the jaw, half severing the windpipe and emerging from the back of the blue neck. Thorn's blow faltered and dropped as he hung, choking and dying, and Kananda was fascinated to see that the blue god's blood was a rich, dark red.

☙

Time froze. The Gheddan aura of god-like invincibility had been destroyed and for most of those watching it took several seconds for this vital fact to sink into their combined consciousness. Kananda had slain a god. The blue gods could die. Raven knew instinctively that only lazers could save them now, for as Thorn slumped and slipped limply from Kananda's blade, the princes Devan and Sanjay were already drawing their swords.

"Burn them all!" Raven ordered sharply, but as he swung his lazer toward Kananda, several things happened simultaneously.

Jahan hurled himself sideways, crashing bodily into the king and the three princes and knocking them all sprawling to the floor. As he did so, he shouted lustily for his archers. Bowmen appeared instantly in the doorway behind him, firing a swift but ragged flight of arrows before ducking back into the shelter of the corridor. The shafts were too hastily fired for any deliberate aim but they distracted Garl and Taron from their intended targets and drew the first bolts from their lazers. One of the ornate, half open doors was split from top to bottom, the white beam bursting it into flame and killing the two archers who sheltered behind it. The second beam lanced down the corridor and exploded huge chunks of masonry from the wall.

Zela had rushed into the room, lazer holstered, sword in hand, distracting Raven from Kananda as she shouted his name. There was a challenge on her lips but Raven had no way of knowing and no time to listen. He registered only a silver suit and golden hair and on the other side of the hall another silver flash as Kyle moved to get a lazer shot through the columns. Raven leveled his lazer at Zela and fired.

Blair had been caught unaware by his commander's unexpected action, but the tall Alphan's reaction was fast and instinctive. He charged after her, shouting her name. His shoulder knocked her to one side as he protected her with his own body. He fired at Raven but took the full blast of Raven's lazer beam in his chest. He spun into Zela again and this time the dead weight of his body pushed her off balance and pinned her to the floor. His own shot had missed and demolished one of the tall columns. Splinters of stone gashed Raven's face and he cursed and backed up to take cover behind the throne.

Garl and Taron had realized that the greater danger was behind them. They turned and crouched at the edge of the dais, exchanging fire with Kyle at the rear of the hall. From this angle, the forest of columns blocked off Kyle's position and the crisscross of white energy beams exploded repeatedly against the stonework. In a matter of seconds, half the columns were shattered and the great dome above them was in danger of collapse. The beam flashes weakened and Kyle retreated to fit a new fuel pack.

The two Gheddans started to make a quick changeover of fuel packs for their own depleted weapons, but now they faced a five-sword attack from behind. As soon as the lazers had stopped firing, Jahan and the princes had scrambled to their feet and, led by Kananda, they fell upon the nearest two of their enemies. Garl and Taron barely had time to draw blades and defend themselves.

The fight would have been swiftly over if Raven had not had the forethought to reserve some of his lazer power. The Sword Lord was not a man to let a situation arise where all of his force could be caught changing fuel packs at the same moment. Because his own men were in the way, he could not get a direct shot at Kananda or Jahan, whom he recognized as the greatest dangers, but he fired past Taron's shoulder. The prince Sanjay was flung out of the fray with his left arm shriveled and scorched.

"This way," Raven ordered. And the three Gheddans backed

up quickly to the side doorway through which Zela and Blair had entered. Raven was first through the door and Gujar sprang directly into his path. The young lord had his sword in hand, but they had collided chest to chest and neither could bring a weapon into play. Raven ducked his head and head-butted the young Hindu full in the face with all his strength. Gujar reeled back out of the way. There were more warriors behind him but Raven fired a last bolt from his lazer and cut a white path through.

The three Gheddans raced down the corridor, fitting the new fuel packs to their lazers as they ran.

Zela lay crushed and shocked under Blair's body. While the lazer battle raged above, her she was unable to move, but once the exchange ceased she struggled clear and onto her knees. There she stared in horror at Blair's blackened chest with its deep, cauterized burn-hole and at his dead white face. She was stunned with guilt and remorse. Blair had loved her, she realized that now with dreadful clarity, and wondered how she could have been so blind to it before. Blair had loved her and he had given his life for her. And it was her own blind folly that had caused his sacrifice.

She wanted to weep, but then Kyle was beside her, helping her up. She became aware of the Gheddans retreating through the doorway and Kananda and his uncles pressing close behind them. She had lost her sword, but now she drew her lazer and snatched up the lazer Blair had dropped with her free hand. She knew that it would take only seconds for the Gheddans to reload and, shouting at Kananda to give her passage, she ran in pursuit with Kyle at her side.

ଔ

Since Namita had been killed, Maryam had been closeted with her mother, both of them trying to comfort and console the distraught queen Kamali. All three of them had at last fallen fitfully into sleep, Kamali prone on her bed, Maryam and her mother on chairs close beside her, when the dread booming of the gong had again roused them into wakefulness. Maryam sat bolt upright, her body stiffening with apprehension. She started to rise but then the two older women pulled her back to her chair and restrained her. They huddled together in fear and uncertainty, the long wait and the tension fraying at their nerves and shriveling their very souls. Then suddenly the night was split asunder by the violence of sword blades, fearsome thunderclaps of sound, the crash of falling masonry, screams, shrieks, shouts and a pandemonium of running movement. It was as though all the demons, minions and monsters of hell itself had been let loose upon the cowering palace.

Maryam shrank within herself, but as the nightmare continued, the agony of not knowing swelled into a driving force more terrible than mere mortal fear. She pushed herself up again, tearing herself free from the clutching hands of her mother and aunt, she ran for the door. Ignoring their wailing cries and pleas, she slammed the door behind her and then ran through the corridors toward the heart of the disturbance.

Raven knew that his game in Karakhor was up. There were Alphans behind them, matching the Gheddan lazer-power, and behind the Alphans were the old war-dog's archers and a pack of blood-thirsting swordsman. All he could do now was to make a fighting retreat out of the palace and the city and back to his ship. Fortunately the frequent twists and turns of the passageways enabled them to stay ahead of any direct line of fire from the pursuing lazer bolts, although both Taron and Garl had by now collected their own minor injuries from the flying fragments of disintegrating stone.

Raven led the way around another corner at the junction of two corridors and ran headlong into Maryam.

She stumbled to a halt, staring at his bloodied face and his torn and dust-smeared uniform. Her mind was full of confusion but her heart was bursting with fear, anguish, and most of all, love. She had been running blindly, without any clear intention, but suddenly she knew why she had been running and who she had been seeking. She sobbed his name and threw herself desperately into his arms.

Raven's first instinct was to throw her aside. But she was a princess of the royal house and might yet prove a useful card to play as a hostage. He tightened his free arm around her waist and hurried her along beside him as he left the palace.

Maryam went without protest. She flung one hasty glance back over her shoulder and saw a glimpse of two unfamiliar silver figures with golden hair and they were using more of the white fire weapons. There were more gods of a different kind! She was caught up in a battle of the gods! But her god—Raven—still wanted her with him! Raven loved her and would not leave her behind.

Her head whirled with that exquisite thought and emotion overwhelmed her. She ran with him willingly, forgetting all of her previous doubts, ready to love him and serve him with undying devotion.

They raced through the darkened streets through the gates in the city wall and out onto the bridge. The Solar Cruiser waited for them on the starlit plains but now there was too much open ground without cover and Raven knew they would be cut down before they could reach it. He stopped on the far side of the bridge, ordering his two companions to take cover and give fire. At the same time he dropped down on his belly, pulling Maryam face down onto the dirt road beside him.

Lazer bolts flashed toward them from the shadows of the gateway. The deadly beams were returned and, for a few moments, the ancient stone archways that spanned the Mahanadi were brilliantly illuminated in streaks of white fire. There was a pause in the display and a flight of arrows sailed out from the city walls.

Raven had his communicator to his lips. He said urgently: “Landis, Caid, destroy the bridge. Use precision targeting. We are uncomfortably close.”

The answer came immediately. “Caid here, commander. Targeting the bridge. On the count of ten.”

They had ten seconds. Raven signaled to Garl and Taron to withdraw, but they had heard the exchange and needed no urging. Raven hauled on Maryam’s shoulder as he wriggled backwards and obediently she kept pace with him.

From the nose of the Solar Cruiser, a single energy beam lanced downward across the plain. Raven and Maryam felt its searing heat as it passed above their heads, scorching their hair and blistering the skin on the backs of their necks and then it struck dead centre of the bridge. In an almighty crack of sound and a violent sunburst of white flame, the bridge disappeared, the archways melted or vaporized. Only at the edges of the impact was there any stonework left to erupt and scatter. The water foamed and boiled in a roaring hiss of steam and terrifying waves surged upstream and downstream along the tortured waters of the Mahanadi.

Raven rose to his feet and smiled briefly at the frustration his enemies must be feeling on the city bank. Any immediate pursuit was now cut off and it would take time for any Alphan or Hindu to pluck up the courage to swim the river or to find and launch a boat. He motioned to his companions and they continued their interrupted run toward the spaceship, moving at a fast trot to take them quickly out of the range of any stray arrows or hand-held lazers.

Maryam ran with them. She did not know what was happening or why. Perhaps the world as she knew it was ending or had already ended? Perhaps the gods were shaping a new universe? Perhaps the stars would fall and the Earth would die? It was all beyond Maryam's comprehension. She only knew that she was running with Raven, that Raven wanted her and that she wanted to be with him. She was the chosen of the god. Her place was at his side.

They reached the spaceship and without pause Garl and Taron scrambled up the steel rungs of the access ladder. Raven stopped to cover them, his alert gaze sweeping the surrounding plain for any unexpected source of attack. Maryam dashed past him and nimbly ascended the ladder behind the two Gheddans. Raven shouted at her to come down.

Maryam did not understand him. She assumed that he was urging her to go faster and so she quickened her speed. Raven cursed and began to climb rapidly after her but, with the agility of a frightened monkey, she stayed out of his reach.

Taron vanished into the airlock. Garl hesitated, half in the airlock, one foot still on the ladder, looking down. Then he swung back and raised one booted foot, ready to kick Maryam in the face and boot her clear of the ladder when she reached his level.

Maryam was unaware of what was happening. Only Raven understood what Garl intended.

Images flashed through Raven's mind; images of their lovemaking, of her almost childish eagerness to please him, memories of the love and trust and vulnerability he had seen in her behaviour and in her eyes.

He had no more need of her. He had not intended to bring

her this far. But a fall from this height would kill her and suddenly he could not permit her to be thrown from the ladder in cold blood.

"No, Garl," he ordered harshly. "Let her in."

Garl shrugged and entered the airlock. Maryam followed him and Raven joined them. Maryam was looking all around her, her eyes filled with curiosity and wonder. She peered through the open doorway that led into the heart of the ship, took a tentative step toward it, and then looked back for Raven's approval. Raven was equally aware of Garl and Taron watching him with questioning faces.

Raven knew that he could make her understand that he wanted her to leave. He could push her back down the ladder. But he could not explain to her the danger she would be in if she did not move well clear of the ship's exhaust thrust. She would probably stand there with that stupid look on her face and wait to be incinerated.

"She comes with us," he said flatly. "We will return to this planet and she may still prove to be of some political value."

It was his decision and there was no argument. Whether they believed him or not, they did not let their opinions show. While Garl closed the airlock door, Raven ran through to the control deck where Landis waited with Caid.

"Immediate launch," he ordered. "Earth escape trajectory and velocity. We return to Dooma. We have no time to waste."

"The Alphan ship?" Landis asked uncertainty.

"We fought Alphans in the city. They will have given our position to their ship. But we do not know their position. We are at the disadvantage and could be hit at any time."

They did not relish the thought of flight but events had turned against them and there was no future in inviting an Alphan attack. All of them could see that every second they now remained on the ground might well be their last. They strapped themselves into their flight chairs. Raven strapped Maryam in the seat that had been Thorn's and then Landis initiated the launch sequence.

The Solar Cruiser slowly lifted upward on its roaring pillar of fire, accelerated into the night- sky and vanished among the stars.

Chapter Fifteen

It was not until the following day that it finally became clear that Maryam had departed with the blue-skinned gods on their return into space. The palace and the city had been searched a dozen times, but there was no trace of the missing princess. Then reports began to filter through to Jahan and Kananda to say that she had last been seen running across the bridge with the retreating Gheddans. Other reports said that as they ran through the streets, one of the blue-skinned men had been pulling the princess by the arm.

Kananda's rage and grief knew no bounds. He was convinced that his sister had been taken by force, kidnapped and dragged to their ship by these loathsome rapists from another world. With five hundred men, he swam across the river to search every crack and rift and furrow of the far shore. They uprooted every bush and turned over every rock, but to no avail. There was no body. There was not a single jewel or a scrap of clothing. There was nothing but the blackened circle of burned earth where the Solar Cruiser had once stood. At the end of the day, Kananda wept and shook his fists at the sky. He cursed every god that had ever existed and then wept again.

Shortly after dawn on the next day, the Alphan Tri-Thruster appeared, landing on the same stretch of open plain. Soon after, Kyle and Zela began making their preparations to leave.

Kananda had mourned and suffered, but at last his spirit rallied. He dried his eyes and went in search of Zela, leading her down to the river's edge where they could be alone. They faced each other and Zela felt the anguish of unfulfilled love and the deep pain of parting. To leave Kananda so soon after losing Blair was almost more than her heart could bear.

But the Hindu prince had no thought of parting. He said slowly, "Your enemy—the one called Raven—he will return to your planet?"

Zela nodded uncertainly. She had expected a warm embrace, a fond exchange of tears and kisses, not this matter-of-fact questioning.

"And you will pursue him there?"

"Yes, I must return to Dooma—that is to Alpha, not Ghedda, they are different continents on the same planet."

"But from Alpha it is possible to go to Ghedda?"

Again she nodded.

"Then take me with you. I know that if my sister is alive then she must be at this land you call Ghedda. I must go there and search for her."

"Kananda, that is impossible."

"Why? I am sorry for the death of your friend Blair. He was a good man—a very brave warrior. But he is with the gods. Without him, there can be a place for me on your starship."

Zela stared at him, words faltering on her tongue and slowly she realized that he was making a kind of sense. Her mission was to learn about Earth and to establish friendly relations with its people. If she took Kananda back to Alpha, then he could answer all of Space Command's questions, and if they could help him to recover his sister, then they would earn the eternal friendship and loyalty of Karakhor. She could easily justify such an action. Some might say it was an opportunity not to be missed.

But was it right for him? She loved him too much too simply make use of him. She did not want him to make a hasty decision which he might later regret.

“What will happen here?” she asked. “Your people still face war with your enemies on this planet. Perhaps they will need you.”

Kananda shrugged. “It will still be many moons before Maghalla can marshal all her forces to attack Karakhor. Sardar is a coward. He knows that even with Kanju and the monkey tribes, he still cannot be certain of victory and so he will seek more allies. When the alliances are all made, they must then gather armies and move them over many days march. Provision wagons and war elephants move slowly. Perhaps the whole circle of seasons will pass.”

“It will take many days to travel to my planet,” Zela warned him. “And I cannot promise that we will go to Ghedda.”

“Take me to Alpha,” Kananda repeated. “And if need be I will go alone to Ghedda. Somehow I will find Maryam.”

Zela smiled at his naïveté, but then her arms were around him and she was kissing him and he was returning her kiss. There was strength and power in his hard-muscled arms that lifted her up from the earth and suddenly she could almost share in his simple certainty. Might not a man who defied the gods defeat the merely godless?

When she could speak again, she said breathlessly, “It is agreed. You will come with me. We will find Maryam.” And then her voice took on the cutting edge of an old anger and a new determination as she added grimly, “Where we find Maryam, we shall also find Raven.”

About the Author

Robert Leader has been a merchant seaman, a retained fire-fighter and a tireless traveler. Twice he has undertaken the overland trip to India and the Far East and has crossed Africa from Tunis to Capetown by Land Rover. He has also found time to run his own business and take a degree in philosophy, social anthropology and politics at the University of East Anglia. Under other pen names he has published thriller and adventure novels exploring the worlds of crime, terrorism and espionage. Robert Leader lives in Bury St Edmunds in England and regularly publishes photo feature magazine articles on the heritage, places and events of his home counties of East Anglia.

To learn more about Robert Leader please send an email to Robert Leader at robertcharlesrleader@talktalk.com.

From the exotic mists of Vedic mythology to the harsh and barbaric Gheddan Empire, the Law of the Sword is carried godlessly into the space age.

The Sword Empire

© 2007 Robert Leader

Book 2 of The Fifth Planet

The first mission to control the Third Planet has failed, and the Sword Lord of Ghedda, Raven, has been driven out of the ancient Hindu Kingdom of Karakhor and forced to return to the planet Dooma. He takes with him Maryam, princess of Karakhor, who sees him as her lover and a possible savior in the coming battle against the might of Maghalla.

They are pursued by Kananda, First Prince of Karakhor, drawn by love for his star goddess, Zela, and his determination to find the sister he believes has been taken by force.

On the Fifth Planet they are all hurled into a terrible arms race between two warring continents. A planetary cataclysm looms as Kananda and Zela undertake a desperate mission into the heart of the Sword Empire.

For Zela, it is a race against time to save her world. For Kananda, it is a matter of love and honor to find Maryam.

And both seek vengeance against the Sword Lord.

Available now in ebook from Samhain Publishing.

Enjoy the following excerpt from The Sword Empire...

After Raven had left her, Maryam lay back in their bed of soft furs and struggled to let her mind catch up with her windswept emotions. The past few hours had been such a hurricane of events and feelings that all her senses were still reeling. She had felt a strong sense of pride as they entered the Council chamber, pride in her handsome blue lover and pride in herself as a noble daughter of Karakhor. Then her whole world had capsized as she realized that Raven was fighting for his life, and even more. Sylve's gloating sneer told her that eventually her life would be forfeit too if Raven lost his battle. After the terrible moments of pure fear had come the elation of Raven's victory, coupled with the horror of Radd's death. And finally, and most recently, the unexpected and most violent bout of love-making she had yet known. She felt bruised, abused, and delighted. His power, strength and virility stunned her, and yet she had matched him. He was her man and he accepted her as his woman. It was, as always, almost too much and too exciting to fully grasp.

She lay with her head spinning and her loins throbbing. Her whole body was still aroused and sensitive and she wanted him to come back. At last, however, she decided that she must get up and get dressed. She washed quickly, and here in these cold rooms, it was a purely hygienic business and nothing like the long, perfumed luxury with attendants which she would have enjoyed at home.

Afterwards, she deliberated for a few moments, and then regretfully folded away her silk shawl and sari, and donned instead the practical Gheddan garments of leather and wool. Her fine Hindu clothes she now kept only for very special occasions. She hesitated for a few more seconds over the studded belt with the sheathed knife, and then strapped it around her waist.

There were four rooms in the block they occupied: the day room, the bedroom, the wash room and the food room. Maryam wandered into the latter in search of some fruit to eat, and made herself a cup of the hot, diluted honey which was all that the Geddhans seemed to drink when they were not consuming beer or wine. She moved back to the tall window in the day room and looked out over the barrack square as she ate and sipped. At this hour of the day, there were several squads of Gheddan warriors drilling, hacking at wooden posts with their swords, or just running round and round the perimeter. She had watched Jahan drilling the warriors and young lords of Karakhor, and although there was less finesse here and the language was more crude, there was a great similarity in that it all seemed to consist of a lot of blind running, stamping and shouting.

She was still watching when she heard the faint click of a key in the door. Expecting Raven, she did not turn immediately. One of the running men had tripped and sprawled on the hard packed earth, and even through the thick closed glass she could hear the choice words of his irate drill master. Many of them were unfamiliar and her imagination was working overtime. She turned at last to teasingly ask the meaning of one particularly illustrative phrase, but it was not Raven who stealthily crossed the room toward her.

Maryam's eyes opened wide in astonishment, and Sylve stopped and gave her a vicious smile.

"You!" Maryam blurted. "How? What?" She was too startled to frame her questions coherently.

Sylve showed her a set of iron keys on their ring and

jangled them in front of her face. “I was Raven’s woman before he brought you back from the third planet. I still have the keys to these rooms.”

Maryam stared at her, and then saw the movement in the outer doorway that Sylve had left open. It was not Raven. Another man stood there grinning. Sylve was not alone.

Sylve saw the shift of Maryam’s eyes and instantly hurled the heavy key ring full into Maryam’s face. Maryam flinched and twisted her face away, bringing up her hand to protect her eyes. The keys smashed into her cheek, and then Sylve followed them up with a clenched fist that hit Maryam square on the jaw. The Hindu princess reeled and fell and the side of her head came into violent contact with the corner of one of the low tables. With the third blow, her senses blacked out with the triple shock and the pain and she slumped in a heap to the floor.

Sylve stood over her victim, breathing heavily but grinning with triumph. The man behind her quickly closed the door, and then knelt to check that Maryam was unconscious. When he was satisfied, he rolled her inert body into the window alcove and then pulled the curtains to cover it.

“Hide yourself,” he commanded Sylve. “The Sword Lord Karn is a sick man and he will not detain Raven for long. He could return at any moment.”

Sylve scowled. She did not like taking orders and this was her plan, but Tighe was a trained assassin and Doran had placed him in charge. She drew the long knife from her hip and then moved to conceal herself behind the tall curtains. It gave her a certain pleasure to hide there, standing over the fallen body of the hated brown bitch. If Tighe did his job properly, she would not be needed, and then she would be perfectly situated to slice the brown bitch’s throat before they left.

Maryam's senses swam back slowly. The side of her face hurt and her head ached and she lay still to avoid aggravating the pain. She felt the wetness of blood trickling down her cheek and remembered what had happened to her. She felt her anger rising, but instinct warned her to remain silent and still.

When her head stopped swimming, she carefully opened her eyes, just enough to give her narrowed slit vision. She saw the bare floorboards, a glimpse of the bottom edge of the tall curtains, and a black leather boot. She could hear nothing. She lay as if frozen and then risked opening her eyes fully. Her head hurt a little more, but nothing else happened. She could see no more than she had seen through her slitted eyelids, just a few more square inches of knotted floorboard and a little higher up the curtain.

Very slowly, she turned her head a little toward the black boot. The black leather rose to a blue-skinned knee, and then there was bare blue thigh flesh, disappearing under a short leather skirt. She realized that Sylve was standing over her, and a glint of steel almost out of range of her vision told her that Sylve was holding a drawn knife.

Sylve was silent and waiting, hardly breathing, and she had not been alone. Maryam guessed that the man who had accompanied Sylve was also silent and waiting, Out of sight from the main door in either the food room or the bedroom. They were waiting for Raven to return.

Maryam steeled herself, and she too waited.

It seemed an eternity before she finally heard movement at the outer door. Raven's key clicked in the lock and she heard the door creak as he pushed it back without any need for silence or stealth. Above her, she saw and felt Sylve go tense.

"Raven, beware!"

Printed in the United States
116734LV00006B/226-246/P

9 781599 988115